Dear Reader,

One of the things that thrills a book editor more than anything else is finding a novel that presents new ideas from a fresh perspective—a work of fiction that isn't like everything else on the market.

Revenge Gifts by Cindy Cruciger is a book like that—a book that excited me from the first. I already knew Cindy had a unique voice; her column for *Romantic Times Book-Club Magazine*, "The Path to Publishing," charted her tale of trying to get this book—and a few others—published. She wrote of the trials and tribulations of writing, the agony of submission and rejection, and the ecstasy of being recognized as a "real" writer.

At some point in life, everyone tries to get a little revenge—deeply personal, highly satisfying revenge. Computer geek Tara Cole is trying to make a living supplying just that, through her small yet effective website. But she's getting far more than she bargained for—people, alive and dead, are drawn to her, hoping to steal, attain, and exact the perfect revenge.

Forget revenge as a dish best served cold—*Revenge Gifts* dishes it up sizzling hot.

Cheers,
Anna Genoese, Editor
Tor Paranormal Romance

D1010422

Revenge Gifts

Cindy Cruciger

tor romance

A TOM DOHERTY ASSOCIATES BOOK
NEW YORK

This is a work of fiction. All the characters and events portrayed in this book are either products of the author's imagination or are used fictitiously.

REVENGE GIFTS

Copyright © 2005 by Cindy Cruciger

Edited by Anna Genoese

A Tor Book
Published by Tom Doherty Associates, LLC
175 Fifth Avenue
New York, NY 10010

www.tor.com

Tor® is a registered trademark of Tom Doherty Associates, LLC.

ISBN 0-765-35225-7
EAN 978-0765-35225-5

First edition: September 2005

Printed in the United States of America

0 9 8 7 6 5 4 3 2 1

Revenge Gifts is dedicated to everyone at *Romantic Times Book Club Magazine*, especially Kathryn Falk, Lady of Barrow, Kenneth Rubin, Carol Stacy, Tara Gelsomino, Ann Peach, and Kathe Robin.

Acknowledgments

In one way or another everything communicates. Humans are the only creatures on earth, with the exception of cats, that are certain of the absolute critical nature of the messages they try to convey. I have found that the only difference between the two is that cats are correct, while humans... eh.... not so much. Ninety-nine point nine percent of the time we are just making stuff up. And some of us have elevated it to a seriously messed up art form.

I blame my parents.

My mother, Sherry Collins Ralph, read some selections of grim literature from her college classes, thus combining the nurturing bedtime stories with *Grendel, Fall of the House of Usher*, and *Rebecca*. My father, Martin Ralph, riffed on life in carefully crafted tall tales based on our everyday world.

My high school English teacher, Jan Pratt, was my very first critic: "How is it possible that someone who writes as well as you *can't spell*?!"

I still can't spell, Ms. Pratt. But I'll make sure everyone understands that you did your best.

My second real critic, Renee Bernard, tirelessly plowed through my first official writing efforts and declared that she adored "the way" I write, but hated "what" I wrote. Author Annette Appollo seconded that sentiment. Determined to prove that I could write something far worse that anything I had previously put to paper, I sat; listed out every evil idea I'd ever stored away for a boring day, and unleashed the story I *wanted* to write. This prompted Ann Peach to ask if I "actually intended to alienate the entire continent of Australia?" I hadn't thought of it that way, but. . . hmm. . . ok.

I discovered something interesting about leaving behind politically correct writing, gathering together wicked thoughts and weaving a world and characters where the usual rules of good behavior are basically ignored. I discovered that a few, very brave souls are willing to take huge risks to put it out in public for the entertainment of everyone. My editor Anna Genoese and agent Cheryl Ferguson are fearless, and I can never thank them enough for taking a chance that no one else was willing to take on my behalf.

If all hell breaks loose as a result, I'll take the heat. . . I expect everyone else to bring the Drambuie and marshmallows.

```
// Thought for the day on the Home Page of
Revenge-Gifts.com, scheduled to load on Friday.
<script language = "JavaScript">
<!-- This figures out what day of the week it
is, and prints a quote. -->
<!--
    Sys_Date = new Date ();
    var DayofWeek = " ";
  var TaraQuote = " ";


    if (Sys_Date.getDay ()  == 5) {
            DayofWeek = "Friday";

TaraQuote = ""Any positive effect resulting
from actions on my part is purely accidental."-
-Tara Cole" ;

  document.write (DayofWeek + " : " + TaraQuote);
  // -->
  </script>
```

CHAPTER ONE

The gris-gris bag

IT'S POSSIBLE THAT the karmic repercussions of running a website devoted entirely to revenge will be massive. I know this, and still I can't see myself stepping off this track. I wonder if the reason I am thirty-three years old, single and childless is actually a reward for having married badly and re-populated a small developing nation while working myself to death as a house-drudge in my previous life. This could be why I'm so uncomfortable around children, then again, maybe not.

I am only certain of one thing. If we are the sum total of our relationships, my balance sheet is bleeding red ink.

I could offer my opinion on why this is so. I could give you advice on how to avoid the crevasse, which I fell into. But, honestly, I can't pull *myself* out, so why should I help *you?*

I guess I just ran out of cheeks to turn one day and, when finally I gave myself permission to get even, a door to my soul blew open with the force of a hurricane. The twisted hinges of that shattered door mirror my now-twisted life. And here's the kicker; once the door was open, it just became that much easier to walk through it again and again.

Some people cope with Prozac. And while I'm never one to discount the benefits of better living through modern chemistry, I chose to take the all-natural approach and cope by getting even.

Does that make me a miserable human being? Maybe. But misery loves company. And, because this is true, Revenge-Gifts.com is doing phenomenally well.

I read somewhere that we attract things to us. We attract certain people and find ourselves in certain situations because we need to work on personal issues. Apparently, I have a lot of issues. At two a.m. last night someone put a gris-gris bag on my car. I guess not everyone is a fan. If that's not enough, my email this morning attracted nothing but trouble.

From: Hpayne@SoFlaInvest.com [mailto:
Hpayne@SoFlaInvest.com]
To: TaraCole@Revenge-Gifts.com
Subject: Revenge-Gifts.com

Dear Ms. Cole,

I was researching small businesses in the Florida Keys and your company caught my eye. I am looking to invest in two, or possibly three, start-up ventures with an eye to combining their strengths for potential growth opportunities. I would like to discuss this further with you in person. I will call to let you know when I will be in your neighborhood.

Kindest Regards,
Howard Payne
South Florida Investments, Inc.
Hpayne@SoFlaInvest.com
(954) 555-6783

I saw a template for this kind of letter\email in a book on business correspondence. Disappointing. I prefer a completely unprofessional approach. As emails go, though, this was a weird one.

    a. How was he going to get my phone number? Last time I checked, it was unlisted.
    b. Why would he want to invest in Revenge Gifts and what other businesses could he possibly have found which would, in any way, shape or form, complement my products?

For the merest second I considered calling him first. Then I thought. Maybe he has caller-ID and it's a ploy to get my number. Maybe he's insane. I Google'd his name, specifying public records—nothing found. If he's slick he could have gotten his records closed. I made a note to research this later.

The shipping invoices for the day's orders finished printing. Business was booming. I spent most of the morning boxing them up. I do not gift wrap. An order for a revenge gift goes directly into the mailbox of the purchaser. If they want to gift wrap the gift before sending it then that's their business. I don't gift wrap revenge. I don't send it to the target directly. Bad karma. There's one exception to this rule. Candy. Not just any candy—a year's worth of candy. The Candy-A-Day is delivered directly to the intended victim.

Of all the gifts I sell, this is the one I treasure most. I hit on this idea, as with most of the others, during a long, dark, soulless night in the computer server room. Aileen inspired it.

Aileen was my supervisor, and the PMS queen from hell. Four of us worked on her team. We played a game. Ask your teenagers about this one, they know it. Every time Aileen would say one of her catch phrases, we would beam a hit to each other's Palm Pilot. At the end of the day, we tallied the hits. Each of us had "our" phrase. The phrase with the most hits won.

If Aileen said, "Jesus people, do I have to tell you your job *every single day?*" the most in one day, Josh bought the drinks that night.

If Aileen said, "I gave up my covered parking space to get CNN. I told you that didn't I?" (Aileen believed we were all completely fascinated by her personal budget constraints), John bought the drinks that night. John was a cheap bastard, though. He wouldn't pony up if we got there after Happy Hour.

If Aileen said, "This is unacceptable," Derrick did the honors. Derrick had certain phrases that annoyed him so much; he started blinking madly if he heard them uttered. Derrick insisted on dragging us to play paintball in lieu of drinks. We played at night with colors that glowed in the dark. Of all the guys I worked with, Derrick was my favorite. The Candy-A-Day? It was really for him.

My phrase? If Aileen said, "Nobody 'gets' your sense of humor, Tara. Please stop posting your snide remarks on the company bulletin board," I bought that night's round.

I posted every single day. For maximum effect, I tortured the conservative geek in the basement by posting opinions so radical he *had* to respond. No one could stop him either. Ehud wrote the code that ran the board. I consistently referred to VP of sales Kimberly Case—a bitchy, corporate ass-kisser who made my life as hellish as she could just for the fun of it—as "Kimmy," thus ensuring a visit from her to Aileen at least once a week to discuss my attitude problem.

I was buying the drinks a lot.

After ten years in Aileen's group, I knew things about her. Aileen had a weakness. Pencil-thin Aileen was addicted to chocolate. She couldn't pass it up. She would forego all food for a day if she so much as whiffed a Dove bar. And Godiva, oh baby, Godiva was her ultimate downfall.

The final straw came on a Wednesday. Aileen harangued Derrick to a head-banging frenzy. I heard her spin up on him. "Derrick. This is unacceptable . . ."

I couldn't help myself. I had an overwhelming desire to defend him. I got up from my seat and headed over to his desk. We were all in one office with no walls in between. By the time I got between Aileen and Derrick he was pounding his head on his desk muttering, "I hate this fucking job,"— over and over again.

I stared her down until she left. She wrote him up for foul language.

The next day, the first box of chocolates arrived on Aileen's desk.

For six solid months, I paid for delivery of Godiva chocolates to her desk. At first, she was gushing. She tortured us by debating out loud who her secret admirer could be. Then, the pounds started creeping on, and Aileen began taking lunch breaks at the gym. Aileen never went to lunch before this. If Aileen didn't go to lunch, neither did we. We celebrated this happy development at Hooter's, at high noon. Score one.

Aileen put on thirty pounds. She was frantic. Her budget was busting wide open at the seams. She replaced *all* of her thousand-dollar suits with the next size up. "I pay a premium for quality. Quality lasts. Over time, quality actually *saves* money." Jesus, I hated her "thrift" lectures. My skin is itching just thinking about it. Score two.

But the final pay-off . . . it was beautiful. Aileen (who never took a vacation) took every day of vacation she'd saved for the past decade and checked herself into the Canyon Ranch in Arizona. During the eight weeks she was gone, we had one last round of drinks, one last game of paintball, one last lunch and left, taking the early retirement buy-out the company offered.

I was onto something.

I have no life. I know this.

It is possible that people purchase this gift with the best of intentions. I feel a twinge of guilt over this and I clearly state on the website that the Candy-A-Day gift is a *very* poor choice if you're intending to give it to the love of your life. I sit down at the computer and forward the order to Key's Candy Shoppe. According to my records, six hundred and seventy-two people are receiving a box of seven candies a week. Mostly chocolates.

This proves at least one thing: I am not alone. There are others like me out there.

And then, of course, there are the stalkers. I read the email from Howard Payne again and it still bugs me.

Is this Howard guy going to call or what?

"Hello?" Kathy was standing outside the screen door trying to see in. My bungalow is one of ten identical buildings on a private beach. The sand is shipped in and the seaweed is carted off, so the beach is picture perfect. I'll never understand why the Keys have to pretend they are a "beach" getaway like the rest of the Florida coast. The Keys are rocks sticking out of the water. Coral lives. Coral dies. We live on the dead coral. Resorts mask the scents of the dead and decaying vegetation and sea life with flowering trees and bushes. This place is no exception. I can smell the frangipani through the screen door. My bungalow is surrounded by the sickly smells of botanical imports. I once asked the gardener if he had ever considered using any native flowering plants. He shrugged. He politely pointed out that the only abundantly fragrant native plant that could tolerate the climate was Spanish Stopper—a plant that smells very much like a pissed-off skunk. Figures.

Yeah. The Keys are a scruffy, prickly place when left to nature. No one wants to see the real Keys. They want the mosquito-free, scruff smoothed off, tourist island.

My friend Sherry rents the other bungalows by the month to tourists. The tourists get what they expect—for an exorbitant price. I get mine rent-free because I run her bar for her when she's out of town. Sherry is out of town a lot. It's a cute little conch-style house with a wrap-around porch and gingerbread latticework railings. I keep the front door open with the screen door closed to let in the sounds of the surf and wind chimes. The AC is on, of course. Packing orders is hot, sweaty work.

"Tara?" She opened the door and slid in around the boxes stacked in the way. "Business is good, huh?"

Kathy is the human incarnation of my conscience, bundled in a five-foot-two, one hundred and ten pound body. She jogs every evening, never colors her hip-length, golden brown hair and conducts spiritual healing sessions at her New Age shop, Reflections, every Wednesday. Her clear blue eyes see things I don't want to know about. Kathy is very nice. I like her in spite of this small fault.

She was already in the kitchen getting her water and me a Diet Coke. "So. What gives? What's with the two a.m. phone call?"

"Someone left a gris-gris hanging over my car." I grabbed the bag containing the gris-gris from the bar and we both headed out to the porch. Kathy won't stay inside my bungalow for more than five minutes at a whack. She says it is haunted. She's right.

My porch apparently isn't haunted. I have rocking chairs and hammock chairs scattered at intervals on each side of the house interspersed with orchids and herbs. The sun is in the front of the house in the morning, so we settled on the shady side in the back.

I handed her the bag. "Have a look."

An expression crossed Kathy's face. Serene, centered Kathy looked concerned. She gingerly opened the paper bag and peered in.

"Why is there salt in this bag?" Her eyebrows pulled together in a deep frown.

"To contain the bad ju-ju?"

Somewhere I remembered reading that salt is a cleanser for bad ju-ju. Kathy's pained expression tells me I got bad information. She held the paper bag out away from her body as she reached down for her backpack. I tried to help her with her backpack once and she nearly had a seizure. I was remonstrated with extreme prejudice. I learned to never, ever touch the backpack.

I waited patiently for Kathy to lay out her supplies. She handed me the paper bag as she gently opened a glass jar full of white sage and placed a handful in a white stone bowl, also from the backpack. She flicked a match out of, what looked like, nowhere and set the sage on fire. She then took the paper bag back, lifted the gris-gris out and wafted it over the smoke.

"What does that do?" I was genuinely curious. This might not be my last gris-gris and I didn't want to have to freak Kathy out every time one shows up on my car. I might need to do this again.

"It cleanses the magic from the area." The fire burned out and, after gently blowing the embers to black, Kathy dipped the bag into the ashes. She then lit a tea light.

"Wouldn't a bigger candle be better?" It's not that I'm superstitious. I *am* superstitious. I'm just one of those *more is better* kinda gals.

She didn't answer. I wouldn't have answered either. I annoy myself almost as much as I annoy Kathy.

She pried the bag open and poured the contents onto the table. She sifted through the spilled contents with cautious hesitation. Grains and grit were grouped into little piles on the glass with careful flicks of her fingernail.

Kathy is meticulous.

She tilted her head to one side and appeared to ponder the mosaic of herbs, stones, feathers, bone bits, ant eyeballs and whatnot spread over the small table. She looked at me, head down, eyes rolled up, peering through her bangs and sighed.

"Tara." She sighed again.

I scratched a spot behind my ear and peered back at her through my bangs. We've done this before.

"Tara." She closed her eyes, as if she's in pain.

My eyebrows were raised so high they had completely disappeared under my hair. I was nodding my head at her as if I can will her to just skip the freaking lecture and tell me what I need to know.

"Is this bad?"

"Damn, Tara. I have told you over and over that this website of yours is bad for your karma."

This is a true statement. I couldn't argue with her on this. She tells me every time I see her that my "aura" is shifting from peachy blue-green to gray.

She tells me my insistence on referring to the bungalow ghosts as "entertaining" only invites more ghosts in. She says this like it's a bad thing. I happen to know differently.

She lectures me on finding my place—the refuge being built by my higher self. She says if I could visit it just once and see what a shit-hole I am creating, I would stop everything I am doing immediately and take up yoga. I nicknamed Kathy after this particular lecture. Marley. She made it sound like I was forging chains of Scrooge proportions. I never call her "Marley" to her face. Kathy hates ghosts. Someday, I am going to have to ask her why. The time just hasn't been right yet. Not that I really care about waiting for the right time. Okay, really, I just usually forget.

Kathy's knee was bobbing up and down as she raised and lowered the heel of her foot, over and over. Kathy has very few nervous habits. Bopping her heel up and down is one of them. She sighed one last time.

"OK. Let's do this."

I tried not to make a face, but I have no self-discipline.

"Don't give me that look, Tara." Kathy shook her head in a way I've seen school teachers do to a student when they know the kid is destined for jail. She began digging in her backpack again. By feel she pulled out a white feather, a small pink quartz stone, a small pair of scissors and a white string. She placed the white feather over the black feather from the bag. She placed the quartz over the obsidian. She picked up what looked like a doll made of straw that came from the gris-gris bag, clipped the black string off and rewrapped it with the white string. She sprinkled some kind of powder over the ant eyeballs and muttered a chant.

"There." She looked up at me, and smiled. "Now let's do your car."

I followed her obediently through the bungalow and out to the car. She carried the tea light and I carried the white bowl.

Bad things had been happening out front while Kathy and I were playing voodoo out back. A man with brown hair, was climbing out of an Alpha Romeo Spider convertible and onto my driveway. It wasn't like I had a premonition or anything, but I knew this had to be Howard. And he made my stomach hurt. He smiled, but it faded as he took note of what Kathy and I were carrying.

"Howard?"

He blinked in surprise and shifted focus from the lit tea light in Kathy's hand to me and my white stone bowl. He put his hand out to shake mine. I shifted the bowls' weight to the crook of one arm and took it.

"Howard Payne?"

Finally, he answered. "Yes." He paused for a second. "How did you know?"

I stared at him, as blankly as possible and, in all serious-ness said, "I'm psychic."

Kathy snorted.

"'Scuse us for a sec. K?" I brushed past Howard to my car and placed the bowl on the hood. My car is a classic Keys Cruiser. It is a 1984 Cadillac convertible, banana yellow and loaded. Everything works but the AC. I bought it at an estate sale in Ft. Meyers. A lot of people retire to Ft. Meyers to die. They have a lot of estate sales there. It has forty thousand miles on it and was only driven on weekends to the store and to church. It's probably haunted, too, but for less than two grand, I can live with the ghosts.

Kathy walked the perimeter of the vehicle waving the candle about and chanting. After placing the tea light on the dash of the car, she went to the bowl, dipped her hand in, wiped out a handful of smudge and dabbed a bit on the car at various intervals. She's all business.

I returned my attention to Howard with the brown hair and arresting blue eyes. My hand kind of tingled where he'd touched me, making me feel much like a fifteen-year-old with her first crush. Not good.

"So." I captured his attention with a direct, slightly rude stare. "Do you really have my phone number?"

He hesitated for a moment, as if he wasn't sure how to an-swer. He looked like he wanted to do nothing more than climb back into his Spider and take off. He looked a little sad and forlorn, as if he'd come here expecting something and got something else. His eyes burned into mine, almost will-ing me to be what he was expecting. But since I have no idea what the vision in his head was, I stared back, pursed my lips, raised my left eyebrow and waited. I was hoping he would listen to that little voice of caution that was telling him to run.

Instead, he squared his shoulders, gave me his most business-like, eye-to-eye contact-look and said, "I do have your phone number, yes."

Howard and I were going to have to talk about stalking laws. As far as I knew, my number wasn't listed anywhere in the digital or print universe.

"Are you . . ."

I looked toward my cruiser where he's pointing and raised my eyebrows in question, giving him time to finish. It's wrong of me to play with strangers like this, but he came into my world uninvited, invaded my privacy—and then he made my hand tingle. I would never forgive him. Howard's jaw was clenched, his lips were parted ever so slightly, enough for me to see his pearly white, clenched teeth and his bottom lip was slightly fuller than the top. It was kind of cute really, for a suit.

"Just . . ." He gritted out.

This was paining him. I could tell. I waited.

"Going to *leave* that candle . . . burning like . . . well. Like that?"

I contemplated the tea light on the car dash for a second. "We have to." I offered no further explanation. He wouldn't understand it if I took days to explain it.

"It *is* small, I guess."

"Yeah." I chewed my bottom lip in genuine consternation. "I wanted at least a votive but Kathy says a tea light should be enough."

Howard seemed to take that answer for what it was worth and just dropped the subject. Not his car. Not his problem. I like him already.

No, wait. I don't.

"Do you need me to stay Tara?" Kathy was heading back to the bungalow with the white stone bowl. She's not asking because she thinks it might be dangerous to leave me alone with a strange man. This is the Florida Keys. Everyone is strange. She just hopes she can use my "personal safety" as an excuse to hear what's going on.

Information. Friend or foe, we've got to know. Gossip hounds, all of us.

I nodded my head, yes. She smiled.

"I'll be right back. Gotta get my stuff."

It didn't occur to her until a few minutes later, as we were settling in at my kitchen table, that she was now trapped inside my haunted bungalow.

CHAPTER TWO

Haunted Bungalow Number Three

HOWARD PAYNE, I suspect is completely devoid of a sense of humor. I suspect something else, too. From the top of his perfectly cut brown hair, six-feet down to his brand new Sebago Docksiders, I suspect Howard is looking for a life. There's no ring or tan line from a ring on his finger. The Alpha Romeo Spider tells me he has no kids. He keeps looking down at his hands and out the front window, but never at me—until he's talking. I'm guessing he's only slightly older than me. I'm betting he was just starting to let go of his corporate identity. The Tommy Bahamas ensemble is as new as his shoes.

He cleared his throat, clenched his jaw (like this is a task he just needs to get through before he can get back to his real work) and started talking.

"First of all, thank you for taking the time out of your busy day to talk to me, Ms. Cole."

My hair is French braided into two pigtails, because it keeps it off my neck and out of my face without giving me a headache. Plus, I like to play with the tails. I curled one pigtail over my thumb, under my index finger, over my middle finger and started flicking the end with my ring finger. Kathy kicked me under the table. I knew from her reaction that my eyes were starting to glitter with mischief. I can't help it. Serious people have this effect on me.

Howard was looking down at his hands and playing with his watch as he soldiered on, "My grandmother can't say enough nice things about you and all that you've done for her club."

Hold one. *Grandmother?*

"Who's your grandmother?" Kathy got this question out before I could. She's always quicker on the uptake than me. My previous employment in the digital world beat the urge to ask first, and deal with the consequences later, right out of me. I listen. I contemplate. Kathy just asks.

"Nana didn't tell you I'd be contacting you?"

That is adorable. *Nana.*

I have few relatives who will claim me. I've never had a relative who would tolerate being called by a name like Nana. I can't help myself. I have to tease him.

"No." I looked up at the ceiling fan as if I was seriously contemplating whether anyone named "Nana" had contacted me. I have to apologize. I know it's infantile of me. After this *one* little fall from grace, I promise to do better. "I would remember a call from someone named . . . *Nana.*"

Jesus, I am *such* a bitch. I have got to work on this someday. I make a note to myself that when I start to really care, I should either work on it or kill myself.

Kathy kicked me again under the table and took over the conversation.

"What's Nana's given name?"

He sucked his teeth for a second and shook his head as if silently wondering how he could have said something like that in the first place. Maybe he's suffering from corporate burnout. God, I hope he didn't get one of my revenge gifts and fall off the deep end.

"I'm sorry. Wendy Grimes. Her name is Wendy. She belongs to the Keys Crafting Society?"

I stared at him. He stared back. It was a pleading kind of stare on his part, a silent cry for kindness in spite of his conversational curse—what's a better term? I pondered it. The word "blithering" fits rather nicely.

He blinked.

I smiled. It wasn't a nice smile, but only someone who knows me very well would recognize that. Someone like . . .

"Oh yeah!" Kathy's thrilled to have the whole situation come clear. Kathy sincerely believes there is a simple answer to every problem.

Yeah, someone like Kathy. Fortunately Kathy was distracted with the puzzle that was Howard and she had just solved it.

How did he get my number and address?

Kathy answer: Nana gave it to him.

Tara answer: He spends months sleuthing the Internet and government files and then more months stalking me. Thousands of dollars go into his search. And anyone who will go to such extremes is up to no good.

I liked my answer better. I'm almost always wrong. One of these days, though, I might be right.

"She does the most beautiful lace work." Kathy's off and running. She's *completely* forgotten her quest for gossip. She also seems to have, at least temporarily, shed her ghost paranoia. Men have that effect, I've noticed. I can be in the middle of a cataclysmic disaster and if a guy is within twenty feet of me, I feel completely safe. I realize this is a terrible thing, but I've never been able to get over it. Now, if they would just keep to that twenty-foot distance, I could have guys around all the time.

By some perverse cosmic joke, I have a look that says to men, "She's huggable!" Men see my oversized green eyes and think: Garbo snuggling a seal pup. I'm not huggable.

I'm not into casual anything. I spent ten years working almost exclusively with men whom I couldn't date and still expect respect from them the next day at work. This is because guys categorize women in three ways.

Way one: I'd do her.

Way two: I'd do her in front of your mother.

Way three: You couldn't pay me to do her.

I've worked long and hard to fall into that last category. It's a hard habit to break once it's perfected.

After two years of freedom, I still have no clue how to let my guard down with out ending up in an orgy at some stranger's house. This is a small island. People talk. I've found it easier to just keep everyone at arms' length.

Howard was looking around the bungalow. "I see you have several of her pillows yourself." He smiled as his eyes lit on the sofa. Two of Wendy's handmade bobbin lace pillows lay casually on top of several other handcrafted pillows. Wendy's design contains a dolphin in the middle. "What are yours stuffed with?"

It's a legitimate question. The uninitiated wouldn't think to ask. The pillows I sell come with the following inserts: cat hair, dog hair, dried strawberries mixed with barley husks, horse hair, dust bunnies, Maleluca blooms and feathers.

Yes. I know Maleluca is the source of the ever popular New Age cure-all called tea-tree oil, a natural antibacterial agent, but its flowers are an upper respiratory nightmare for the allergy jet set here in South Florida. As the trees suck the wetlands dry, the flowers kill off countless numbers of asthmatics. I buy bags of them from the farmers along Krome Ave. Krome is a dividing line. It cuts like a knife through the cancer that is Miami and the lethal beauty of the Everglades.

Until the 1980 Mariel boat lift, when Castro opened the prisons and mental hospitals and an exodus of approximately 125,000 Cubans came to the shores of South Florida, no one had ever heard of Krome Avenue and its infamous

detention center. Now, commuters trying to avoid the tolls
on the Turnpike, die in head-on crashes every week driving
it. It's lined with so many Maleluca trees that the sun is almost permanently blocked from reaching the swamp below
and developers are eagerly awaiting the inevitable ruination
of the wetlands. Once the swamp is gone, the houses will go
up. It's an avenue of despair on every possible level. I love
driving Krome. Whenever I am on it, I hear the line from the
movie *Men in Black* in my head.

"Your world is about to end." Yep. In the meantime, it's a
great source for the Maleluca blooms I use as one of the fill-
ings for my allergy pillows.

A customer can special-order a filling and I try to find it.
That's how I happened on the Maleluca blooms in the first
place. Special request. The buyer goes through an extra
screen before the order is processed, requiring them to swear
on their first-born child's toes that the intended recipient of
this gift is not *lethally* allergic to the substance in the insert.
Believe it or not, this seems to stop some people from order-
ing. They are either stopping to think for a minute if they
really want to do this, or they are kids who just think the disclaimer is hysterically funny and are coming back to that
page over and over to read it. It pains me a bit to think that
people are probably buying them for their own beds and so-
fas. Down is my most popular seller. But what can I do.
Some people are just willing to pay a small fortune for handmade lace.

"Cat hair." I smiled back at Howard. Precious was wrapping herself around his feet, just as I said it. "Hers, mostly."

"And the urns? Are they . . ." Howard pointed to the set of
seasonal urns on the windowsill behind me. They were the
Mother's Day set of the Elegant line. If you didn't know better, you would think it was just a ceramic tea set and vase full
of silk flowers.

"Great Uncle Lester. He despised holidays."

This seemed to stop the conversation dead for a full minute. I anticipated the kick-under-the-table and moved just as Kathy tried to land it. She kicked Howard instead.

"Ohmygod." She groaned. "I am *so* sorry."

"'sokay. Ok." He rubbed his shin. "I should have moved out of the way, too."

Howard's shoulders slumped a little, his chin dipped nearly to his chest and he sighed. He spoke without looking at me—a first for him.

"So. You use the urns for a little revenge of your own."

It was a flat statement of fact. Uncle Les had hated holidays and he went out of his way to ruin every one of them for the entire family. When he'd stipulated that no one would inherit his money unless I kept his ashes in my home, the seasonal urns just serendipitously seemed right. The man had spent his entire life trying to get the last word and manipulating everyone he knew into doing things his way. Putting his ashes in the holiday urns should have given *me* the last word. But Uncle Les wouldn't let a little thing like death slow him down. Some people are just a force of nature, unstoppable.

The light above us flicked on and off, quickly, almost like Christmas tree lights except the pattern was three quick blinks, pause, and then another quick blink. Usually Lester leaves them on after that. This time? No.

Kathy's spine stiffened up. I could see the hair on her arms stand on end. Kathy just remembered why she doesn't stay inside my bungalow for more than five minutes.

"UPS!"

In the nick of time, Nick, the cute UPS guy.

"Hey, Nick. It's right there inside the door."

"Business is good, eh?"

I got up from the table to help Nick haul the boxes out to the van. Kathy managed to get out several apologies as to why she couldn't stay longer and raced past me and through the front door. Howard followed us awkwardly, as if not sure what just happened.

We were all out in front of the bungalow, which is more reaction than Great Uncle Lester's little display deserved. As I got to the UPS truck I felt a spray of water hit me. Not alot of water, just a drop. Kathy was shaking her bottled water out on the ground all around her car before getting in and driving off. I felt that this tactic might or might not work. Ghosts, I am told, will not cross water. I do not think a drizzle of Evian is going to stop a determined phantasm.

Great Uncle Lester isn't going to leave me anytime soon in any case. I suspect he is seriously ticked off about the seasonal urns I keep his ashes in. He's not going anywhere until he gets his point across. He's going to have to do a lot better than flicking lights on and off if he wants to accomplish that.

Howard was still looking at the water soaking into the sand where Kathy's car had been parked, as if he can't quite reconcile this new behavior with the nice young woman he had just been talking to.

I looked at the damp sand and then at Howard, "She has issues."

He glanced at the tea light still burning on my car dash. Point taken. I have a few issues too.

"I don't believe we've met Mr. . . . ." Nick let the question hang in the air as he forced Howard to shake his hand.

Where the hell are my manners? I attempt to salvage the faux pas.

"Nick. This is Howard Payne." Part one accomplished. "Howard. This is Nick Sams, my incredibly cute UPS guy." Ditto, part two.

Nick really *is* cute, in a way only a UPS uniform can set off to perfection. As guys go, Nick's all right in my book— nosey as hell, though. But, aren't we all?

"Howard Payne." Nick said this like he's thinking. He might be for all I know. I give him a minute. He has that

Palm Beach Country Club look with bangs just touching his eyebrows. I've already teased him about his perfect eyebrows. I accused him of plucking. He swears to me they are naturally that shape. There are only two ways to know this for sure. I could keep him locked up in my bungalow for two months and see if they grow out or I could have a kid with him and see if the kid has perfect eyebrows.

Whatever he was searching his brain for surfaced, "*You* just bought the old Sells place up the beach. You two are neighbors!" If Nick were a dog he would definitely be a Labrador. Everything is great news to him.

Howard lives less than a mile from me and he drives it? Sheesh. I have found my soul mate. He must hate walking almost as much as I do.

"I have a delivery for you. Hang on a sec." He leaned into the truck and plucked a package off the top of the stack. They went through the usual, polite UPS procedure where Howard signed the electronic screen and Nick, clicked a few boxes on the screen to indicate the delivery is complete.

"Wish I could stay and chat, but I've got other deliveries to make. You working at the bar tonight, Tara?"

"Yeah, until the night crew comes in." Part of the reason I am here in the Keys and not somewhere else is to help out a friend. Well, and the free rent—which I only get because I help out a friend. See? Altruistic. I can feel my karma getting fluffier by the second.

Sherry, a sorority sister from better days, called me a little over a year ago in a deep blue funk after her divorce, complaining that she inadvertently won custody of Crusty's Bar and had no desire to run it. I was at loose ends. I can run a website from almost anywhere, and the artistic and culinary resources for making my revenge gifts are first rate here in Islamorada. I would have done it for her if she lived in Siberia. She is that good of a friend. Plus I bartended my way through college and therefore I'm qualified.

And they say we don't use anything we learn in college once we graduate. Live and learn.

Nick was leaving. "Maybe I'll stop in later." He might just. He wants to know *all* about Howard Payne. For that matter, so do I. Hand-tingling and stomach-hurting aside, he's yet to tell me why he's living next door and stalking me.

"Bye."

Howard and I waved him away politely. He came perilously close to backing into Howard's Spider. We held our breaths. Missed it. Life is good. I returned to the business at hand.

"I have to get going as well. Perhaps we can discuss your idea on another day?"

"Where do you work?" I'm thinking that if Howard were a dog, he would be a hound dog. Nosey.

"Don't be offended, Howard, but I need to chat with Nana before I give you my life's history. Nothing personal."

CHAPTER THREE

Bad Omens

Crusty's Bar. Ocean Side, Islamorada

I HAVE ONE customer.

"Hey Sam." I give him the same greeting every afternoon. And in return—yeah, there's the wave. He brought his thumb and middle finger to the rim of his Costa Del Mar sunglasses and tipped them down to the end of his nose, gives me the look—like I forgot to dress today and he's enjoying the show.

"You know what I want, babe."

Sam leaned toward me in his usual effort to look down my shirt. Higher education was completely wasted on this man. Sad. I hate being called Babe.

"Kir Royale?" Kir Royale is a "poofter" drink. Ten years ago no respectable bar south of Miami would have served it. Hell, no one south of Miami would have known such a libation existed. Times, they are a-changing.

"I knew you loved me." He flipped his sunglasses back up to cover his sky blue eyes and started to run his fingers through his streaked blond, shoulder-length hair. He caught himself, just in time, looked around to make sure no one saw that, and flipped his hair back using his most macho shrug. One of Sam's finer qualities, and the reason I don't flame him outright, is that deep down, he is as close to a girl as a guy can get. I, on the other hand, lean more toward the guy end of the girls' scale of feminine qualities. We make a cute couple, Sam and me. I poured myself a shot of Drambuie after I fixed Sam's drink.

Sam has it all. Looks. Money. But for all his finer qualities, he is currently unattached and someone is tired of banging him. It's a common story here in the Keys. I gave him my best smile as I slid his chardonnay and crème de cassis onto the coaster in front of him. I should use a sparkling wine, but Sam doesn't know the difference. The smile is a wasted effort on him. His eyes were fixated on the mirror behind me. He is watching the guys walking in from the street entrance. A string of Harley Davidson cycles are now parked in view of the bar's front window. Men are so fickle. But, interesting. I wonder if it's the bikes or the bikers that grab his interest. I'm guessing both.

A view in the Keys is everything. In a bar on the best dock in Islamorada—which is where Crusty's is—no expense is spared on windows and mirrors. You can see the water from every angle of the room. Ceiling fans are on high to give the illusion of a tropical breeze. Years ago, the windows would have all been wide open and the bar patrons would have enjoyed a real ocean breeze. Now, however, tourists coming straight from Disney World expect air-conditioning.

No one sweats anymore.

"What can I get ya'll?" I handed them menus and placed coasters in front of each of them. There are five of them seated so far. I can see a few stragglers puffing on cigarettes outside. I'm guessing they're Europeans and the bikes are rented. Americans with enough money to buy a Harley don't smoke.

"Ya got any real beer here?" The accent was Australian. I'm off by a few continents. Sue me. I'm also screwed out of a tip.

Australian men treat women like crap.

Razzing American beer is only the beginning. Of this fact, I am certain.

I have express permission from the owner, my best friend Sherry, to—and I quote—"Treat squids as badly as I like." And, as far as I'm concerned, almost everyone on the planet qualifies as a squid at some point or another. As with their oceanic equivalent, human squids come in all sizes and can be found all over the place, are quite tasty to sea creatures and some gastronomically adventurous humans, serve a useful purpose in the general eco-socio system, but at some point or another extrude an ick-factor that impels me to comment. It's an all-inclusive insult. I try not to discriminate, naturally, but some people just demand the moniker more than others, customers for example.

Don't visit the Keys for stellar service—at least, not in the summer.

This is not a chain of resort islands. It's a chain of islands settled by wreckers, smugglers, pirates and people who don't want to be bothered. In the winter, northerners who believe service is a professional career take up residence, four to a condo on the ocean side, and shock regulars by providing five-star service.

But right now, it's summer. The summer servers—or locals—prefer that you get behind the bar or go into the main wait yourself and get it. It is not unheard of for an establishment to post a self-serve sign on an unlocked door, because the owner/proprietor is out fishing or running in a load of drugs and/or illegal aliens. Fishing and the tourist trade are the skin that covers up the real business of most locals. If fishing is the skin, drugs are the blood that flows through the veins of these islands pumping life through their heart. Most people couldn't afford to live here otherwise.

Over the main door into Crusty's is a sign. PEOPLE WHO BITCH WILL BE SHOT. Crusty's is not kid-friendly. For that matter, as you might have already guessed, neither am I.

"There's a list of all the beers we have available on the back of the menu." I'm guessing he can read. I could be wrong. If he were American I would read it to him. Make of that statement what you will. Since he's not American, I headed for the bar and another shot of Drambuie.

I *could* close early—Sherry doesn't need the money. She just keeps the bar open to annoy her ex-husband. She got the liquor license in the divorce and he had to sell her the bar at a court-appraised cost.

Her ex, Dennis, is a regular. He keeps hoping he can close the place down, the spiteful little shit. I caught him last month with a Ziploc full of roaches and the county health code inspector's home number displayed on his cell phone. I have carte blanche to be rude to him. It's one part of the job description I consider a real pleasure. As he was reaching for the Ziploc in his front pocket, I inserted, set off a small bug bomb inside his boxers from the back, and got out of the way. He sent Sherry a bill for his therapy sessions after that little episode. She paid it. She paid me a bonus.

I would have done it for free.

"Oi, Girlie." The koala crew was motioning me back to their table. The rest of the group had arrived. Six men. Two women. Aussies having a hard time getting even numbers for the boy-girl line up? Go figure. "We'll have three pitchers of this an' eight orders of ceviche with extra crackers, *if* you would be so kind."

Our Haitian cook, Riqué, refuses to prepare ceviche for reasons he has yet to articulate in any language but Creole.

Of everything they could have selected, they pick the one item that I have to fix. Good menu choice. I stare at the sign above the door behind them. I need to change it to "Customers" instead of "People" because I seriously want to bitch.

I brought them the pitchers of beer, chilled mugs and crackers. After checking to make sure all was well in the guest area, I slid back into the main wait to set up eight ceviches. Riqué watched me suspiciously. The only word I understand of his mutterings is *morte*. Death.

Ok. Yes, it is possible to get ciguatera (along with numerous other hellish diseases) from raw fish, but I figure the lime juice kills most of the really nasty bugs and the rest is just Darwinian roulette. Cooking doesn't kill ciguatera anyway.

I mix up the ceviche myself with key limes and cilantro from my garden twice a week. And no, I'm not nature girl. I just happen to have a key lime tree, and cilantro is the only shrub the local insects will leave alone. I've tried everything else.

Sometimes I even catch the fish that goes into the mix. Since this is highly "illegal" (almost everything is nowadays), I don't advertise this small fact.

I sanitized the scoop with very hot water from the tap. This is also the scoop I use at the bar for anyone annoying enough to order ice cream drinks. I douse it with vodka before dipping. This kills any lingering germs. I think.

Eight of Sherry's cute glass fish plates from the fridge with healthy looking leaves of zero-nutritional-value iceberg lettuce and two scoops of ceviche each, covered with thinly sliced red onion and wella. We have koala chow.

Puddin, one of the three bar cats who live in the main wait, gets a scoop as well. Puddin has an eating disorder. He refuses to eat cat food. If human lips won't touch it, neither will Puddin's. I really can't blame him. Puddin weighs in at over twenty-six pounds, gargantuan by cat standards. Puddin could stand to do a few laps in the pool. Not my cat. Not my vet bill. Not my problem.

Puddin meows polite thanks and attacks the ceviche. Spoiled rotten.

Bad things have happened while I'm in the back doing Riqué's job.

"Hi, Tara, how's business?" Dennis's new wife, Kerry—and yes, I know it rhymes with Sherry. Dennis is a sick man. Did I mention he's in therapy? Anyway, Kerry was tapping perfectly manicured nails on Sherry's mahogany bar.

Kerry only comes in when Dennis is serious about starting trouble. I should've closed early.

"Business is great as always, Kerry, 'scuse me?" I have a huge tray with many dishes of ceviche stacked on it, balanced on my fingertips and shoulder. I made sure it dripped a little juice on Kerry as I bumped past her.

"God's sake, Tara!" She scooted behind the bar, grabbed the soda spray gun and, as delicately as possible, spritzed soda water on the affected spot. She alternated spritzes with dabs from a clean bar towel.

I set the tray stand down by the Aussie's and set the plates on the table. Ladies first.

Kerry hit me with her mission as soon as I put away the tray behind the bar.

"Um. I don't mean to bother you while you are working."

But, of course you do, Kerry. Why else would you come in while I am working if not to bother me?

There's something wrong with me. I know this. She's younger than me. She's far more beautiful. Even if some of her beauty is bought, it doesn't detract from the fact that she could pose for *Playboy*. God, for all I know she *has* posed for *Playboy*. I went to college. Kerry didn't. I wasted ten years after college working for IBM because I thought I was building a life, but I had no real goals. Kerry's eye has been on the ball since she was born, I bet. I am still looking for the ball. I want to dislike her. Really I do. She fits into so many categories and clichés I find unappealing. But, there is something about her that I like.

Why does she irritate me again? Oh, I remember. She's married to Dennis.

"Dennis mentioned that Sherry's gone on retreat again and he wondered when she would be coming back?"

a. How did he find out Sherry's gone?

b. No way in hell am I saying when she's due back.

Information is gold in this town. With the right information, a person can be ruined, lose a business, miss a court date, be fined, fail to pay it and be assessed a penalty. Dennis is a snake. Why the hell doesn't Sherry take out a restraining order on these two?

I lied. "I expect her back tomorrow, Kerry. Check back with me then. Can I get you a drink?" Kerry is a closet alcoholic. She usually doesn't touch the stuff—but when she does, watch out. It's horrible of me to push alcohol on her, but I need to know what Dennis is up to. "On the house."

"Oh, well then. That's very sweet of you. I'll have a blush wine, whatever is open." Kerry sincerely believes that blush wine is what wealthy people drink. Someday, if she ever attains human status and grows a soul, I will tell her that wealthy people drink whatever the hell tastes good to them. I will point out that Mad Dog 20/20 was probably the original blush wine—that and Boone's Farm.

I poured her a glass of Sutter Home. Kerry choked down a sip and reached for the bar crackers. I don't blame her. I prefer Gallo.

Bad omens are all over the bar. I snagged out my Tarot cards and shuffled. A quick lay out under the rack of clean glasses, where the squids couldn't see, even if they hauled their lazy asses up and walked over instead of yelling at me. My sense of foreboding only increased with each card.

I know you're wondering why a skeptic like me reads

Tarot cards. Well, it's a mystery to me, too. I guess I took one too many trips to Casadega in college and now I can't shake the whole New Age thing. Casadega is a small town just off I-4 on the way to Daytona. Every house has a psychic or two in residence who will tell your fortune. Some require an appointment. I always thought they should know I was on the way and pencil me in anyway. They're psychics for Christ's sake. I think the last psychic I visited doubled her fee when I made that joke. I can't blame her. It's what I would have done. I'm a pain in the butt.

By the third gulp Kerry had sat down on the leather barstool and found her drinking rhythm. She glanced down at my Tarot cards and rolled her eyes. Was that liner tattooed on? It was too perfect for the casual morning makeup pencil sweep.

Dennis did well by himself in the divorce from Sherry, who has more money than any god or goddess you can think of, but not well enough to keep up the lifestyle he and Kerry were living. Some of the diamonds on her could be faux, but knowing Kerry, I seriously doubted it. I was beginning to wonder if Dennis had taken a walk on the dark side. If so, he was slimy enough to grease his way all the way to the top—if he didn't get himself killed. What a happy thought.

I scooped up the cards and shuffled again, this time thinking about Dennis. I drew the top card. The Devil. I drew the second. The Fool. Interesting. Dennis had to be The Fool—so who was The Devil leading him down the brimstone path to badness?

"Where's Dennis?" I refilled her wine glass.

She shifted on the barstool and leaned in toward me like what she's about to say is some big secret. I ignore the fact that Sam has turned on one of the bar TV's on, to CNN. I hate TV. "He's at the kick off party for the Holiday Isle Dolphin Tournament."

I leaned into her and my voice lowered an octave in sympathetic, girl-talk mode. "And you didn't go because?"

"It's the kick off party." She downed half the glass in one gulp.

Oh yeah. No cameras yet. The press doesn't take pictures until the trophies are being handed out, after the tournament ends. Not to say that Kerry is vain. Well, no, she *is* vain. But she has her priorities. Dennis is a jerk. Dennis is a fairly rich jerk. Kerry's job entails mitigating the fact that Dennis is a jerk. This includes showing up for all public events that involve photo ops. More on Kerry's job description later. She has one firm rule as far as I can see. No Cameras, No Kerry.

"His boat or charter?" I was making polite, distracting conversation. I call this circling my prey.

"*Our* boat of course." She leaned back on the stool and glared at me.

I forgot. Community property. I topped off her glass. She took a few delicate sips and just kept the glass cradled in front of her face.

Dennis never uses a charter boat. I asked just to be mean. He has his own 42 foot Bertram, a captain and mate, an arsenal of custom made matching rods and reels, numbered, and a full wet bar for when the fishing sucks.

Dennis never touches a rod himself. This makes it necessary to employ a captain who can beat a lie detector test. Most tournaments are based on the honor system. Sometimes there are actual fish dragged into the dock for a weigh in. In bill fishing, the captain takes measurements and releases the fish. Independent observers sometimes travel on the boats with the anglers. When this happens, Dennis usually loses. When there is no observer, the winning captain takes a lie detector test to confirm the veracity of his reported fishing results.

"Anyone selling pinfish or pilchards this time or is Dennis going to have to go out at four a.m. to net his own bait?"

"He's buying bait. He always does." Yeah. Any captain who can consistently pass a lie detector test probably isn't overburdened with the desire or inclination to get up at four a.m. to catch bait. There is the cost of the captain. And then, there is the cost of the captain's specialties. Dennis probably doesn't even notice. I like that about him.

"Any idea what he wants with Sherry?" I find that a direct question gets the best response if it follows a pointless exchange of pleasantries. There's no time for the person to drum up a fake answer. If Kerry says nothing, I fill the silence with more small talk and try again in a few.

Nothing. No answer. If it were anyone else, I would say it was caution causing the lack of response. With Kerry, it could just be that she has no idea.

"He probably wants to load up with free ice again." Kerry was going to have to respond to that. She hates it when I intimate Dennis is a mooch.

"You have the worst opinion of Dennis, Tara. And, I'm sure I have no idea why." Kerry downed the rest of her wine in two gulps and carefully placed the glass on the bar. She held the base in place as if it might get away from her. Kerry is on the road to being hammered. Light weight. She probably hasn't eaten in days . . . sucks for her. I refilled her glass.

"What did I say?"

"You know perfectly well what you said. You just implied that Dennis only wants to see Sherry to load up on free ice. Well. For your information, he bought his own ice maker a month ago."

"New or used?" It's a legitimate question.

"God's sake, Tara. You know we only buy new. And is it any business of yours anyway?" Kerry grabbed a hand full of bar nuts and proceeded to munch. Damn. Food might slow down the effect of the alcohol. Why the hell do I put out bar snacks anyway? I considered snatching the bowl away. Kerry grabbed the bowl with one hand and scooped out a handful with the other. She tried tossing one up in the air and catching it with her mouth, but missed. It hit her smack center in the eyeball. Hand-eye coordination is usually the first thing to go. Tragic. I almost felt bad for her. If she had spilled the information I wanted on Dennis, I might even have helped her out. As it was, I simply backed out of the way and let her flush her eye in the bar sink with shot glass after shot glass full of bottled water.

If the cornea's scratched, she's going to have a very red eye for the fishing trophy pictures. Dennis is going to be pissed. Not my spouse. Not my problem.

The closing crew was straggling into the bar. They all have on clean and pressed Crusty's polo shirts, shorts that cover almost nothing, sneakers, bobby socks and the trusty Crusty's hat. I wear none of these articles of clothing. I made certain stipulations when I agreed to fill in the shift gaps during the slow hours. One of the stipulations was that the uniform was a no go. I am not twenty-one. I was never twenty-one. I do not wear shorts that require surgery to extract them from the crack of my ass at the end of the shift.

I noticed that Kay had beaded strings hanging suspiciously down from the waistband at the side of her shorts. A fad. The undies have tassels, or something, with beads, which the wearer untucks for show on the outside of the outfit. Don't make me explain further. It's too painful. I wondered if this makes peeling the shorts off her body any easier at the end of the shift.

"You figure out what that was on your car last night?" Kay reached around Kerry to tuck her purse under the bar. She keyed her employee number into the register to clock in. "What's with her?"

Nothing escapes Kay's notice.

"Attacked by a bar nut. And it was a gris-gris bag. Why do you ask?"

Kay pulled an apron out from under the register and tied it around her waist. "Ya got another one out there, bigger." This last bit came from over her shoulder as she hustled to a table to take an order. "It's moving."

```
// Thought for the day on the Home Page of
Revenge-Gifts.com,
scheduled to load on Saturday.
  if (Sys_Date.getDay() == 6) {
                DayofWeek = "Saturday";
                TaraQuote = "
```

I had an epiphany last night. During a phone conversation with my one and only sister, during which she accused me of never calling and of avoiding her calls, I realized why our parents never beat us as children. It had nothing to do with modern parenting methods and the belief that hitting a child only teaches that child to hit. It had nothing to do with parental affection for adored offspring. Beatings just weren't needed.

Why?

Because Little Shit and I beat on each other enough to satisfy any parents requirements for daily child abuse. Mom and Dad never had to lay a finger on us. My sister and I pounded on each other every hour, on the hour.

New Bumper Sticker: Every parent's dream. Galapagos. Only people who read Kurt Vonnegut will understand it. They are the only people who matter anyway.";

```
  document.write(DayofWeek  +  " : "  +
  TaraQuote);
  // -->
  </script>
```

CHAPTER FOUR

Zeke

IT'S SUNDAY.

I used to savor Sundays. Now? It's just another day in paradise.

Kathy and I were doing the usual, lazing on Sherry's boat down at the dock and drinking ice-cold Corona's. Sherry bought hammock chairs and mounts for under the Tuna Tower just for Kathy and me. Carlos, her boat captain, says they ruin a perfectly good fishing boat. Sherry had Tamarind Welding through-bolt two recessed hooks to hold the chairs. A stainless steel flap covers the hooks when the chairs are taken down.

Carlos is a whiny pain in the ass.

Just thinking about it makes me want to call him and make him take us out on the water for the day. He's under Sherry's orders to do whatever I ask when she's out of town. If Sherry were a guy I think I would have to marry her. She's the perfect spouse. She cooks, too.

I am now the proud owner of one adorable ball of fluff. Precious is beautiful. This is true. Precious is gorgeous in a way that only a white, ten-year-old Persian can be. We know each other well, Precious and I. But, little black-haired, blue-eyed Zeke and I are going to be buds.

In the second gris-gris bag left on my Keys Cruiser last night was a tiny, black Persian kitten wearing a solid gold collar that said "Zeke." If I am on someone's shit list, I hope it's forever. I love this cat.

"You realize, of course, that you can't keep him?" Kathy was trying to rain on my sunny day.

"I'm keeping him. Just look at him." I had a sleepy little Zeke cradled in the palm of one hand with his tiny legs interlaced between fingers and his tail wrapped around my wrist. He was half-heartedly clawing at my index finger and biting the nail polish off. This could be bad for him. If true, then Zeke and I will be going down together because I am constantly chewing off my nail polish. Bad habit. Zeke understands.

Precious was crashed out on the gunnel over the transom.

Ok, I hear the non-boat people bitching from here. The gunnel is that wide shelf that runs around the perimeter of the boat. People sit on it when there are no chairs and risk falling overboard when the boat accelerates. The transom is the back wall of the boat. For more than this, you are going to have to buy a copy of Chapman's.

Where was I? Oh yeah. Precious is whipped. She and Zeke raced all over the bungalow last night, all night. I finally had to put them outside the bedroom and close the door.

"Tara, you can't keep him. He could be seriously bad news."

Zeke is purring so loud I think they can hear him in Key West, a hundred miles south of here.

"You think he's a shape-shifter?" I said this in all seriousness. I don't discount any weird possibilities these days.

"Are you mocking me?" Kathy looked hurt. Damn.

"I mock you not. I swear."

Sometimes I wonder how people delineate what is reality and what is fantasy. In Kathy's case, I always guess wrong on where the line is drawn. She is fully into witchcraft and the occult and yet she can't even entertain the possibility that Zeke is a shape-shifter. You wouldn't believe the things she *does* believe in.

I personally set zero limits on what's possible. For all I know, Zeke is an alien life form sent to Earth to report back on why Precious never calls her mother.

"Did you ever call Wendy?" Kathy knows I'm not giving up the cat, so she moved on to a different subject.

"I did not."

"Aren't you even a little curious about her grandson?"

"I am not."

She snorted. Kathy knows I am lying.

I compound the damage by lying further. "I *swear* I'm not."

The suspicious sound of a cell phone dialing brought me out from under my sunglasses and I stopped spinning the chair around in circles to see what Kathy's doing now.

"Mrs. Grimes? This is Kathy." You can hear the smile in Kathy's voice when she talks. She's like a warm feather mattress. I could hear Wendy admonishing Kathy to call her Wendy. She hates being called a "Mrs." anything. I always wondered what her husband was like. I've never noticed any pictures of him in her house.

"Yes, Miss Wendy, she's here. No, ma'am, we are not drinking alcohol before noon." Kathy paused for a second to listen. I searched the sky for clouds and lightning. That last whopper was a scorcher. "Yes. He came by yesterday. You called him 'Muffin' when he was little? That's so cute. Yes. He's a very handsome boy."

Boy? Nana. Nana. Nana. Your little muffin grew up into one hot set of buns.

Kathy is now glaring at me. Sometimes I think she can read my thoughts.

"He used to work for Disney? The Big Red Boat. I see. He hates boats? Oh. *Kids*." Kathy laughed. "He worked for the rat for ten years and he hates *kids?*"

She paused to listen for a minute and then stared at me again.

"No, ma'am. I don't think that makes him a bad person. You know Tara hates kids too, and I love her to death."

People will talk about you here, to your face. It's the most amazing phenomenon.

"Yes. They are perfect for each other."

Matchmaking. I knew it.

"Oh you mean their businesses?" She scrunched her face and smiled at me as if she knew exactly what affect that last sentence had on my nerves. People are just plain rotten sometimes.

"Yes."

I was getting annoyed at only hearing one side of the conversation and Zeke was making my hand sweat uncomfortably. I shifted him to the other hand and dipped the hot hand into the bucket of ice water holding the beers. I lifted one out and handed it to Kathy. She automatically popped the top for me, thus insuring that Wendy heard the beer bottle opening and now knows Kathy is a big fat liar.

Kathy handed the beer to me and glared.

I smiled.

"Well maybe they can work out a deal. I'll tell her." She listened some more. "I'll tell her." Another pause. "Ok." She sighed. "I love you, too, Miss Wendy."

Kathy means this.

She really does love Wendy. She loves almost everyone she knows. If angels walk among us, I think Kathy might just be one of them. Why she hangs out with me is a complete mystery. I count her as proof positive that if God exists, he's as warped as I am.

"What'd she say?"

"She said her grandson is a great catch and that you could do worse."

"Did not."

"Did."

"What did she really say?"

My other hand was sweating and I struggled up out of the hammock chair to put Zeke on the gunnel next to Precious. Zeke stretched for a minute and then walked around to her head to snuggle there. They are so cute.

My getting up rocked the boat a little and Precious got up and resettled herself with Zeke practically underneath her. Both of them are purring so loud I think people in Cuba can hear it. I settled back into my chair and hooked my toes onto the fly bridge ladder.

"She said he used to work for Disney."

"Figures."

"She said he retired early because they were transferring him over to the Big Red Boat."

"Poor guy."

"Yeah. Anyway. She says he hates kids and he is philosophically opposed to trapping adults on a cruise ship with their kids for a week, even if it's Disney-ized."

"Amen to that." Cruises are for teenagers on spring break and retired adults wanting to be waited on hand and foot. Cruises are not for young families with children. I can see the liabilities all over the place. Physical damage. Psychological damage resulting when Mom is seasick, the kids are crazed like trapped weasels and Dad says to his wife, as she hurls up her guts for the millionth time, "What do you expect me to do with the little rodents?"

I am seriously considering producing a series of subliminal tapes for kids that play when they are asleep, which teach the kids to always ask Dad first. Renee, my child psychotherapist friend, refuses to help me with this project. Renee concedes that there is a real need for just such a product, but she is concerned about unforeseen repercussions.

As if I care.

As if any mom truly cares about repercussions when the kids treat dad like a piece of furniture and make a beeline directly to Mom for anything and everything. I have a hypnotist friend who is in the process of renting studio time in Miami to create the test tapes. I just need a few kids to beta test them on and we are in business.

"You've got that look again, Tara."

"What look?"

"That evil look."

"Did I say anything?" I tried to look as innocent as possible. I failed.

"You don't have to *say* anything. I *know* you."

I can't argue with that. She does.

"Interesting." I decided to distract her. "So. Aside from our mutual dislike of kids, what else did Wendy have to say about Muffin?"

Kathy blew out a frustrated breath. She knows all of my tricks. She knows she is being sidelined from her true purpose in life, which is reforming me. She allows it—for now.

"She says he's invested in a shipping company in Key West and wants to set up a funeral at sea service using your urns."

"Oh lovely. Anything else?"

"She says you should do business with him. He's a good kid."

"I'm sold."

'You're not even going to consider it. Are you?"

"You know me so well."

"Why? Why won't you at least consider it?"

"Why should I?"

"Well for one thing, it would be a nicer use of your artistic talents and a far more ennobling pursuit of the almighty dollar. You would be doing a service for people. A real service."

Oh, Kathy. Will we ever see eye to eye on the human race?

"Revenge Gifts *does* provide a service."

Kathy said nothing. We've argued this out before.

"So. What are we talking about here?" I pretended to consider it. "He's going to want me to design fancy urns for people, to put ashes in, to dump off the side of a boat, three miles out."

"I think it's twelve."

"You can dump your head at three miles, are you saying ashes are worse?"

"Ok, three."

I could see she didn't want to debate human waste dumping versus human ashes dumping with me on a Sunday. Sad. Maybe Muffin will be up for that discussion. Kathy glared at me again.

"Stop reading my mind. It's creepy."

"I'm not reading your mind. I just know how you think."

"Oh yeah? And what was I thinking?"

"You were thinking about debating dumping with Howard Payne. Later."

"You're *so* wrong. I was thinking about . . ."

Kathy gave me that look, the kid-going-to-jail look.

"Well *you* lied to Wendy about the beer."

She stared at me harder.

"Ok. I *was* thinking that."

"I thought so."

"That's just creepy." I can't help shuddering. "You like him, right?"

"I think he would be a good influence on you."

"Did you ever consider that I might corrupt him? If you like him, you can't possibly want my bad karma rubbing off on the man."

She pondered that for a minute. "There's something kind

of sad in him, like he's not altogether here among the living. People come here to run away from the real world. I think Howard is here to escape. You would be good for him."

"Oh yeah. I'm a little ray of sunshine. Hanging around me will definitely cure whatever ails him." Sarcasm, who me? Kathy is one of the few people on this island who doesn't do drugs, but sometimes I wonder.

"You are so full of life. He was fascinated by you."

"Not happening."

"It's already happening." And maybe she's right, but I'm not going to tell her that.

"I don't think Howard hates kids." Kathy had that thousand-yard stare that usually means she's seeing something besides what the rest of us mortals see. I could feel a chill enter the warm tropical breeze.

"Why do you think Nana would kid about something like that?"

"Because it's how she deals with bad things—like you do. She makes a joke but with her it's so far off that it sounds wrong. With you . . ." She looked at me and sighed. "You *really* find bad things funny."

"Because it usually is bad . . . but funny."

"I think, in Howard's case, it's just bad."

"He looked perfectly normal to me." The minute I said the words I knew I was screwed. There is no such thing as normal. Not in my world anyway. By saying that, planets align into some hellish portent of bad omens, stars form patterns in the sky that take up the challenge of proving to me just how not normal Howard Payne probably is and my life goes a wee tad further down into the abyss. Shit.

There was a steady wind and the wires on the outriggers were clanging against the metal bars of the Tuna Tower. Small waves were slapping against the hull of the boat and I could hear the high whine of a jet ski, not too far off. I was suddenly cold in the 98-degree heat. Kathy shivered too. It's

like a falling sensation, only you never move a muscle. Both
Precious and Zeke hopped down from their snuggle spot and
began wrapping themselves around my feet.

"Let's do lunch today."

"Where?"

"Sushi?" I never know if Kathy is in the mood for raw fish.
Usually she wants pizza. I always ask anyway. Doesn't hurt.

"Sure."

"Deal with the beer bucket and the chairs?" I gathered up
the cats and headed to the bungalow. Talk of Howard had
brought in an ill wind. The subject was dropped for the fore-
seeable future as far as I was concerned.

"Got it." Kathy's a good boat person. Very organized, neat
and tidy. Probably planning her next "Howard" assault.

I grabbed her purse and mine from just inside the door,
slipped on my shoes and we met at her car. She hates mine.
Not because it's cursed—or haunted—but because it's a
convertible. She thinks it's dangerous. When Kathy and I go
anywhere together, she drives.

She got to the highway and waited. "Which way?"

"North."

There are a few sushi bars in Key Largo and I have absolutely no preference for one over another. I left it up to
Kathy. She picked the one with booths adorned with plastic,
shoeless, crossed legs. The glare from the sun outside
blinded me for a second after we stepped into the gloom of
the restaurant. At first, it looked like we had the place to ourselves. We didn't.

Sitting in the booth closest to the bar was none other than
the Muffin man himself. He had a dining companion.

"Is that a guy or a girl sitting over there with Howard?"
Kathy is way *mo bettah* at determining the male-female
thing than me.

"Guy." She didn't hesitate.

Howard was facing us, but his companion had his back to

us and all I could see was a ton of jet-black hair. It's braided down past the back of the seat, so I can only guess that his hair is longer than mine. Mine hits me at midwaist when it's down. It's almost never down.

I lingered a moment too long on the staring meter, trying to ascertain how Kathy could be so sure that is a guy sitting there, and Howard caught my eye.

Damn. He waved us over.

"I'm not joining them." I whispered as quietly as possible to Kathy as she swept past me to get to Howard's table. If I could only be certain about Kathy's ability to read my mind I would be projecting all kinds of STOP thoughts at her. I think her clairvoyance is selective though. She only hears my truly evil thoughts.

I followed. Reluctantly.

Howard stood up as we approached.

This one act of gallantry alone raises him ten notches in my book.

"We were just talking to Nana!" Kathy hugged him like he's her long-lost brother and Muffin seemed to handle it well.

People who are comfortable with hugging alarm me somewhat. I have a personal no-touch zone and I prefer that it not be casually violated like that—icky—minus one point. It's possible he isn't the huggable type and is just being polite. It's something to keep a close watch on in any case. Kathy knows not to hug me, ever.

"Did she give me a good rec?" He reached past Kathy to shake my hand. Eye contact, very important to him apparently.

"She did." Kathy glows when she talks to people. Did I mention that?

"This is Jack." Howard politely indicated the other man in the booth. "Jack. This is Kathy and Tara. Tara Cole."

"We were just talking about you, Miss Cole." Jack did not get up, but did, at least, turn to face us. "Please join us. We haven't ordered yet."

Jack has an accent. I can't place it right now. It's not Spanish.

"We wouldn't want to intrude." I started to decline.

"We'd love to." Kathy accepted at exactly the same time.

She's going to owe me for this. Jack smiled at me like he knew I'd rather dine with dogs. She's going to owe me—big time.

Somehow, Howard managed to tuck me in next to him, with me on the inside. Trapped. Kathy got the aisle seat next to Jack with the knowing eyes. He's staring at me and it's beginning to get on my nerves.

Howard took up two-thirds of the booth and I am scootched as far in as I can get without moving the salt, pepper, and cocktail ads to another table. He smelled faintly of coconut. I love that smell. The day was just going from bad to worse. It was the "Howard is normal" comment. I know it. I should not be sniffing the man like a bitch in heat. It's *so* not me. Not me in public, anyway.

I eased slightly out of the corner and Jack's smile widened. His eyes are a fake green, that can only be achieved with colored contacts, and his skin is perfectly tanned to a deep, golf course brown. The Tag-Hauer watch on his wrist screams money and, if I weren't sure, the Monte Blanc pen in his shirt pocket would clench the deal. The polo pony logo could be a knockoff, but I'm betting it's not. Jack lives on the rich side of U.S.-1. He shifted his gaze from me to Muffin and looked like he could eat us both for dinner. I get the distinct impression that both Jack and I are attracted to the same man. I hope I'm wrong, but I'm usually not.

"So, How do I get to be the subject of choice for the dinner conversation, guys?" I go on the attack when I'm uncomfortable. It's a nervous habit.

"Jack runs a catering business in Key Largo and in Key West." Howard picked up a business card from the table and handed it to me. I glanced at it politely. It said: Crêpe Makers.

And below it gave the usual information on how to contact the business. A small Eiffel Tower sat forlornly off in the top right corner of the card. Jack is Jacques. Jack is French. The French are second only to the Australians in treating women like crap. I'm not prejudiced. I have first-hand experience in these matters.

"He's agreed to handle the food arrangements on the cruises we book."

"What if the customer doesn't want crêpes?" I deliberately pronounced the word *crêpe* as if it rhymes with grape. I can see it's like fingernails down a blackboard to Jack. Now, *I'm* smiling—safely out of range of Kathy's feet.

"I've had their cuisine." Kathy jumped into the fray. "It's delicious. They set up at the last Pigeon Key Art Festival, and the line was wrapped around the island. They do way more than just crêpes."

Damn. She said it correctly. I felt slightly let down by this, but I forgave her.

"I am a regular customer of yours, Miss Cole."

"Call me Tara."

"Tara, then. Your seasonal urns are magnificent."

I mentally went through all the past orders and wrack my brain for more than one order from a Jack person. I drew a blank.

"Which set did you order?"

"All of them."

"All of them?" I suppressed the urge to whistle.

"Oh yes. I give them as gifts. You have a style for every kind of taste."

"Gifts." Why in the hell would someone give them away as gifts? I mean, I know the AIDS epidemic is bad in South Florida, but really . . .

"I don't use them for ashes."

Well that cleared that up.

"I put candies, cookies and treats in them and send them.

I have a gift for each season to send to my mother, aunts, uncles, and friends. They are perfect."

"And they can recycle them when one of them dies." I had to say it. I have zero self-control when staring such absurdities in the face.

I was nearly under the table wanting to laugh. The pillows I can overlook. If people order the lace "allergy" pillows because they like handmade lace pillows, there is nothing I can do to stop them. But this—this is just subversive. Using my seasonal urns as cookie jars damn near borders on sacrilegious. I may have to sue this man on principle. "Aren't they a wee tad expensive to be used as glorified cookie jars?"

"Quality is always expensive. I buy quality whenever and wherever possible. Quality lasts. Your products are all top of the line."

I suddenly had a thought: *What line?*

"Cookie jars." Kathy was grinning from ear to ear. I could see the visions of redemption dancing around in her head and it depressed me.

"Yes," Jack agreed with an even bigger grin.

The "quality" speech nearly gave me Aileen-style hives and I suddenly wanted to be anywhere else but here. I started to excuse myself, and placed my hand on Muffin's arm to indicate that I needed to exit the booth, when the waitress arrived and blocked all of us in. I was trapped.

"Miss Cole!" The waitress knows me. "The usual for you?" She knows me real well.

"Yes. Thank you, Tina."

"And to drink?" She politely hovered over her order pad and waited.

"Mineral water please." I don't have to ask for the lime. Tina knows her business.

"Battling a hangover today, Miss Cole?" Tina knows me a little too well. I am now considering taking my business to another sushi bar. Unfortunately, everyone on this island talks to everyone else. I'm guessing this appalling familiarity would be the same no matter what sushi bar I frequented.

"Nope. Just a little too much sun." So? I lied. The company I'm in is giving me a bad stomach. My nerves are starting to stretch uncomfortably under my skin. Muffin smells good enough to eat and Jack is still staring at me with that look. Kathy is glowing, as usual. I would much rather have a shot of Drambuie and Tina probably knows it. Tina would draw her own conclusions anyway.

The fact that Kathy and I were doing lunch with Howard and Jack will be all over the Keys before sunset. Kathy is impervious to this kind of gossip. I, unfortunately, am not.

I was so wrapped up in my own personal meltdown, I completely missed what everyone else ordered. I was focused on one thing and one thing only. Getting out of the booth.

CHAPTER FIVE

Bad Deals

EVERYONE EASED BACK into the conversation after Tina departed.

"I must have chosen well if you frequent this place often enough to have a 'usual.'" Howard is now prying. Just a little.

"I order take out."

"I thought you got free dinners at the bar, Tara?" Kathy doesn't know me quite as well as Tina does, at least not when it comes to food.

"I don't trust Riqué not to doctor the food if I order it for me."

Kathy does know that I don't keep anything more than basic breakfast items in the bungalow. One of the ghosts, not Great Uncle Lester, likes to throw food around. Great Uncle Lester would die before he wasted food. Bad analogy, but you get the picture.

"Riqué is the cook at the bar where you work?"

"Yes."

"Why would he want to poison you?"

It's a fair question. I just wish it hadn't been Jack who asked it.

"For reasons known only to Riqué, I rate somewhere between roaches and fish guts on his popularity meter. He hasn't liked me since the first day I set foot in his kitchen. I think he dislikes the fact that I got Sherry to put ceviche on the menu. With Riqué, ya just never can tell."

"I love a good ceviche. What kind of fish do you use?" This is from Howard. Jack was looking like breakfast might come up. Did he order sushi or cooked food? I missed that. Maybe Jack likes raw fish less than Riqué. Maybe they belong to some nature group that frowns on carnivorous consumption of raw fish flesh. It bears looking into.

"I mostly use whatever is in season. No grouper or barracuda for obvious reasons, but any other mild fish is great."

Polite conversation ensued and I nearly settled into a Z'd out stupor where my answers were on autopilot. I knew the signs. Boredom was setting in. Jack's food arrived, cooked, and Muffin ordered that horrible sushi roll with the whole shrimp tempura'd and rolled in rice and nori. The Japanese have a whole lot to answer for with that dish. Who, in their right mind, eats shrimp heads? Disgusting. Muffin's not getting a good-night kiss until the shrimp head is digested and out of his system. I can't watch.

Jack watched and looked distinctly green. This could be interesting. I contemplated stirring the situation up a bit when Kathy caught my eye. She shook her head once. No.

Damn. Busted.

I am the only one eating with chopsticks.

I try very hard not to suck the soy and wasabi off of the wooden sticks but it's a challenge. I love wasabi.

Where was I? Oh yeah, in hell.

"You seem to have reservations about this business association, Tara. What are your objections? Perhaps they can be easily addressed." Jack was trying to focus his attention away from the shrimp heads. I can appreciate this. I have used this distraction device many times myself in gastronomically unpleasant situations.

"What do you know about the shipping company you've signed with?"

I don't know about Jack. Jack may know exactly what kind of people manage to stay in business here in the Keys with nearly invisible sources of income. I was pretty sure that Howard had absolutely no clue.

Howard answered. "I had my accountant go over their books. Their expense and income appear to be solid. They operate in the black, just barely. They have new boats and licensed captains. They have good dock slots in Marina's that do not require more than the slip fee and a booking percentage when they send customers their way."

"Do you or your accountant know much about boats?"

Howard looked puzzled. Jack looked interested, finally, in something other than me sitting next to Howard.

"Not really, no. They have the purchase receipts and documentation. I checked with their insurer and it appears to be good coverage."

"Do they own the boats outright?"

"Yes."

"How did they pay for the boats?"

"I don't know." Howard was starting to follow where I was leading.

"I don't want to bust your bubble, Mr. Payne, but I would want to run the company and every member of its crew through a background check before I signed on."

"What difference does it make to us if they are not hundred percent above board?" Jack understands what I am saying, but in typical French fashion sees no reason why laws and business need affect each other in any way, shape or form.

"One word. RICO."

"What is that?"

It's possible he doesn't know, so I take the time to explain.

"It means that if our new best friends are smuggling, the government has the right to seize their assets and the assets of any partners associated with the business in question. It means that I don't do business with people I don't know here in the Keys."

Jack bristled at that. I'm not sure if he is insulted because he is smart enough to realize that I include him in the category of people I don't know, or if he doesn't like being lectured by a woman on business. Not my problem.

"You would be a full participant in all decisions where this venture is concerned Tara." Howard took a reasonable tack.

I can be reasonable.

"I would want my own accountant to look over the books of this firm and Jack's company."

"Do you offer your own books in return?" Jack was looking for a reason to bitch. I could tell. We were not going to make very good partners. Not that I was even considering it. I wondered for a moment if Howard had started to re-think this deal of his.

"Of course."

"You're not a public company. You don't have to reveal anything you don't want." Howard sounded strained.

"But now you understand why I am so reluctant to consider your proposal. If I join this venture, my books are no longer private between the taxman and myself, my assets are out on the line to be seized if one of our group is doing something illegal. I can't see that it's worth it for me. Are you just running an idea or do you have a market study for me to look over?"

"I had a study done. I can bring a copy by, along with the books of the other business. Are you considering joining us?"

"That depends." Kathy was giving me her thoughtful

look, like I just did something she hadn't expected and she likes it. "Are you married to this shipping company?"

"Married?"

"Do you have contracts? Or, can you walk away and find someone else if their operation isn't kosher?"

"I have a contract."

"Then I am considering it, but I have reservations."

"Understood." Howard really is a reasonable guy, naïve as hell but reasonable. Maybe I can train him.

The bill arrived and Howard took it without hesitation. He put cash on the table to cover it and the tip and I was free, finally.

Someone left another gift attached to the gingerbread latticework on my bungalow.

CHAPTER SIX

The Black Rooster

"THAT'S A REALLY, really big bird."

Kathy and I are standing with her car between the front porch of my bungalow and us. Standing on the porch is a four-foot tall black rooster. Its foot is leashed to a wire that has been strung from one end of the front porch to the other, giving it the full run of the entire porch and preventing us from getting to the front door.

I noticed two things.

a. The rooster is very angry.

b. The rooster has pooped all over my beautiful front porch.

"I'm going to get the hose."

"You can't blast it with water. That's cruel." Kathy loves all animals.

I only like cats.

"Assuming we can subdue a twenty-pound ticked-off rooster, I would rather not slip and skid on my butt on bird shit."

"Oh."

"Yeah, oh." I headed over to the side of the building, keeping a close eye on rooster-zilla. As I rounded the corner, I came up with a plan.

"Go get the boat hook off the boat!" I shouted back to Kathy.

"Can't we just call Animal Control? Or the police?"

"No."

"Why not?"

"Because I don't want this to hit the papers. I do not need this kind of publicity and it's only a little rooster for crying out loud. We can handle it. Get the filet knife too. Oh, and the wire clippers."

"K." Kathy didn't sound thrilled by this plan.

Animal control would take the rooster away in any case. I want to keep it, maybe for dinner.

We met back up, out front, and I handed Kathy the hose. She handed me the tools.

"OK. Here's what I need you to do. Hose down the patio and scootch Kentucky Fried there to the end of the porch. Don't hit him directly with the spray, just scootch him. Got it?"

"What are you going to do?"

"I am going to catch his leash with the hook and cut it. And then I am going to run like hell. I suggest you do the same."

Kathy looked at me for a minute, both eyebrows scrunched down and she pursed her lips as if I just made her eat a key lime.

"Is this the best plan you can come up with?"

"Do you have a better one?"

"He's a rooster."

"What's your point?"

"Roosters don't just fly away. They tend to hang around. This rooster might be chasing you to your car every day till it dies. You may never get a chance to pen it again. If you let it go now . . ." She left it unsaid but I got the gist.

"It just needs some hens to keep it occupied."

"Ya think?" She looked doubtful, and rightly so. I had no idea if hens would tame this rooster.

What the hell do chickens eat anyway?

"Hose it."

The plan worked right up until I cut the leash and Extra Krispy flew at my face startling Kathy into hosing us both nearly to death. And, of course, I fell on my ass. As soon as the water hit it, the rooster changed directions and headed straight up.

Great. Now it will poop all over my roof.

I was sopping wet and I had feathers and bird poop all over my butt.

"I'm good." I tried to reassure her.

"Really?" Kathy turned off the hose and rushed over to help me up. "Yuck."

"Just hose the porch off for me. I'm going in to shower."

"I'll hose it off, but I have to get going." She started at the other end away from the front door.

I turned around with my hand on the screen door handle. "Kathy?"

"Huh?" She's in the hosing zone.

"Why are you afraid of ghosts?"

She looked up at me, finally, and thought for a minute.

"I'm not afraid of all ghosts." She released the handle on the sprayer and the water stopped.

"Then why my ghosts in particular?"

"Your ghosts are free roamers." She shivered as if she thought they might be listening in, and they might be.

"What's the difference?" I really wanted to know, even though I had bird shit on my butt.

She sighed and stared at the ground and then up at me with a very serious expression. "Some ghosts aren't aware that they have passed on. They follow a pattern of something they suffered in life that haunts them until they're freed. They don't know you and I are even there. Free roamers, they know they are dead. They go where they want, sometimes to a person they have issues with or to a place that holds memories for them. But, the fact is, they can act and react to things going on around them. They have focus. Usually, they aren't dangerous. Not lethally, but they are capable of doing damage."

And that, answers that.

"They haven't done any real damage."

"Not yet."

"Fair enough."

"Will you let me bring someone in to at least talk to them and find out why they are here?"

"I know why."

"You do?"

"I do."

"Oh."

"Don't worry about it Kathy. I promise they will behave."

"Tara, you can't make that promise for them. I can tell they are angry. At least one of them has real rage issues against you."

"Relationships are a bitch, even in death." I snorted. I can't help it. My ass is wet and icky and I seriously want a shower. I can hear the cats yowling inside and Finger Lick'n up above is probably wanting to come down on someone's head.

"I don't know how you can joke about something like this." She pressed the handle of the sprayer and got back to it.

I went inside to a nice warm shower. If the bird gives me any trouble Zeke and me will just go on a rooster hunt later.

After cleaning up I headed in to work by way of the animal shelter. I had to go in before five or they would be closed and I would have to wait till tomorrow. They are not technically open on Sundays but someone is always there to take care of the animals. I picked up a big, fat, brown hen—we have lots of them here in the Keys. Unfortunately for me, they did not have any white hens. I need a white bird to counter the bad black rooster ju-ju. I am forced to rescue Sunshine from the boarding pokey.

Sunshine is Sherry's Malaccan cockatoo. Sunshine is, quite possibly, the single most annoying bird on the planet. But, Sunshine is nearly white, ok, peachy-white, and a very good anti-curse color for the black rooster. If the rooster stays, I need Sunshine, simple as that.

Sunshine has a roost in the bar and, if you look around carefully, you will see that she has chewed her way through almost every wall and piece of wood within a twenty-foot radius of her perch.

Sunshine demands non-stop affection. She likes the weirdest foods. She is loud. I am starting to dislike being on this person's shit list. Maybe we can come to terms.

I heard Riqué bitching as soon as he caught sight of Sunshine. He hates her almost as much as I do, too bad. The hen stays in the crate out back until I go home. Two hours more or less wouldn't kill it.

After I settled Sunshine on her perch I went back and checked on Riqué and the hen.

"Don't butcher the hen out back."

Riqué didn't even blink. "Why you got that bird."

"The hen or Sunshine?"

"Both."

"Someone left a black rooster on my porch today. He needs a girlfriend." I realized the crate was sitting near a damp spot that might turn into a puddle before the night was over from the AC drip and hike it up to move it over a few feet.

"Black rooster was alive?"

I set her down as gently as possible but between her and the crate she weighed a ton. "Yup. Alive and ticked."

"How big?" He looked thoughtful for a moment.

"'Bout four-feet high. Why?"

"Make good dinner." His face was a closed book and this was the most he'd ever said to me in two years.

"You want him? I might be convinced to give him up."

"Bad ju-ju." He headed back into the kitchen shaking his head.

I followed. "What kind of bad ju-ju?"

"You got no loa to tell you these things? I told you. Let me take the head off that cat last night. But you not listen. Bad ju-ju. Now you got black rooster. That why you got Sunshine, I bet."

"You bet right."

"You believe."

"I'm hedging my bets."

"I don't know 'hedging bets.' I know you believe and that make you vulnerable. You no believe. Nothing can hurt you. You believe, It *all* can hurt you."

"You know somebody who can help me?" It never occurred to me before to ask Riqué for assistance. I never thought he would help.

"It cost you money. You pay?"

"I'll pay."

"I send someone tomorrow. She's good voodoo. You treat her with respect. She helps you." He turned his back on me and headed for the men's room. And that, as they say, is that. It's the most I have ever gotten out of Riqué ever. Probably best not to push my luck. I just hope Miss Good Voodoo isn't too weird.

Bad things had happened out in the bar while Riqué and I were talking in the kitchen.

"Tara." Dennis had smarmed his way in and was eyeing Sunshine with distinct distaste. On this one thing, we agree. Sunshine is a pain in the ass. Her best quality is that she bites Dennis every chance she gets, hard. "I stopped by Sherry's house and it looked like she's still away, but if Sunshine is here she must be somewhere nearby.

Dennis mistakenly thinks that I won't take care of Sunshine if Sherry isn't here. Yesterday, he would have been right. Today, however, I will brave Sunshine's beak and whatever else she does in order to counteract the rooster juju. I do not correct him. I do, in fact, lie.

"Yup, she's back."

"Where's she at?" He was trying to peer behind the main wait to catch a glimpse of her in the kitchen.

"She stepped out for a few minutes. Would you like a drink while you wait?" I have a special mix I keep ready, just for Dennis.

"No." He looked disappointed. "No. I have to get to a party."

"How's Kerry's eye?"

"She looks like shit." Now he looked annoyed. As if it's my fault his wife is a klutz. "What the hell did you do to her?"

"Me?" I looked as innocent as possible. "Not a thing." I paused for effect. "She was attacked by a bar nut."

He stared at me for a full minute as if he was trying to ascertain if I was making fun of him in some way and then, finally, "Right."

"I swear."

"She said the same thing."

"Ok, then, why are you accusing me?" The roach thing did not endear me to him. I know this. But to accuse me of every bad thing that happens is colossally unfair in my opinion. Asshole.

"You're just rotten, Tara." He had that holier than thou look now, like butter wouldn't melt in his mouth.

"And you're a choir boy, Dennis? If you're not drinking or eating I would appreciate it if you would haul your ass out of here."

"No need to be vulgar." He was smiling. Dennis is one of those sick puppies who like it rough. I forget this to my own detriment sometimes. Damn. I have a sinking feeling that I somehow have a starring role in a number of Dennis's fantasies.

I needed another shower.

With any luck, he really did have a party to get to. I ignored him. Sam was there.

"Hey, Sam."

"You know what I want, babe."

"Kir Royale?"

"I knew you loved me."

I leaned over to him and whispered in his ear, "You have no idea."

His usual ten-thousand-watt smile widened and he gave me another once over.

"Slut." Dennis muttered to no one in particular.

Sam's smile froze for a minute and faded as he turned to stare Dennis down. Dennis looked somewhat contrite, but not nearly enough for Sam. "I ever hear that outta you again and I'm going to wipe the floor with your ass, Dennis."

Bars can be rough places. It's nice to have friends.

Dennis looks for all the world like he wished he had the balls to take Sam on, but the fact of the matter is, Dennis has locked horns with Sam before. Sam always wins. Boys have a pecking order. Dennis is at the bottom of this particular heap. He departed with a lovely F-you and slammed the door to the bar behind him. The windows rattled but nothing fell.

Sam looked at me expectantly, like a puppy wanting a treat.

"Thanks, Sam." God I wish he were straight.

"My pleasure, beautiful."

I placed his drink on a coaster and blew him a kiss. "On the house, handsome."

Life is good.

"Is Sherry in?" He and Sunshine were eyeing each other like long-lost sweethearts and Sunshine was climbing down off her perch to get luvins.

"Naw. I just decided to rescue Sunshine from the bird jail for a few days."

"You're a good soul, Tara." He scratched her just above

the shoulders and she fluffed her feathers up so he could reach skin. They will spend the entire evening like that, until I take her away. It's true love. I wondered why he didn't get a bird of his own. For that matter, he might have a million of them and I just don't know about it. But he's never mentioned them if he does. He seems content to get a bird fix whenever Sunshine is in residence. Watching the two of them made me miss Precious and Zeke. I wished I were home instead of here.

"Dennis up to something again?"

"Most likely."

"I stand ready as your council." Sam's megawatt grin was back. Thank god.

"Sherry has a lawyer, but thank you anyway."

He tried feeding Sunshine one of the bar nuts. Sunshine hates the bar nuts. I pulled out a packet of sunflower seeds, unsalted, and handed it to him. Sunshine tried to help him open it and Sam let her have the bag. They've done this before.

"*You* don't have a lawyer." Sam looked up from Sunshine and the bag of sunflower seeds with a suddenly serious expression.

"I haven't needed one." I risked beak damage to ruffle Sunshine behind her ears.

"You might need one now."

"Dennis is not my problem. Dennis is Sherry's problem." I'm deliberately being obtuse in the hopes that Sam doesn't know as much as I think he knows about my current problems.

"Word has it, you are on someone's shit list."

Ok. He knows.

"Someone gave me a cat."

"A *black* cat *and* a gris-gris bag." He dragged out the "and." Sigh.

"So what? I accuse someone of stalking me with cuddly, loveable creatures?" I was hoping he hadn't heard about the rooster.

"Think it's Dennis? I hear he's been making new friends. If he's looking for Sherry to do business, tell her she doesn't want anything to do with Dennis's new partners."

I hadn't considered Dennis. I wondered why.

"Can I get you anything from the kitchen."

"Actually, yes. Gimme a burger platter, medium, and a side of coleslaw."

I wrote this down and took it back to Riqué.

When I returned, I had the feeble hope that Sam would be ready to move on to a new subject. Could Dennis be the gris-gris guy? It seemed unlikely. For a moment I contemplated Riqué, but his offer of help sort of put him off the list of suspects. He hates me, true, but he's had a year to do something like this and hasn't. If it were Riqué I would have to thank him for the cat and that would be an unpleasant chore, to say the least. The gold collar is probably out of his price range. For that matter, so is a Persian cat. I'm on a well-to-do shit list. In South Florida, this doesn't narrow the list of suspects by much. I think only Idaho has more millionaires per capita. Dennis wouldn't give away something that expensive, even for revenge. Cheap bastard.

I'm going to have to change the subject. I like Sam; point-in-fact, I lust after Sam, but I swore off men after the last loser dumped me for a high school drop out. He said I used too many big words on him and it made him itchy.

Sam found Sunshine's nirvana spot and she's now making that cute kissy sound cockatoos make when they are happy.

"Sherry would probably give her to you if you asked."

Sam looked like he was considering it for a moment. "Too much responsibility."

And *that* is why Sam would make a bad boyfriend. If vacations were a guy, Sam would be the number one destination spot. He'd be a Club Med. Gay, straight, bisexual . . . if it's fun, he's up for it, as long as it ends in under two weeks.

I handed him the TV remote and headed outside to sweep

the front walkway and pick up trash. I hate being inside on a day like this if I can help it.

Sam knows how to grab his order from the pass through when Riqué puts it up.

It rains enough in the summer that I don't need to water the plants, but I watered them anyway. For a few minutes I contemplated weeding more than the planters and decided against it. The lawn guys would know. Every time I do yard work around the bar they ask Sherry if she still needs their services. Paranoid. They do the property around the bungalows too. Sherry rents the other bungalows out by the month. My rent and utilities were a package deal for managing the bar. Sherry's house is two bungalows over from me. She offered free cleaning service, but there are things I would rather not have to explain to a cleaning crew, so I passed on that perk.

Customers started arriving as Kay and the night crew clocked in. I packed up the hen and Sam brought Sunshine out to the car for me. It's been a long day.

"Want me to ride home with you and hold her? I can walk back for my car." My bungalow is only a mile from the bar, but I managed to get Sunshine here from the Birdy Boarding jail. I can get her a mile more to home.

"Thanks Sam. That's sweet of you, but I can handle her."

She immediately tucked herself under my arm and started making kissy sounds. If she weren't so freaking loud and destructive I could fall in love with a bird like this.

"I know where you live." Sam smiled. He says this a lot.

"I know that you do." I grinned back and started the engine.

"What's with the chicken? Starting a farm?"

"I ran out of eggs. I'm determined to never let that happen again."

He accepted this as an answer even though he knows I'm full of shit. "You're gonna need more chickens."

```
// Thought for the day on the Home Page of
Revenge-Gifts.com,
scheduled to load on Sunday.

<script language="JavaScript">
<!-- This figures out what day of the week it
is, and prints a quote. -->
<!--
  Sys_Date = new Date();
  var DayofWeek = "";
  var TaraQuote = "";

  if(Sys_Date.getDay() == 1) {
          DayofWeek = "Sunday";
```

Occasionally, I get an email asking why I don't stock anything decent to get revenge on an ex-boyfriend. I clearly state on the default.htm page that almost all effective forms of revenge in a romantic dispute are illegal.

New bumper sticker: The best revenge against a man is to marry him.";

```
  document.write(DayofWeek  +  " : "  +
  TaraQuote);
  // -->
  </script>
```

CHAPTER SEVEN

True Confessions

SEVEN P.M. IN the Keys in June and the sun still hasn't set completely. We get really long days. I dropped the chicken off in front of the bungalow and opened the crate for it to fly free. The rooster was nowhere in sight. Maybe all of this work was for nothing.

I headed up the path to Sherry's house to steal her smaller outside cage for Sunshine. Sunshine's hitching a ride on my shoulder and gripping with uncomfortably strong claws. As soon as she saw her cage she was one happy bird. She hopped off my shoulder and onto her cage and immediately started investigating all of her toys. I grabbed a bag of Sunshine's food from the porch closet and set it on top of the cage. A few bumps down the steps and Sunshine, Sunshine's cage and I were rattling our way down the path through bungalows one and two to haunted bungalow number three.

Bad things had happened while I was stealing bird supplies from Sherry's house.

The Muffin man was sitting in his Alpha Romeo Spider with the top down and the black, four-foot rooster perched on top of his windshield. As usual, the rooster looked pissed.

Here's a question: Do I rescue Howard or do I subject him to a rooster test and see if he can handle it on his own? Granted, in Howard's defense, this is a devil rooster. Ordinary tactics might not work. But if Howard is going to be visiting me, he is going to have to handle these kinds of problems on his own. I can't be running to his rescue every time he has a problem.

The hen was sitting quietly, still in her crate. Once I got Sunshine and cage up the steps to my front porch I stepped back down and kicked the crate. The hen flew out like a fox was on her ass and the rooster immediately followed. The two of them would be busy sorting out domestic arrangements for the next hour or so. I'm hoping it's not on my roof.

Howard looked grateful.

By the time I got Sunshine in the house, fed, tucked and covered, Howard was at the door.

"I brought those papers for you to look over."

"How'd you know I'd be home?" Howard was starting to worry me a bit. For a new guy in town he'd managed to get my schedule down pretty good.

"Nana told me you're usually home by seven."

Zeke raced over and started to climb Howard's leg like he's a tree. Howard gently pried the kitten away from his slacks and held him out to me by the scruff of his neck.

"Between the rooster and the kitten, you seem pretty well protected."

"Sorry about that. I just got them and they haven't learned proper greeting techniques." In fact, chances are nil to negative nine that they will ever learn *any* acceptable social skills from me. Can't teach what you don't know. I'm now feeling kind of bad about this. Precious made it up to him by rubbing against his leg and purring. I took Zeke from him and set the kitten in front of his new food dish. He started eating like it was his last meal. Domicile protection duty is exhausting work for a little cat.

Howard handed me a leather binder and I set it on the kitchen table.

"Can I get you something to drink? Wine? Soda? Beer?"

"Beer would be fine." He picked up Precious and started prowling around my bungalow, stopping to look at artwork and novels strewn over every surface in the living room. He passed by the computers without a word and headed through to the bedrooms.

I met him with his Corona and mine at the entrance to the small hallway and forced him to come back out to the living room to get it from me.

Precious looked happy. He had her cuddled on her back like a baby. She usually hates being held like that.

"This is a very nice little bungalow."

"Thanks."

"Did it come furnished?"

"Furniture and utilities included. Want a tour of the property?"

He set Precious down and brushed fur from his shirt.

Taking the beer from my hand he stared at me and looked for all the world as if there were things he wants to say but doesn't know how to say them. The silence dragged for a little too long and I nervously took a swig from my bottle and started babbling like an idiot.

"This property has been in Sherry's family since before Flagler came through with the railroad. All the bungalows were built with the same design as the homes on Pigeon Key."

"It's charming—very comfortable." He smiled as if he was actually saying that he thought *I* was charming and comfortable. I guess you can take the boy out of Disney, but you can't take Disney out of the boy. Howard's going to be ever so disappointed when he sees me out of my character costume. I should let him down easy.

"Thanks. It came that way. I've tried to fix it but surly and prickly is taking more time than I would have expected. By next year the place should be completely uninviting and uncomfortable."

He laughed.

"What?"

"You can do my place next . . . if you like. Start a business. You would win the affections of everyone living in Florida who is sick of friends and relatives visiting for prolonged vacations."

I thought about that for a minute. Yeah. People would pay for that kind of decorating service. Howard is as screwed up in the head as I am. No good can come of us continuing any kind of social association—or business association for that matter. Clearly, he's gotta go . . . after the tour.

"Maybe." I conceded grudgingly. If I encourage him there will be no prying him off me later . . . so I tell myself. "Ready?"

I have no idea if I should lead him outside for a walking tour or flop down on a chair and settle in for a cozy chat. No guy has made me feel this awkward since high school. I don't like it.

"I'd love a tour."

"Great." I turned my back on him and headed out the front door.

He paused for a minute at the doorway. "You don't lock it?"

"Never."

"Why not?"

"I lost the key."

He sighed, heavily. For a moment I worried that I was in for a lecture. I contemplated telling him that the ghosts guard it fairly well, but decided against it. If he hasn't noticed, then I'm not going to make waves.

"Rooster gone?"

I looked around and saw no sign of either bird. "Yep."

Finally we were on our way down the path to the docks.

"There are ten bungalows, all identical and the caretaker's house. Up at the entrance to the property is Sherry's house. She's off in Sedona for a while. Sunshine is her bird. There are twelve slips on the dock for guests who bring their own boat and Sherry's boat sits on the end of the dock."

"Do you have a boat?"

I laughed. "Heck no."

"You don't like boats?"

"I love boats."

"But you don't want to own one of your own."

"Nope. I have free use of Sherry's. She hates boats, but she got it in the divorce and maintains it to tick off her ex-husband. If I don't use it, it will rot. I don't have time for two boats."

"You run it yourself?"

I shook my head no. "She has a captain who runs it."

"Interesting."

"You have no idea."

"Did her ex get another boat?"

"He bought the sister ship of Sherry's."

"Even more interesting. Why would he go to the trouble of getting an identical boat?"

"He told everyone he got the original in the divorce and that Sherry's the one who was pathetic enough to buy its twin."

"Are the names the same?"

"Yup."

We were at the end of the dock and the name of the boat was clearly visible in three-foot high letters on the transom: Till Death.

"It was a wedding gift."

Howard seemed transfixed by the name. "Very romantic."

I could tell he was kidding. Howard just made a joke, a little lame but cute.

"Marriage should be to the death. Divorce should be non-survivable by one partner or the other. Make it a true battle to the death, people will be a lot more careful who they marry."

"Have you ever been married?" His tone was serious.

"Nope. You?"

"Yes. Once."

"Still?"

"Good question. In a way, yes."

"And what does that mean?" I have a feeling I've just stepped into a minefield.

"She died." He suddenly looked so sad I wanted to break one of my cardinal rules and hug him. I am very bad when faced with actual death. It's not something I've ever come to terms with in my own life and I am of little use to anyone else when the subject comes up. Death is one of those loose ends I can't tie up in a neat bow of platitudes yet—my problem, not yours.

I wanted to say something stupid like, "So. You won." I managed not to, thank god.

"I'm very sorry to—" I barely got the words going and Howard cut me off at the pass.

"Don't be."

I shut up and waited. We don't know each other well enough for this kind of conversation. How the hell did the subject come up anyway?

He sighed and stepped onto the boat, sitting down on the fighting chair which I've always felt was in the way, there in the dead center of the back of the boat. "She killed herself and our soon-to-be son three years ago."

No way am I saying "sorry" again.

Normally, I am a master at getting information out of people when they know something I want to know. But this . . . I'm not sure I want to know about this. Everyone who ever died on me went down fighting. Not one of my now deceased

friends or relations wanted to go—especially Great Uncle
Lester who isn't even gone yet.

Howard took my silence as a sign to continue.

"I'd been at Disney for almost seven years. We met there.
The pay is low but the perks are phenomenal. There's a social order to it, parties, cookouts, you can't imagine it if you
haven't worked there. I felt completely taken over. It wasn't
what I wanted to spend the rest of my life doing. I had a job
offer for an investment firm in New York and I was going to
take it. She said if I did she would end it—all."

I do understand the fantasy world that Disney creates. People buy season tickets and go back year after year to live in it,
for a little while at least. Anyone who can rewrite the story of
the Little Mermaid with a happy ending can make the worst
life imaginable bearable.

"And she did."

"She did."

What do I say to *that?* Nothing appropriate comes to mind.

"But you stayed?"

"I was on autopilot for about three years after that. By the
time I finished with the funeral arrangements and settling
her affairs, the offer from New York was gone and I just
didn't have it in me to look for another. Her parents died a
year after we married in a car accident. Artists and perform-
ers I'd hired and become friends with, were dropping off
like flies. The AIDS epidemic burst into full bloom. I felt
surrounded by death."

"So now you are going into the funeral business?" It
seemed a little masochistic to me, but I have no room to talk
about bad career choices.

"I know a lot about funerals."

Irony. I can relate to that.

"Do you know how far off shore you have to be to dump
ashes?"

"Three miles." He answered without hesitation.

"I knew it!"

He smiled again, finally. "Someone debating that fact with you?" Howard is an astute guy, even when he's in sad-mode.

"Kathy thought it was twelve."

"Kathy is incorrect."

"I will be happy to tell her."

Crisis conversation averted. Close call. The subject is bound to come up again. Muffin is going into the undertaker business. Everyone has issues. He's haunted by his dead wife and kid. I'm haunted by my Great Uncle Lester. It looks like Muffin and I have a few things in common— except he didn't put his dead wife's ashes in a Mother's Day urn. He didn't, did he? I wracked my brains for a moment trying to remember if I'd seen his name on any orders.

"You've never bought any of my revenge gifts, have you?"

He took a few seconds too long to answer. "Nope."

"Nana told you about my website?"

"Yep. She wanted to show me her new lace design." It was a reasonable answer, but not a complete one. I was digging now. Perfectly normal Howard wasn't so perfectly normal. I wanted to know just how far from normal he had roamed.

"So you surfed a little, saw the urns and had an idea?" Fishing, but I was using the right bait. I could feel it.

"Something like that. Yes." He wasn't looking at me anymore. He was looking everywhere but at me. Hmmm.

"With so many funerals, you must have considered at least one of the urns for someone you knew?" I dug harder. "Maybe for your wife? Some of the designs are perfectly innocuous—elegant—no one would even know it was designed for any specific kind of revenge. The Mother's Day urn, for example, it doesn't say what it's for, it's just flowers." My mom used to say that if a guy hasn't married by the age of thirty-five then he isn't fit to be married. I thought she was talking about space on the bathroom counter issues and closet space. Easy stuff. I am finding out that she was talking about a whole lot more than counter-closet territorial problems.

It's Sunday. Damn. I didn't call Mom. I bet Little Shit called her. Some day Mom is going to admit I'm adopted.

I stepped onto the boat and sat on Precious's favorite spot. The water is tinged pink and purple from the sun setting on the bay side of the island. Night falls very quickly once the sun is down and the dock lights automatically click on when the gloom sets in.

"I thought about it." Howard sighed heavily. "You knew that already though, didn't you?"

"I suspected."

"Think she'd come back to haunt me like your Uncle Les?"

"I think she's gotten her revenge and has moved on to the next victim."

Howard stared off into nothing. "Maybe, but she still haunts me, just the same."

"Literally?" Maybe Howard and I are soul mates.

"No."

I hate heart to hearts with people I know. With Howard, it was freaking painful. But I did dig into the subject, hoping maybe he was as bad as me, hoping someone else out there finally put death in its proper perspective. Death doesn't en-noble the soul that occupied the corpse. If they were rotten in life then there's no reason to pretend anything different after they are dead. His wife's ashes *should* be in the Mother's Day urn. It was a good instinct on Howard's part. But some people never get in touch with that inner cruelty that lurks in all of us. They think that, if they are nice enough, they can counter balance the cold, cruel world. Be-ing nice just attracts more people to you, most of them mean. Mother Nature has a sense of humor that way. It's sort of like "nice" is a vacuum waiting to be filled with bad things. Howard is wide the hell open.

"You know, part of living is learning to live with your

demons. Some demons you create, some just come to you uninvited. The thing is, once they are yours, they're not returnable. This one is a little of both, I think. Whatever you have to do to make it comfortable to live with, do it. Get it boxed away so you can move on. The next demon is just waiting to move in."

"I can't."

"It's not like you bought one and put her in it. It was just a thought. Everyone travels that dark path in their head at least once in awhile."

"What is it like to walk it in the real world?" He was looking at me again. I guess that's something—except he was looking for me to put his demons in a box for him. He was in the land of the living dead and hoping I could bring him back to life.

"You want to walk it with me, Howard? I'll donate the urn for free."

He laughed. It was a deep rumble low in his stomach, so I knew it was real. "Tempting, but then she would probably haunt you. Trust me, you don't want to invite that demon into your life."

"The more the merrier." Whew. Will I never learn to mind my own damn business? It's not even as if I'm hoping for any kind of relationship with the man. True. I desperately want to jump his bones, but only once. More than that and I'll end up with cavitities. "Nana says you hate kids?"

This question really startled me. Kids are the last thing I expect Howard to want to talk about after what he just revealed to me. Should I tease him?

"Nana says the same about you." I couldn't help it. I had to say it.

"I just tell her that when she asks me about great-grandchildren. She's relentless."

"It's not that I—" we are deep into sharing mode and I am not sure I want to go any farther. The one up-man-ship abyss of *I tell you something personal so you tell me something personal* is opening in front of me like the Grand Canyon. I want to put the brakes on right now, but Muffin is staring at me like I'm his last meal. I am breaking my second cardinal rule: Men you do business with are not potential dates. Never ever socialize with them. I am somehow in it now and I can't gracefully back out until I take a few left turns. I just know this is a bad idea, but I dive in and swim.

"Have you ever heard the phrase 'Water, water everywhere, nor any drop to drink'?"

"*Rime of the Ancient Mariner* by Coleridge."

Damn. He's literate.

"Yeah. Well. I spent ten years as a computer engineer, surrounded by men. Tack on the five years before that in college and I basically—" How the hell do I say this without looking like a complete geek. "It's like this. As a woman in a guy's field, dating within my species was career suicide. Does that make sense?"

Howard smiled, got up from his chair and walked over to me. He stopped just inside my personal no-touch zone and leaned against the gunnel with one hand braced on the boat behind my back. "Guys have a more graphic way of describing your dilemma, but I get the gist. You can't possibly be trying to tell me that you've never had a date."

I scootched a little to the side, away from him and stared him right in his left eye.

"I've dated—outside my species. Non-engineers. Non-computer geeks. It was disastrous. I quit, cold turkey, after college."

"You haven't had a date in ten years?" His voice went an octave deeper on the word "ten."

"For the most part, yeah." I had to scootch a little farther to the left. "In any case," he closed the distance I'd created, "All my friends, sorority sisters, relatives, they all got married, had kids. The usual. While I—."

Why the hell had I started this?

"I sort of fell off the map." That sounded wrong. What's a better word? "I was a third wheel. I didn't know how to handle kids and it was a strain to go out places with my friends who *had* kids and I just sort of started resenting kids in general. I mean I understand the witch in Hansel and Gretel. Here she is, a perfectly normal person with a life and everyone moves away to get married and have kids. She's left completely alone for centuries. It's perfectly *natural* that she would want to eat the first kids who show up at her door looking for an afternoon snack."

"Well, what if you were to have kids of your own? Would you eat *them?*"

Howard was finding this amusing. I spill my guts and he's amused, very nice. Yes, as reasons go it's a lame one. But it's all I've got right at the moment. I'm one of those people who should never, ever have kids. I would ruin them. I would suck as a mother. I would love them and they would suck the life out of me and then leave home and never call. Shit. Why didn't I call my mom? I am a horrible daughter. There's no *way* I am genetically related to my sister. She, at least, calls. This is Dad's fault. He was supposed to keep her company after we left. Jerk. And that's the other reason I never want kids. "Under no circumstances would I have children without a guy to take on half the workload. And the guy doesn't exist, who is willing to take on half the workload of raising kids."

"You seem pretty sure about that." He looked miffed, like he wanted to volunteer to be the first guy in the history of the human race who would hold up his end of the parenting pole.

"I am one hundred percent positive."

"Really?"

"I could tell you stories that would curl your hair."

"Let's back up to that water metaphor instead."

He's now inches from my ear and I am in real danger of falling backwards off the boat.

"What do you mean?"

"Has it really been ten years?" He blew a warm breath just past my ear and into my hair. It wrapped around to the nape of my neck and I started shivering.

Aw, crud. I did *not* just tell Muffin that I haven't had sex for over ten years. I should just call the IRS and beg them to audit me. I am that stupid.

I pressed my hand firmly to his chest and shoved. He backed up enough for me to get to my feet and get around him. My legs were shaking and I was breathing so hard I sounded asthmatic.

"I am *not* that desperate, Howard."

"Did I *say* you were desperate?" His eyes were gleaming, even in the dark. I could see that look creeping over him, the look that says, she's ripe for the plucking.

I will beat my head against a wall later. This is what comes of intimate conversations. I inevitably say something that gets taken out of context.

Why do I hate kids? Because I haven't been laid in ten years and I resent all evidence that points to the fact that others have. Gawd. There's no fixing this one. Howard *has* to go.

I said the first lame thing that came into my head. "I need to get up early tomorrow."

This is social code for; *it's been lovely, but you must leave, now.*

I emphasized this by scrambling up onto the dock and walking to Howard's car. He followed. I didn't look back. I didn't want to see that gleam in his eyes. I could feel him staring at my ass as I tried my best not to sway it. Intolerable.

As soon as we reached his car I stopped, turned and held out my hand to shake his.

"It's been an interesting evening. I will read over the papers you were kind enough to bring by. Please drive carefully going home."

If he understands half of that, we are doing well. I said it so fast I could barely make out what I said myself.

He seemed to understand.

"Thank you, Tara."

I wanted to say, *For what?* But I was afraid he would tell me.

"My pleasure." Is that worse than, *For what?* I have a sinking feeling it is.

I swore I could hear him laughing as he drove off. Did I just fall for the oldest ploy in the book? Did he just play the sympathy card on me? The, "My wife and child are dead, please feel sorry for me and take me to bed?" ploy? This is what staying out of the dating game for ten years will do to a girl. Men don't need newer and better lines. Hell if it worked on Cleopatra, it's still good for Tara Cole. She's never heard it before.

I bet he's never been married.

Squid.

I am embarrassed. If I want to lay all of the blame on Howard, I will.

Damn.

CHAPTER EIGHT

Nighttime Visitors

It is four-fifteen in the morning and Zeke is bouncing all over my bed like he's in a pinball machine. I do not want to wake up.

Precious is purring loud enough to wake the dead and situated at the head of the bed on the top of my back pillows. She's such a good cat. Zeke must die.

I kicked at the last location on which he'd bounced in the vain hope that he'll get the message and take his Tigger routine out into the living room. He doesn't. He settled down a bit though and started rubbing back and forth against the bottom right bedpost. Weird cat.

I slowly opened my eyes to place a better kick, and froze.

Standing at the end of my bed, petting Zeke's furry little head is a woman. At least, I think it's a woman. The room is dark and my eyes are still fuzzy from sleep.

No matter how many times I blink, I can't quite bring her into focus.

For a moment, it looked as if she was going to say something, but a loud pop exploded behind me high and left and she disappeared, like an electrical static discharge. The light next to the bed snapped on.

"Dammit, Uncle Les, she was about to *say* something."

I lifted Precious up and over and turned her face-to-face, nose-to-nose with me.

"As a guard cat, you are completely worthless."

She just purred louder.

The phone rang. For a minute, I considered letting the computer answer it.

Someone might be dead. Damn. I have to answer it.

I snatched the phone off the hook and held it somewhere near my ear. "What?"

I am understandably cranky. Whoever it is will just have to forgive me.

"Tonight is the first time I've seen you with another man."

"Who are you and why are you calling me at four a.m.?" I am not the sharpest knife in the drawer at this hour of the morning.

"I am," the voice paused. "Disappointed."

Click.

I was now in a cold sweat. Afraid to move a muscle in case someone is watching me through the window. I need a dog—a big, big dog.

Outside I heard the freaking rooster start to crow. I snapped off the lamp and rolled out of bed. I swear I am going to unscrew every light bulb in the house if Uncle Les doesn't cut this crap out. This kind of crisis requires Diet Coke.

I've never been afraid of the dark. I always felt that problems and bad things look far worse in the cold light of day than they do at night, in the dark.

Diet Coke in hand, I headed to my computer to check email and reconnect with the real world. I sifted through the sex spam, saved off the personal emails and opened the first email to Customer Service for Revenge Gifts.

Dear Sirs,

*I realize it is out of season, but I am interested in order-
ing approximately thirty of your Key Lime Fruitcakes. I
was wondering if you offered any bulk discount for
large orders, in which case I will purchase the correct
amount to qualify.*

　*My fiancé and I want to serve it at our wedding re-
ception July twenty-first.*

Kindest Regards,
Sidney Cerulio

I am under some kind of hellish curse. Or maybe, this is a
nightmare and I just haven't woken up. The ghost, the phone
call, the rooster, this stupid email are all part of some weird
voodoo induced dream and I just need to wake up.

I am going to sue Sidney and Jack for improper and subversive use of products purchased under false pretences
from Revenge-Gifts.com. Squids. I wonder how much Sam
charges for this kind of case?

I blasted off an email to the Key Lime Bakery and asked
Sheila if she could whip up thirty or so fruitcakes and if she
could give a discount. I calculated the approximate weight
of the cakes and looked up the UPS overnight shipping cost
and told her that the customer could save twenty dollars in
shipping if we send them all in one box. I do not tell her that
the thought of my two-thousand-year-old fruitcake, complete with a family tree detailing who has received this fruit-
cake, with special note of how many years it lay dormant in
cellars and attics, all the way back to the woman who originally cooked it in 42 BC for her husband in an attempt to kill
him, so she could be free to marry her personal body slave
Chorn, for a snack at a wedding reception is going to kill me.
It's a run-on sentence. That's how I think. It's now five a.m.,

I am slightly afraid, very annoyed and I have just chugged down an entire can of Diet Coke in less than two minutes. I can run on if I want to.

I got up and got another one.

I'll answer Mr. Romance after Sheila gets back to me with an answer. I should just tell him a flat no. The website clearly states that it can only be ordered between November first and January thirty-first. It's not even that great a fruit-cake, no offense to Sheila. I should tell him that they cost extra out of season.

At some point in time roosters do shut up. Don't they? I have a headache.

Who can I share it with?

I turn on my Palm Pilot and cruise through my address book; maybe someone in England. They're up now. Most of them. I look at the list, but no, all of them are at work now. Sigh.

I can't wake Kathy up after the two a.m. gris-gris call the night before last. She'd kill me. OK. That's an exaggeration. She would be really annoyed. But worse, she would be worried. She would insist that I call the police. If you've never been stalked before, calling the police might seem like a sensible solution to you. It's not.

A serial killer, who had a hatred of blond-haired, green-eyed twenty-year-olds, once stalked me. His name was Robert. He got my name and address from the university phone book, which the college gave out at the admissions center, free to anyone who asked. He called every day with a report on what I had done that day and expressed his dislike of my boyfriend and roommates.

I thought I caught sight of him once in a car parked in front of my building. I called the police to say that some strange guy was parked under my window and to please come ask him what the hell he was doing there. They came three hours later. He was, of course, gone by then. As for dealing with the seven a.m. wake up calls, they suggested that I change my number. He murdered eight women before they caught him and the police report described the car I had reported parked beneath my window.

Say what you want, I have no faith in the police in a situation like this. It would just result in really bad publicity for my business and no help whatsoever.

Caller-ID on the phone says "Unavailable." I can't block his number. Do I just let the computer answer the phone from here on out? I'm thinking this is too cruel for my computer. I go to my phone company's website and put in an order to change my phone number and keep it unlisted. I wish I knew how he got my number in the first place. Maybe Nana gave it to him.

Web person,

> *I think my boyfriend is cheating on me and I need to find out for sure. Can you help me crack his email password?*

Thanx,

Sigh. No name.

There is, of course, no good answer to this and it's not what Revenge-Gifts.com is all about anyway. Do I answer and commiserate and tell her that, when I was dating a decade ago, all but one of the guys I dated cheated on me. Do I tell her about the night my French boyfriend stood me up for a date? That was a banner night in my dating career. I had never been stood up before. I could have called any one of a dozen guys and had one take me out that night, once I established that Gervais was not coming to pick me up.

I didn't.

Should I tell her that I took my bottle of champagne out of the ice bucket (I had aced a particularly hard exam that day.)

and drove to his house at three a.m., sat in my car until dawn, grabbed his newspaper when it arrived on his doorstep and read it, drinking champagne until the squid came out in his robe looking for it.

"What are you doing here?" He lived in a normal neighborhood. It couldn't have escaped his neighbors' notice that I was sitting in my little blue convertible reading the paper and drinking champagne from the bottle. He seemed upset. He had nothing on me.

"I am waiting for you to get up so I can ask you what happened last night." I knew what happened. I just wanted to hear it. This was the first time I suspected that I might truly be psychic. Somewhere during the course of the night, I zoomed in on Gervais and ran a film in my head of what he was doing and with whom. I could see blond-haired Janet with the boyish figure draped on his sofa half dressed while he lit candles and poured wine into the crystal glasses I had given him for Christmas.

"I met up with some of the guys from the fraternity and they kidnapped me. They wouldn't let me call you. I am so sorry. I didn't think we had firm plans for the evening. I didn't think it would upset you."

"You have no idea."

"Yes. Well. Sitting here and getting drunk, reading my paper is over-reacting a little bit, yes?"

I pretended to consider this for a moment. "You're right of course. I should sober up. Invite me in for coffee?"

He was so flustered he completely forgot how much I despised coffee. "That would be—" he paused to look behind him at the front door of his house. "A bad idea. Some of the guys, they are still here."

"Gervais." I looked at the front door for a moment too, wondering how I was going to worm my way inside just to prove what I already knew was true. "I'm a little sister to the fraternity. The guys won't mind."

"I would mind." He looked genuinely jealous for a moment and I wondered if it were possible he was telling me the truth. Perhaps the house *was* full of frat boys—and then Janet opened the front door. She had a towel covering her front and nothing else.

I sighed.

"I need my paper, Tara."

People say the stupidest things when confronted with hideous situations.

Do I tell my anonymous emailer that I kept his paper? As revenge ideas go, it was spur of the moment. It was lame. It was over, obviously. I don't have that level of forgiveness in me. Do I step into a box of Fruit Loops and tell her that I was more alarmed over the psychic revelation than I was over him cheating? He was a business major anyway.

I learned more in college than just academics. I learned that men cheat, and there is nothing you can do to stop them. So I didn't even try. And while, in theory, I understand that if the guys are cheating, there must be women helping them, in my heart, I think they are all cheating with Janet.

I delete the email without answering it.

Dear RevengeGifts,

I use your seasonal urns as jewelry safes. Honestly, you really should advertise all the wonderful uses there are for these beautiful urns. Anyway, I wondered if you ever considered creating a locking mechanism on the inside brass canisters?

. . .

I can't read any further. The adrenaline rush is gone. The caffeine hasn't kicked in yet. I am exhausted, demoralized and I have a headache. I am going back to bed.

```
// Thought for the day on the Home Page of
Revenge-Gifts.com,
scheduled to load on Monday.
<script language="JavaScript">
<!-- This figures out what day of the week it
is, and prints a quote. -->
<!--
  Sys_Date = new Date();
  var DayofWeek = "";
  var TaraQuote = "";
  if(Sys_Date.getDay() == 1) {
          DayofWeek = "Monday";
```

TaraQuote = *"People make bad choices every day. Thank you for choosing Revenge Gifts. — Tara Cole";*

```
  document.write(DayofWeek + " : " +
  TaraQuote);
  // -->
  </script>
```

CHAPTER NINE

Miss Good Voodoo

SOMEWHERE ALONG THE line—and by line I mean one of the Richard Bach, life-altering decision threads that make up the weave in this rag of a life I am living—I must have inadvertently killed a nun by breaking several mirrors over her head. My luck has been that crappy lately.

Once I finally got out of my own way and going for the day, the orders started pouring in for Revenge Gifts. I am running out of stock. I had been on my cell phone for two hours with my artists and suppliers negotiating. Fortunately, it's summer. Business is slow all over the Keys. The company that makes my brass canister inserts for the seasonal urns also does welding work for boats. He's got a few weeks of down time before his winter customers start calling with requests for work on their boats before they arrive for the season. The ceramics shop is also slow right now but they need to order more materials. Ditto on the brass for the canisters. The craft club can't make lace any faster for the allergy pillows, so I have been on the phone to a club in Puerto Rico. They actually charge less for their work than the Keys

Crafters but the mail from Puerto Rico is slow and iffy. Worse, they are not especially fond of the use to which I put their lace. So, I just don't tell them what I'm using it for, problem solved.

This is probably more than you wanted to know, but I felt the need to share. I hate suffering alone.

I am about to start the process of raising the price on almost everything I sell. It's Monday and therefore the perfect day to raise prices. Since bad news is inevitable in life, I've always felt that it should only be allowed on Mondays. This sets a nice tone for the rest of the week.

When I first put Revenge-Gifts.com online I used the most basic HTML set up I could manage and sent customers to a canned site that handled the credit card transactions. A few pictures, descriptions and a simple form to fill out that linked to the bank service to process the order form. I paid the Verisign fee for the little lock on the order page and that was pretty much the whole shooting match. Since those early days I've transformed it to have a database backend with Active Server pages and I access the products, prices, pictures and descriptions via SQL. The main pages, which the customers view, are dynamically created around what's in the database. I have a few back door pages, protected by passwords and 128-bit encryptions to maintain the data files. My password is PerniciousSquid. Or at least it was until I just told you.

I amused the hell out of myself at four in the morning writing Java scripts that cause all kinds of weird things to happen on random pages. I am very fond of abusive alert boxes. I wrote one that forced the user to swear they're not currently residing in a state penitentiary. Those of us living on the Web like to evoke a reaction and pretty much any reaction will do on a slow day. That particular alert box brought me death threats. In my world, I call that a success.

"Hello?"

Apparently my guard rooster is now sleeping, worthless bird. People just drop by without so much as a call for warning. I'm not even dressed and someone is tapping on the screen door. I debated getting dressed. I've got on last year's Victoria's Secret jammies with the shelf bra tank top and silk pants. I'm more dressed than most people get these days so I decided against changing. I can see it's a woman. She can handle it.

I hit save on my computer and told it to sleep.

"Can I help you?" I asked as I opened the door and slid out onto the porch to join my unexpected guest. At first glance she looked normal, so I looked a little harder. And there it was, an earring shaped like a dagger dangling from one ear. Gold. It stood out like a stop light against her chocolate brown skin. Dreadlocks? No. She just had a lot of hair in a lot of braids, so, not a Rastafarian. Voodoo then.

"Riqué send you?"

"Yes." She smiled so wide I swore I could see even her back teeth. Then she did something that sent a chill up my spine. She shook her braids, covering her stiletto earring and backed off my porch so fast I almost missed it.

"You got a ghost problem in your bungalow." She looked spooked and she was breathing so hard I thought she was going to pass out.

I played dumb. "What makes you say that?"

"That man," she pointed behind me to the screen door, "he tell me to shoo. Nobody tell Miss Good Voodoo to shoo. You ask me to come. You tell him that."

"You want me to talk to Uncle Lester?" It seemed to me he probably already heard her and that should save me the trouble of having to talk to him directly. A task I abhor because I think it thrills him to no end when I acknowledge his presence. He used to "shoo" me when he was alive. I hated it too. "I prefer not to talk to Uncle Lester directly if I can at all avoid it."

"Sweet Jesus, there's more of them in there. Riqué, he tell me you got a curse problem, not say nothing about spooks and spirits."

"I don't need help with the ghosts. At least, not that I'm aware of anyway."

"You need help I can't give." She turned away and started to walk down the path, barefoot. I stopped and pondered that for a moment. The fact that I didn't note the barefoot thing as odd is, well, odd. I can't let her leave without at least some clue as to what I am dealing with.

"Someone's putting curses on me," I shouted it at her retreating back. She's wearing a backless sundress. White cotton.

"How you know that?" She stopped and turned halfway back, just her head, and I could see the earring. The sun hit it and it looked like it was glowing. Her almond-shaped eyes were barely open and all I could see was the white part. I combined all this with the fact that she saw the ghosts and heard Uncle Lester and I figured she's the real deal. I felt a headache coming on.

"I've gotten a gris-gris bag, a black kitten named Zeke and a black rooster left on my car and my front porch respectively."

"What was in the gris-gris bag?"

I told her.

"You got a reversal of fortune curse on you. What you do so far to fix that?"

I told her.

"That all you can do then. Some of the curse bound to leak through 'cause that bird not all white. Nothing you can do 'bout that. You know who put this on you and we can do work on them. Stop them from doing more."

"I don't know who is doing it." I slumped onto the porch railing with my head down for a second. I have a splitting headache now and sweat is breaking out on my forehead. I looked up and Miss Good Voodoo smiled like she knew I was in pain. The fact that her only offer of help is for revenge is not lost on me.

"You call me when you know."

"You have a phone number?"

She smiled wider at that and laughed. "You just call Miss Good Voodoo and I come. I hear." And with that she headed down the beach, around the corner and out of sight. I hate people who walk everywhere, and barefoot no less. Gawd, my head hurts bad.

You know how you prefer not to know that certain people and certain things exist in this world? I put Miss Good Voodoo at the top of that closet shelf. I'm not sure, but I think she scared the shit out of me. Once my headache's gone I will reassess that feeling in depth. I went in and grabbed another Diet Coke.

What the hell is a reversal of fortune curse anyway?

I looked it up online. I found a bunch of stuff, none of which was useful. It's time to get dressed, grabbed my Mundillo (for making lace), and headed over to Nana's for the weekly meeting of the Key's Crafting Society. It's time for a little lacemaking therapy.

MISS WENDY'S SECOND floor balcony overlooks a canal. The canal leads out to the bay side of the Keys' chain of islands. A vast majority of the bay side is designated National Park Wetlands. The Everglades spill out into the bay and, if the weather's bad on the ocean side of the Keys, everyone stays out on this side—in the backcountry. It's the perfect nursery for juvenile fish, crustaceans and kids. From my rocking chair I could hear the first strains of Hoobestank's *Crawling in the Dark* resonating on the still water. Miss Wendy grabbed her portable phone and stood at the railing.

I had my feet up on the railing but I had a pretty good view of the boat coming around the corner from the other canal. It's nothing special, just a simple flats boat with a forty horse Johnson. The kids captaining it caught sight of Miss Wendy at the rail.

"Shit, man, put it on!"

One of them fell back off his seat and came up with his life vest.

"She's got her phone out!" the other kid hissed. "Buckle it!"

There's a mad struggle to get the buckles latched. Dean and J.G. smiled beatifically up at Miss Wendy as they passed under her balcony. Miss Wendy checked her watch.

"It's summer, Miss Wendy. No school!" Dean shouted up.

She just smiled and waved.

"How old are those kids?" Howard asked from behind me. I hate it when people sneak up behind me: Minus one point for Howard.

"Dean is twelve and J.G. is eleven." Miss Wendy answered.

I bet she knows their birth dates. I bet she was there when they were born, in fact.

"Where's the adult that should be driving that boat?" Howard is about to get a lesson in Keys culture and I couldn't concentrate on weaving another knot of lace. He's like a wall of testosterone at my back. Again, he is inside my personal space and I am positive he knows it. His hand settled on the back of my chair as he lowered himself into a chair he'd pulled up.

My chair was cornered between his knees, stopping me from rocking for fear of rocking back into him. I felt his other hand on the seat behind the bars of my chair as he looked over my shoulder at the Mundillo box on my lap. Howard has no business looking at my lap, or anything on it. Squid.

Miss Wendy answered.

"Kids here get a boat years before they get a car. They can get a captain's license at twelve. Some don't"

"Yeah, but what if something happens?"

I turned slightly in my seat and stared at Howard. "Did

you not just see your grandmother make them put on their life jackets?"

He thought about it for a second. "She did. Didn't she?"

"Yes. She did. And you know what else?"

"What?"

"All up and down the canals and out on the bay, people are keeping an eye out for them. Retired rich people from the shore with their telescopes and binoculars, the back-country fishing guides out running charters, older kids, everyone. No one escapes notice here and the kids—they get the closest watch."

"So. It's safe."

"I didn't say that."

"You just said . . ." He's not quite acclimated but he will get it in a second.

"No one is all that safe. They just have space to grow up. They have a little breathing room."

"I see." This he said directly into my ear—on an exhale of breath. And now, *I* couldn't seem to breath. Intolerable, the effect he's having on me. It must stop. Worse, I think he knows it.

"Are you playing with me?" I finally asked. "Because, I have to tell you, if you are in any way attempting to mess with my head, I will have to hurt you."

"It's your perfume."

"Come again?" An unfortunate choice of words, I know. But, Howard's proximity has shut down my linguistic database and I have no fail-safe back up.

"Opium."

That's it. That's all he said. As if it explained everything.

"Opium?"

Howard lowered his face into my hair and pulled a deep breath. "Uh huh."

"Miss Wendy!" I caught Howard's grin out of the corner of my eye. "Muffin is bugging me!"

"Did you pick up lunch on your way over, Howard?" Wendy had settled back into her chair at the patio table and her bobbins were clacking softly as she worked the lace on her pillow. Wendy does traditional bobbin lace. I make Spanish style lace. She can weave an entire pattern from the center out on her pillow whereas I use a Mundillo, which looks like a padded wheel perched over another padded surface. The bobbins and the thread are the same, but our patterns are created differently. Mine starts from the top and I work down. I can rest mine in my lap. Because the pillows aren't rigid, Miss Wendy has to work at a table.

Howard scooted back from my chair to get up. Finally. "I did. I'll get it."

Miss Wendy smiled a little as he brushed past her with a kiss to the top of her head. "It's so nice to have him close by again."

"A little too close." I grumbled.

"He always loved to snuggle up when he was little."

"He was a snuggler?"

"He was."

And here we arrive at the crux of our communications logjam. Miss Wendy is talking about a five-year-old boy. I am talking about a full-grown man. We are using the same words, but talking in different languages. It's cute, but pointless. I want to snuggle Muffin, as in wear him as a coat. Miss Wendy's talking about the caring little kiss he laid on her head and the fact that he just got her oil changed and four new tires put on her car. We're not on the same planet.

I shut up and worked on my lace.

The rest of the craft club arrived as Howard brought out the deli trays he picked up from the Islamorada Deli loaded with deli meats and fresh fruit. Miss Wendy cooks, but usually not for lunch.

Soon the balcony filled with sounds of bobbins clacking and gossip.

"Can I get you something, Tara?" Howard leaned in from behind me, again. Someone had taken his chair so he was forced to stand—or lean as the case may be.

I didn't look up. I just shook my head no and kept on weaving my bobbins back and forth. Muffin came around to lean back against the rail in front of me, next to my feet.

"Would you like to come over after work tonight and review the paperwork for the deal? I've already ordered your favorites from the Sushi Bar. Tina helped me."

"You already ordered?" For a moment I couldn't place my finger on what was really wrong with what Howard just said. Oh yeah. He asked me over for dinner but he's already made arrangements as if it's a done deal. Damn. I'm a sucker for sushi.

"I'm working tonight."

"Only until seven. I told them I'd pick it up at six forty five."

"You're pretty sure of yourself." I still hadn't made eye contact with him.

I was suddenly aware of the profound silence that had fallen all around me. No one is even pretending not to listen.

"If I say yes, will you leave now?" I finally looked up. Howard's blue eyes captured mine in his smile.

"Yup."

"Then yes. Now go away."

The conversation picked back up all around us as Howard strolled away. Howard doesn't know it yet, but he is a dead man.

CHAPTER TEN

My First Date in Ten Years

I KNOW WHAT you're thinking. You're thinking, Tara hadn't been on a date in ten years and there is no way she has anything to wear. I am staring into my closet. I have casual clothes. I have work clothes. I have boat and beach clothes. I have nothing to wear.

Actually, that's not true. I do have one off-white linen skirt and shirt, slightly see through. The idea is to wear white thong underwear and an interesting bra underneath. This has the effect of causing people to do a first glance where you look properly dressed then a second glance when they realize you are definitely not properly dressed. I bought it at Island Elegance. It's a Keys thing. When body paint can pass as clothing, my little linen number is a mere speck surfing on the local shock wave. I wore it for Christmas at Crusty's last year. The tips were phenomenal, but it took me weeks to live it down. For a thirty-three-year-old, I have a pretty good body. It is not exactly a Barbie Doll body but I have curves in all the right places. And no, I am not going to give you my measurements. That's none of your business.

I do not work out as much as Kathy, obviously, and I hate walking, but somehow between the bar and Revenge Gifts I am getting plenty of exercise.

I've already called Kay and asked her to open Crusty's for me. I am not working tonight. Howard doesn't know every little thing, now does he?

I know I should work tonight but, quite frankly, I haven't had a date in ten years and this may be a one-shot deal. Me being me, I can almost guarantee this is a one-shot deal. I am not going to go from Crusty's to Howard's house. Not happening, not ever. I need time to get dressed and stressed, not necessarily in that order.

The Sells house is an old conch style made of cement block with floor to ceiling slat windows that crank open. If you open every window in the house you have the illusion that there are no walls separating you from the outside. Once a month, Mrs. Sells would take down the screens from the windows and hose them down. I used to help her out on window day.

She made the chainmail boxer shorts for Revenge Gifts.

Her husband was an avid diver and bought tons of chainmail when the first dive suits were tested against sharks. He had been diving since the fifties and never been bitten by so much as a damselfish, but still, it was his deepest fear. He tried to make a go of making them and selling them in the dive shops but they never caught on. The water temperatures just don't encourage you to want to layer on more gear than you absolutely need when diving off the Keys. And, honestly, yeah they keep the teeth from ripping your flesh away, but it's the jaws crushing your bones that you really want to avoid. Rumors of Old Moe, a fifteen-foot hammerhead living under the Bahia Honda Bridge, crushing the hulls of small boats, while completely unfounded, demonstrate the our real fear of sharks here in the fishing and diving capitol of the world. Besides, chainmail wet suits just aren't manly.

You don't dive because you want to live a long life. You dive because you live, breath and dream the ocean. The less that separates your body from the water you've immersed it in the happier you are in the water . . . if you're a real diver. Think I lie? One local dive shop runs a yearly nude dive trip with no difficulties booking the boat to capacity. But what do I know. It's entirely possible chainmail dive suits sell like hot cakes in France. They didn't sell here in the Keys, unfortunately for the Sells.

When I saw all the special equipment and the soft-as-silk, runs-like-water-through-your-fingers steel material, I knew I had to put it to use for something. Serendipitously, a patron at Crusty's had just been complaining that her bra under wire set off the security alarm at Miami International. She went through a humiliating secondary search as her husband alternated between laughing and griping that they were going to miss their flight because she was "busty." There are drawbacks to being busty. This is one of them.

Anyway, this material, laid into the seams of real silk boxers—the heavy, burnished weave—would not only hang perfectly when worn, it would set off every metal detector on the planet. Unless you told the wearer that there was chainmail mesh in the seams, he would never know. At sixty dollars a pop per pair, they don't exactly fly off the shelves, but I sold enough to keep the Sells comfortable in their retirement years. Their daughter took over the business after they died, but she didn't want the house.

It has no air-conditioning.

The breeze off the ocean is pretty consistent. Ceiling fans in every room and all along the outside patio keep the air moving too. The Sells family has lived in the Keys since before the 1935 hurricane. They weren't rich by any stretch of the imagination and they were the most god-awful neighbors you could ever ask for. Like all natives they had no interest in socializing. One seldom saw them unless there was a hurricane approaching. Then they would jump in the action and go from house to house boarding up and tucking treasures into sheds and garages.

I could see into every room of Howard's house. I saw boxes stacked and furniture still covered. Before I could even ring the bell, Howard was at the door, because Howard could see me as well. My lips were dry. I hate how I wish I could just crawl back into my own haunted bungalow Number 3, snuggle up with Precious and Zeke and hide. Already, I was miserable.

As if sensing how nervous I was, as if anticipating that I might bolt, Howard pressed a glass into my hand. The fumes hit me. Drambuie. How the hell does Howard know I love Drambuie? I am positive Miss Wendy never served it at her house and Miss Wendy never came to the bar. Something to ponder later. I took a huge swig and nearly choked to death. Drambuie is a very strong drink.

The only room set up in Howard's house is the dining room. He has, what looks like, a hundred-year-old mahogany table and ladder-back chairs. Howard had gone to my pottery shop—the one that makes the seasonal urns—and bought the entire set of my favorite sushi dishes. Sitting in the middle of the table was a huge tray of all my favorite kinds of sushi. Also, in the middle of the table, was a chill bucket with a bottle of wine.

"It doesn't look like we're going to be talking about business, Howard."

"We can talk about everything."

I felt the heat rising in my face. "Uh huh." A full on seduction scene was laid out in front of me. I could feel my stomach start to hurt in a way I was affectionately beginning to call 'Howard pain.' Ha ha.

I blinked a few times and shook my head. "Look, Howard, while I appreciate you slitting your own throat and serving yourself up on a platter for me, I am really not that hard up.

I could go, maybe, three or four more years without sex, more with enough Drambuie. You don't have to treat me like some kind of public service charity case. Could you forget we ever had that conversation on the boat and let us move on like normal adults and not hormonally crazed adolescents?"

An unholy grin spread across Howard's face like he just saw Santa Claus.

"That little speech is exactly why I am going to ignore your request."

I know my eyes are narrowing down to battle mode and I can't help it. Howard is being perverse. I turned my back on him and headed to the table. My steps faltered when I heard Howard draw in a pained breath and I realized: He noticed the skirt. He noticed the thong underwear. My speech was now road kill.

"That speech *and* that dress." Howard said matter-of-factly as he walked around me to pull out a chair.

"I have a few hard and fast rules relating to business and dating, Howard." I turned my head just enough to see his face over my shoulder. "I haven't broken them in a decade and I'm not breaking them now."

"I think you are going to break a lot of your rules tonight Tara," he said into my ear as I sat down and he adjusted the chair in to the table. "I think we are going to draw up a whole new rule book, in fact."

I looked out through the dozens of open window slats and realized that, even though we appeared to be completely alone and isolated by Gumbo Limbo trees, by the Jamaican Dogwoods, and Mahogany, we are never alone.

"Howard," I said, "I am very flattered. But. You don't know me. You don't know anything about my life. You don't know what you're getting into."

"Tara. You'd be amazed at what I know. You have no *idea* what I want to get into."

I looked up at Howard. His eyes caught mine in a long stare.

The breeze off the ocean set tree leaves rustling and I listened hard for the sound of wind chimes. Mrs. Sells had placed wind chimes, large and small in the branches of almost every tree on the property. I remembered thinking that the squirrels and birds couldn't be thrilled with the constant noise, but they forgave her because she fed them better than anyone else on the island. I guess her daughter must have taken most of them because I could only hear a few in the far distance.

The cloying scent of night-blooming jasmine wafted in through the open windows, so thick you could wring it from the curtains. The smell only lasts a few hours. When the darkest part of night falls, the scent fades. The first time I smelled it I sent the gardeners on a hunt and destroy mission. Mrs. Sells asked me to just have them dug up and delivered to her house. I was happy to oblige.

The silence stretched between Howard and I, but it wasn't uncomfortable.

He poured the wine. We made our selections from the platter of sushi. I over dosed my soy sauce with wasabi. We ate in a companionable silence, listening to the sounds of the night for a few minutes. It couldn't last.

I, for one, don't have the ability to sit in quiet solitude for more than ten minutes. Kathy tries to get me to meditate with her; I lack the Zen gene. I could see that Howard was having entire conversations in his head as well. As much as I would like to be able to read minds and converse telepathically, I can't. And, I suspect, neither can Howard.

"Where did you learn to make lace?" Howard broke first—like I knew he would.

"I learned over a summer in Puerto Rico. I went home with a sorority sister of mine and her mother taught me. After that, I took lessons in Little Havana from a Puerto Rican lady. She runs an ad every six months offering free lessons.

Puerto Rico pays her to give them so the art won't die out."

"Why didn't you just have Nana teach you?"

"I didn't know Nana at the time. I'd just moved here. I had a design for my allergy pillows in mind and I wanted to know how to make them. I wanted them to be something special. You want the person to keep it out in full view, not in a closet or worse—a plastic storage bin. It lets whatever the pillow is stuffed with get into the air a bit better. A converted discount store special wouldn't fill that bill. I considered ribbon pillows—I love those. But, the ribbons are color specific, usually, and less likely to stay on display if they don't match the décor."

"And lace always matches?"

"Lace always matches."

"You are a seriously diabolical businesswoman." Howard was smiling again so I took it as a compliment. "You could use a little work on your social life though."

"Are you questioning my interpersonal skills, Howard?"

"I am questioning your interpersonal skills, yes." He quirked an eyebrow up and then winked in the cutest way. Squid.

"You're not the first person to mention this lack in my skill set."

"I can see you give it a great deal of consideration, when the subject comes up."

"I give it all the merit it so richly deserves."

"Which is?"

"Zilch." I blew Howard a mock kiss and then popped a teka maki in my mouth.

"Are you going to eat that?"

He had one of those horrible tempura'd shrimp heads wrapped in rice and nori clenched between his chopsticks. It paused, inches from his lips. "Why do you ask?" He set it back down on his plate with a thunk.

"No reason."

Now it was Howard's eyes that narrowed. He bit his bottom lip, ever so slightly, in consternation. Yeah. He'll figure it out. "Off putting?"

"Way."

"That *is* a shame." He plucked it back up and chomped it in half.

"That is foul."

"To each his own." Howard finished off the first one and picked up another.

"You have no idea how amazingly disgusting that is," I choked out as I chugged down a full glass of wine in an effort to keep my own dinner down. He poured me another glass. "How can you eat that? It has eyeballs, for god's sake."

"You should try it. I bet you would like it."

"I bet I wouldn't." I concentrated on finishing my own plate full of food as if the fate of the world depended on it. No way in hell am I going to let those lips anywhere near mine for at least twenty-four hours. Yechth.

One glass of Drambuie, and two glasses of wine, and I am feeling no pain. My nose is numb and it is only a matter of time before I say something stupid and make an ass of myself. Some of you might think I have already done that. Some of you should set the bar a wee tad higher.

"I've always loved this house." And it was true. This house was a slice of the old Keys. It was like warm memories of summer nights listening to the frogs sing and the trees rustling in the breeze off the ocean, waiting for the fan to make its circuit around the room, back to the small body laying above the covers in the bed, craving the cool breeze.

"Thank you. I haven't exactly finished moving in." His eye swept the half-unpacked living room. "But, already it feels like home to me."

"You need one thing."

"What?"

"Before you do anything else, you need to get a pet. Are you a dog person or a cat person?" I looked around for any indication of preference one way or another and found nothing obvious.

"Actually, I had a dog. A Great Dane named Sally."

I hated to ask. I was learning that Howard never has a happy answer for anything,

"Sally died about a week after I moved here."

"Oh, Sad." And I really meant that. Moving is traumatic enough. Having a pet die just adds to the suck factor of moving.

"She was my wife's dog."

Oh, God. Here it comes.

"I had her cremated."

Well, that solved the disposal problem. It's nearly impossible to dig a decent hole in the ground here because six inches down is caliche rock. That also makes it expensive to install a pool.

"Where on earth did you manage to find a crematorium that would ashify a one-hundred-twenty-pound dog?"

"Miami."

"Naturally."

He nodded his agreement. If you want anything, anything at all, Miami is the place to go. Sometimes I wondered if there were limits to this bounty of weirdness. I have yet to broach anything resembling limits.

"Did you scatter the ashes at sea?"

"No. Not yet anyway. My boat is in the shop for repairs."

"Ain't it always the way?"

"Yup. I've decided to put her in one of your seasonal urns."

"Don't tell me. Let me guess. Dogs supposedly don't have souls so you want the Atheist Collection."

"Correct."

"The Dog Days of Summer?"

"Correct again."

"You know, I've never been overly fond of dogs but that piece is one of my favorites."

"When we launch, we're offering services for pets too. That was another reason I wanted your urns."

"It all makes perfect sense now." My nose was numb; my head was just starting that nice little spin thing it does when I've sipped one sip over the line. Suddenly, Howard's idea sounded brilliant to me. "Give me the papers. I'll sign them."

"We can do that tomorrow."

I tilted my head slightly to one side and dropped my chin an inch or so as I puzzled this new mystery. "Why tomorrow?"

"You'll be sober then. And, we'll have a lawyer present to notarize the documents."

Good plan. "Fine then. Anything else?"

"Not that I can think of at the moment, no." Howard was having a little trouble following the conversation. I could tell.

"Then I'll just be on my way." I scooched the chair back and started to get up. "Dinner was great. Next time we'll do it at my place—my place being Crusty's. Can't go having real food in the bungalow or the ghosts will get twitchy again." I snorted and laughed at the same time. Classy, it was not.

Suddenly, Howard was behind me, helping me stand up. "You can't drive home like this, let me walk you and I'll bring your car over tomorrow morning."

"Fine." Howard smelled of coconuts, again. I turned into his shoulder and took a deep whiff. "Hmmmmm."

"What does that mean? Hmmmm."

"It means I want to know how you know that I like Drambuie." I plucked that one right out of thin air.

"It was on your kitchen counter and half empty—so, I guessed."

"What else did you guess?"

"I guessed you like Diet Coke. Want one?"

"You have Diet Coke?" I practically squeaked, so embarrassing.

"Yup."

"Yes. Please." I followed him into the kitchen. "No glass." I caught him just before he got the glass down from the cabinet.

"They're not cold."

"That's ok. I don't mind." He handed it to me and I took a sip, trying not to sway as I did it. I leaned on the door jam. "I was just about to leave, wasn't I?"

"You don't have to leave, Tara. The night's just getting started."

I contemplated the mystery of night starting and wondered what that meant, exactly. "But we've agreed to do business. That was the whole point of my coming over here. You've strong-armed me. I caved over sushi. We're done." I waved the Diet Coke can in a circle eight for added effect. Hey, I'm not completely wasted.

"We don't have to be done." Howard was looking at me like I was dessert. That look . . . that look was doing things to me. Should I tease him, mess with his head, or both? I think, both.

"That shrimp head thing, Howard . . ." I let the sentence trail off deliberately.

"What about the shrimp head thing?"

"Off putting."

He grinned a ten-megawatt grin and started walking toward me. I backed out into the dining room and then to the front door. Just as I decided to turn around to walk front ways, his hand gently touched my waist.

"Let's walk." He grabbed a throw blanket from the back

of the partially uncovered sofa as we went out the door. His hand steered me to the dock.

A full moon was rising over the ocean and small waves were lapping against the rocky shoreline. The dock was one of the few things about the property that received anything in the way of real maintenance. Old Mr. Sells used to bitch that if one single mangrove took root near his dock, he would lose his land to the tree huggers. Thus, he scraped the shoreline daily and eradicated all plant life within fifty yards of the dock.

"You have a hammock?"

"I do."

"Nice." And I meant that. I love hammocks. Mine broke about a month ago and I hadn't had time to pick out a new one.

He took the soda from my hand and held the bar on the hammock steady. "Have a seat."

I eased bonelessly back into it, sideways. Howard handed me my drink and settled in next to me. It was so high off the dock; my toes barely touched the planking. Howard took over the task of rocking us back and forth. I decided to just go along with the ride, kicked my shoes off, and tucked my feet up next to me. This moved me a little closer to Howard, but hey, it's a hammock. He draped the thin cotton blanket over me. I was starting to feel my nose again, but I was also getting a little tired. Stress knocks me on my ass every time. It took me years to understand why I was so exhausted all the time after work when I worked for Aileen. It wasn't like it was physical labor. Computer geeks don't even break a sweat on most days. I was exhausted more on the days I didn't go to the gym.

Eventually it dawned on me. The more stressful the day, the more tired I was when I hit the front door step of home. Judging by how tired I am now, I'd have to say Howard has Aileen beat by a mile. But the fact that I can relax now kind of scares me.

Howard sighed and I wondered if he knew that I'd compared him to Aileen. Doubtful.

It seemed as if hours passed but it couldn't have been—could it? Howard finally spoke. "What's it going to take, Tara?"

"What's it going to take for what, Howard?"

"To break this ten-year curse of yours."

I considered his question sleepily. Curse? Was that what it was? I had countered all the reversal of fortune efforts except the one that was leaking because Sunshine is peachy white and not all white and wondered what else the evil Voodoo Queen could throw at me to break the ten-year celibacy curse. "Sacrifice a goat?"

Howard was silent for what seemed like forever. As I was just about to fall asleep I think I heard him say, "That's doable."

```
// Thought for the day on the Home Page of Re-
venge-Gifts.com,
scheduled to load on Tuesday.
<script language="JavaScript">
<!-- This figures out what day of the week it
is, and prints a quote. -->
<!--
  Sys_Date = new Date();
  var DayofWeek = "";
  var TaraQuote = "";

  if(Sys_Date.getDay() == 2) {
          DayofWeek = "Tuesday";
```

TaraQuote =" "In an interview, Evan says that his life isn't glamorous or easy, and that he needs a woman who can take a tough situation and be able to laugh about it. So in other words, in twenty years when he's still faking the back injury that brings in his workers' comp check every month, he needs a woman who can laugh while she heats up his turkey potpie. Got it." —Kim";

```
  document.write(DayofWeek  +  " : "  +
  TaraQuote);
  // -->
  </script>
```

CHAPTER ELEVEN

The Morning After

DISASTER STRUCK AT Bungalow number three while I was napping on Muffin's hammock. The food poltergeist managed to get the fridge open, again. Because I had just stocked it with breakfast staples, there were enough eggs for it to get creative. The word "bitch" was spelled out in eggs on the kitchen counter with a knife through the egg that dotted the "i." No biggie. Seen it before. Usually it doesn't have enough eggs to do any real words. I've learned not to stay out all night with a full fridge—unless I happen to get hammered and pass out on someone's hammock. Under those circumstances I think I can be forgiven.

And yeah, it could be a human. I thought that at first myself, so I'll forgive you for thinking it too. After all, I don't lock the doors. I called the police the first two times it happened. No fingerprints. All they found was this icky spooge on each of the eggs. It's a kind of clear gel that dried sticky. I asked them if they were going to have it analyzed to see what it was. They said I should watch less TV. I quit calling the police after that.

Anyway, the reason I knew it was not a human doing it is

because I saw the fridge door opening all by itself as I walked in late one night. No one was around, just me, the fridge and whoever was opening it. I apologized for coming home late, like a complete moron, closed the refrigerator door and went to bed. So, no, I don't think it's a living, breathing human being doing it.

It's a waste of eggs, if you ask me, but you didn't. I tossed them in the garbage and washed off the knife.

"The knife's a nice touch, ghost." I won't talk to Uncle Lester, but the food poltergeist I occasionally acknowledge.

I actually noticed the egg art when I stumbled in at about six a.m. this morning. Muffin walked me home after letting me snore all over him in the hammock last night. I am completely and utterly humiliated. I am also ashamed to say that, as it was my first ever all-night snuggle session, I loved it. Muffin was warm and comfy; the night was cool and slightly breezy. No rats or mosquitoes chased us inside. It was bliss. My cruiser is still over at Muffin's house. The plan is for him to pick me up this afternoon in it, take me to Crusty's and he'll walk home from there. It sounded like a brilliant plan at six a.m. At four p.m.? Not so good. My Crusty's grunge clothes are completely unacceptable for Howard viewing and anything dressier will draw comments from the Crusty's regulars.

I have pulled everything out of my closet and drawers and actually started a bag for charity of things I haven't worn for two years. It looks like I am going to have to go with the khaki Capris and standard GAP T-shirt with my trusty brown Sebago Docker deck shoes. Zeke has taken up the task of softening the laces on the left shoe. Precious is draped over the right shoe. I have less than an hour to iron my outfit, shower and restore my bedroom to its pre-chaotic order.

My cell phone was ringing. I ignored it and took my shower. People rude enough to call when I am about to take a shower deserve to be ignored. I suds'd off last night's make-up and vowed never to put on mascara again—after tonight. I lost the mascara removing stuff a million years ago and soap stings. Precious and Zeke are just outside the shower door yowling. It's a cat thing. I'll never fully understand it. It's as if they see you getting wet; something they would never do voluntarily in nine lifetimes, and want to save you. I don't know what Zeke's deal is. He's not old enough to even know what water does to a cat's fur. Precious is breaking him in.

My cell phone was ringing again as I stepped out of the shower. I ignored it again to braid my hair. Me and phones have a love-hate relationship going on. The phone has a need to direct calls at me, I have a need to ignore them. Since I pay the bill that keeps the phone alive, I win. I decided on one diagonal braid and a brass dragonfly hair clasp to hold it wrapped to my head. Very tropical, I think.

I started reapplying mascara and make-up and—you guessed it—the phone started ringing again. And again, I ignored it.

I got dressed. The phone rang. Someone better fucking be dead, is all I have to say about it. I answered it with out looking at the caller-ID.

"What?" If it's someone who knows me, they are used to it. If it's not, they better get used to it or lose this number.

"Is this Revenge-Gifts.com?" A very masculine, very French accented voice, which I don't recognize, is talking on my cell phone at me. Now I am really pissed. Jack? I swear to God if it's Howard's friend Jack I'm going through the trouble to block this number from him. Does the man not know I am minutes away from . . . from . . . what the hell am I minutes away from anyway? A date? Nah.

"No. This is not Revenge-Gifts.com. Revenge-Gifts.com does not have a phone number where you can talk to a real human being that I am aware of." I sounded pissed. I was pissed. I didn't try to hide it. "Is this Jack?"

"This is not Jack." Now the caller sounded pissed. Good. "I got this number from the web host for Revenge-Gifts.com

and I would like to talk to the person in charge of that abom-
ination of a website."

Oh, I *so* don't have time for this shit. My name and number are not supposed to be listed on that site. I pay extra for
that. What changed? I should have never used a local hosting
service. Squids. Damn.

"Your website is garbage."

I hung up. I saved the number under the name "Loath-
some Ferret" and made a mental note to have the number
blocked when I have time. In the meantime, I turned the
phone off and decided to leave it at home. No one needs me
that badly that I need to have a freaking phone hanging on
me 24\7. It's time to break free of the phone.

I heard Howard drive up in the cruiser and so I snatched
Sunshine out of her cage. We met him at the door. She made
kissy sounds all the way out. Howard actually got out of the
car, came around, opened my door and waited to close it
again, without making a comment on Sunshine. I tried to
hide a smile but I haven't had a door opened for me since
high school. I now realize that I kind of miss it. Is it worth
rewarding him with sex? Maybe.

The lunch crew had all but left as I got in but there were
no customers. Sunshine settled in nicely on her perch and I
handed her a bag of sunflower seeds. She can open a tin can
with that beak; a plastic bag is no struggle. Keeps her busy
and out of trouble. Howard settled into a seat at the bar.
Howard doesn't get a bag of sunflower seeds. I'm not sure
why he's decided to hang out and I put off asking until I'm
organized and oriented. Awkward.

"Can I get you something?" I finally asked Howard after
I'd settled in to bartender mode.

"What are you having?" He nodded at the glass of ice I
set up on the bar. I'm on autopilot. The soda spritzer is
already in my hand and my thumb is on the "S" button for
soda water. I fill the glass.

"Hangover cure." I shook a good dose of bitters in the glass and topped it off with a piece of lime. Stick in a straw and it's ready. I took my first long sip of relief. I didn't realize it, but I'd been craving this all day. "Want one?"

"Thanks, but no."

"Something else then?"

Howard sighed softly and scanned the bottles behind me.

"You know what I want, babe." Sam dropped into the barstool next to Howard.

"Kir Royal?"

"You secretly lust after my body. Admit it." Sam blew me a kiss as Sunshine snuggled up under his hand for her feather scratching. I have no good answer for this so I fixed his drink in lieu of a response. Howard turned to stare at Sam, then stared at me. I raised my eyebrows and dropped my chin in my best *what are you looking at* stare.

"Heard you spent the night over at the Sells place in a hammock," Sam said. Then he leaned into me and whispered—loudly—"With him." He gestured at Howard with his free hand. "How was it?"

"None of your business." There's no use in denying it. If Sam knows then it's all over the islands.

"Yeah, I heard no actual action was reported. Shame."

"We haven't been introduced." Howard offered Sam a hand to shake. Sam shook it. "I'm Howard Payne. I just bought the Sells house a mile or so south of here. And you are?"

"Sam." He grinned at Howard with a genuine smile. Generally Sam only gives the genuine smile when it's someone he's not interested in sleeping with. Howard is safe . . . for the moment anyway.

"You a regular here? Or just passing through."

"I live here. Work here . . . Attorney at law, mostly criminal defense. Ever need me, just give a call." Sam whipped out his business card and handed it to Howard. "I eat here at

Crusty's most evenings. I hate cooking. Nice view. Good company. Is that a new shirt, Tara?"

"Nope."

"Looks good on you." Sam dropped his Costa Del Mars just a smidge to ogle my chest. Either Sam is jealous of Howard, or he is trying to get a reaction out of Howard to judge what stage our relationship has reached so he can report back to his source. I could flip a coin as to which, but I bet I'd be wrong. I let it go.

"Howard?" I had to break his gaze because his eyes drifted with Sam's to my chest and he seemed to have stopped thinking for a moment. "What would you like?"

He pulled himself together enough to look back over my shoulder at the bottles. "Seven and Seven."

I handed both of them menus and got Howard his drink. He tentatively scratched Sunshine under her wing under Sam's tutelage. If these two become friends, I am going to have to move to another island.

"I'll just have the usual," this from Sam, who never opened his menu.

"Is the ceviche fresh?" Howard took a sip from his Seven and Seven after I handed it to him.

"She hates it when people order the ceviche." Sam is being helpful, point for him.

"Good to know." Howard went back to studying the menu. "I'll have what Sam is having."

"You sure?"

Howard looked at Sam for confirmation, a nod to acknowledge that it's not going to be rat poison maybe? Who knows? I punched in separate tickets and put it up for Riqué. It's gonna be a long evening.

"So. How long have you known Tara?" Howard had a hopeful gleam in his eye as he began pumping Sam for information. Like Sam knows anything about me—he wishes. I excused myself and headed back into the kitchen to make up a fresh batch of ceviche for my dinner. There was a receipt from the fish company for a delivery next to the register. I felt eyes on my back as I disappeared into the kitchen.

"You sleeping with that man?" Riqué was all over me before I could even open the main wait fridge.

"Nope."

"Word is, you slept all night with him."

"Technically, that is correct. But I am not 'sleeping' with him. No."

"Yet."

"You sleeping with anybody, Riqué?"

He blinked at that for a minute and shut up. We're not going to have share time tonight. Darn. Riqué cooked the burgers and fries while I chopped fish, cilantro, onions and limes. He was finished before me and rang the "order up" bell with a wee bit of attitude. I ignored it to finish the ceviche.

Once the ceviche was all stirred in together properly, I scooped a dish for Puddin, who was waiting patiently under my feet, dished up a scoop for me and put the rest in the fridge. The theory is that the lime "cooks" the fish as the ceviche ages. Eating it before this mythical transformation takes place is just one of the many karmic stones I use to pave my own little road to hell. I was originally looking for the "road less traveled," found it and then started paving it for everyone else. Revenge-Gifts.com is the sign up ahead. I am amazed every single time someone else makes that turn.

I carried everyone's food out on an arm and one hand. It took me all of three days to learn that particular balancing trick. No one had come in to the main dining area while I was in the back. Good. Sam had poured Sunshine a glass of something and she was slurping it down happily.

"Want anything to go with this, guys?" I pulled out catsup and mustard from my apron and grabbed three wrapped silverwares from the pile left by the day shift at the end of the bar.

"Looks good." Howard reached for the catsup and proceeded to drown his burger and fries.

"Mine's fine." Sam puts nothing on his meat or fries. I'm not sure why. He also eats it in pieces, onion first. There's probably a ream of information to be gleaned about a person by the way they eat a burger. I've just never been interested enough to do the research. Or more truthfully, I don't want to know that much about my fellow man. But I bet you can tell if someone is a serial murderer just on the burger thing. Someone should check.

"Are you eating ceviche?" Howard had just noticed my dish.

"Yup."

He looked at Sam who shrugged. "Women. Can't predict a damn thing."

"Apparently not."

"Want a dish?" I asked to be polite, although the thought of ceviche mixing in Howard's stomach with all that catsup started mine churning. Howard looked to Sam for guidance.

"Don't go there, man."

"Thanks, Tara, but I'll just stick with the burger." Howard smushed his burger in one hand and chomped a goliath-sized bite out of it. I picked at my food. Ceviche really needs to settle for an hour before it's edible, but I felt the need to eat socially with the guys. Sunshine stole a fry off of Sam's plate and raced back to her perch. She knows Sam doesn't share the fries. They've had this fight before.

The front door to Crusty's opened and a perfectly normal couple walked in, and the man held the door for the women to precede him. We don't get many of those in here. I hurried over with menus and sat them as far away from the boys as humanly possible. They wanted a bottle of wine and two glasses of water. I got it for them and took their order with as little fanfare on the wine bottle opening as I can get away with and still expect a tip. Crusty's is not a fine dining experience but we can manage opening a bottle of wine at a table. We even have the clay wine chiller things. Sherry bought them in California. She brings the wine back with her every year from there as well.

Business picked up after that and I found I could completely forget the weirdness of Howard hanging out with Sam at my bar. Before I knew it, Kay was punching in at the register and donning her apron for the evening.

Had it been four hours already? Time flies.

"You ever figure out what was in that bag last time?" Kay had a different set of tassels hanging down from the back of her shorts this time. New.

"It was a black Persian kitten. Why do you ask?" I like Kay, and she doesn't generally engage in information gathering so I'm willing to provide her with answers to the few questions she chooses to ask of me.

"Because you've got a black goat tied to the bumper of your cruiser out back. Just thought you should know." She paused. "In case you didn't already."

I stared at her. I stared at the boys. Howard looked poleaxed and guilty as hell. "I was kidding when I said that about the goat, Howard."

"I had nothing to do with it, I swear."

"When you said what about the goat, Tara," Sam asked?

"Nothing, Sam." I was ripping off my apron as fast as I could. I started a mad search for my cell phone in my purse under the bar and remembered that I'd left it at the bungalow. "Give me your cell phone, Sam."

Sam, bless him for not asking why, handed it across the bar. They all followed me out through the main wait to the back of the restaurant. There, munching peacefully on hay spread on the ground behind the cruiser was an honest-to-god black billy goat.

"I swear to god I didn't put it there, Tara." Howard was pale as a ghost and almost pleading. I kind of believed him.

"Riqué?"

"Boss?"

"You still know that guy who butchered and roasted the pig for us last Christmas? The one who charged fifty bucks and a bottle of rum?"

"Yes, Boss. You want me to call him? We gonna have a goat roast?"

"Yep and yep. Spread the word. Tomorrow's dinner is on me."

"You're going to kill it?" Howard's complexion grew even paler if that was possible. No goats are actually killed in the making of a Disney product. It's time Howard realized he's not in Disney anymore. Sam just looked gleeful as hell. Kay went back to work with a snort.

"You are looking at tomorrow night's menu special, Howard." The goat probably weighed slightly over sixty pounds. It should be enough to feed a few people with all the "go-withs." Which reminded me, I started dialing Sam's cell phone.

"Tavernier Deli. How can I help you, Sam?" Marl's cheery voice blasted from Sam's phone at top volume. I clicked it down two notches.

"It's not Sam, Marl. It's Tara over at Crusty's. I need bread and go-withs for about fifty people delivered here at one tomorrow. Can you handle that?

"What kind of go-withs and what's your price limit?" Marl is all business with big orders.

"I don't know." Deep down I was pissed and the list of consequences for sacrificing this goat were starting to run through my head one by one. "Whatever you think will go well with roast goat. Set the cost at $400."

"You footing the bill or is this one on Sherry's account again?"

"I'm paying this time."

"Damn, Tara. I heard you got laid last night but I didn't believe it."

"Excuse me?"

"I always said you'd unclench from that pocketbook of yours if you ever got lucky and here you are paying for a feast. Rumor has it you spent the night with that new boy over at the Sells place. He do you up right and proper?"

"You want my business, Marl, or not?"

"I'll take that as a yes, and yes indeedy I do want the business."

"Spread the word that there's a goat roast at Crusty's tomorrow afternoon." I hung up.

Howard was petting the goat on its head. "You know what this means."

"Yes, Howard. I know. Stop petting the food." I dialed a local band and made arrangements for them to play a few sets. It was their day off and the weather forecast sucked for fishing. No jokes about my sex life from them.

"Will someone please tell me what the deal with the goat is?" Sam asked as I handed him back his phone.

"No." Howard and I both said it together.

"Answer enough for me. I get it." Sam grinned and headed back inside. Sunshine was probably chewing up the bar by now. She never lets an unsupervised moment go to waste. Sam would deal with it.

"You gonna put up flyers or call more people?" Howard was finally looking at me. He had a slight gleam in his eyes that suggested all kinds of bad thoughts were chasing through his brain. I secretly wanted a starring role in every one of Howard's bad thoughts.

"Don't need to."

"Am I invited?" He asked.

"Howard. You are the guest of honor."

"I hoped you'd say that."

"Well I said it."

"I didn't leave this goat here." He still looked kinda guilty, but I believed him.

"I'll drive you home."

```
// Thought for the day on the Home Page of
Revenge-Gifts.com,
scheduled to load on Wednesday.
<script language="JavaScript">
<!-- This figures out what day of the week it
is, and prints a quote. -->
<!--
  Sys_Date = new Date();
  var DayofWeek = "";
  var TaraQuote = "";

  if(Sys_Date.getDay() == 3) {
          DayofWeek = "Wednesday";
```

TaraQuote = " "In June of this year, an "amorous" dolphin
named Georges began making sexual advances on divers in an
English town, so efforts were made to relocate him to France
(logically enough)."— Miss Allie";

```
  document.write(DayofWeek  +  " : " +
  TaraQuote);
  // -->
</script>
```

CHAPTER TWELVE

Goat Roast at Crusty's

WORD SPREAD, AS it always does here, about the goat roast and at least a hundred of my nearest and dearest showed up for the impromptu party. I bought a yellow linen A-line dress similar to my semi-see-through linen number in honor of the occasion. Kathy showed up, even though I knew she felt she was just contributing to the badness by being present. She'd called me at midnight in tears begging me not to kill the goat. She said we could fix the bad ju-ju if I just gave her a chance to do a little research into the matter.

I told her that a girl had to draw the line somewhere and my line gets drawn at goats.

If someone wanted to curse me bad enough to sneak in and tie a goat to the back of my cruiser, then I was just going to have to suck it up and take the curse. I didn't want to know what came after a goat. How many years could roasting a goat get me anyway? Two, max? Fine by me. And, it had the added benefit of taking away my guilt for lusting after Howard's body. I mean we just met. I should technically wait for the third date before even considering sex with him.

This way, I can have him tonight with no guilt involved. It's out of my hands. Blame it on the curse and the goat.

Things were going great. The crowd was happy. The band didn't suck too much. The food was holding out fine. It couldn't last. Dennis and Kerry arrived.

"Christ, Tara, I heard you got laid but I had no idea you'd completely crossed over to the slut side." Dennis was eyeing my dress up and down as if I'd forgotten the underwear. Good thing for him Sam wasn't around to hear him say that. Kerry just whacked him on the shoulder and I turned my back on them both to walk away. Dennis got an eyeful of my backside and sucked in so hard he choked. Wheezing hard he tried to get me to come back. "Is Sherry here tonight? I need to talk to her."

I shouted over my shoulder, "Nope." And kept on walking. Let them fend for themselves. I wasn't putting up with Dennis's shit tonight. I was in too good a mood.

I had the doors and windows wide open to Crusty's and Tiki torches lit everywhere. I'd rented hurricane stand fans and placed them where the natural breeze might not hit. It was a cool, comfortable evening inside and out. People were dancing and drinking. For a Wednesday night, no one seemed to worry about having to work sober tomorrow. A hand slipped around my waist and I smelled coconuts. Howard.

"It's going to be a late night, Howard. You sure you want to wait around here?"

"I'm staying for the long haul. Why don't you let me fix you a plate? You haven't eaten anything yet and the food is half gone." He spoke low into my ear as he guided me over to the fire pit and food tables Riqué had set up. Howard grabbed a plate and started filling it up with some of everything. Mercifully, the head of the goat had been removed before they laid it out on the table to carve it. Howard forked up a few slices of meat and we headed to a quiet table by the water.

Privacy, as you already know, is an illusion. A hundred pair of eyes gauged our progress from the food table to the dining table and took note of Howard's proprietary air. They would note that I did not give Howard a hard time as he skillfully steered me through the crowd of people in the dance area. I ignored all of them. Tonight was all mine.

Howard and I spent the better part of the evening just getting to know each other a little better. Kay and the rest of the staff worked the party and raked in the tips since the food and drinks were free. I was paying them handsomely on top of the tips to handle any problems. Kay kept bringing Howard and I refills on our Seven and Seven and Drambuie so we never had to actually get up. Kathy and Sam joined us for an hour and then drifted off to dance. Dennis tried once more to annoy me and was headed off at the pass by pretty much every guy at the party. Everyone knows how much I hate Dennis. They hate him, too.

As parties go, it was a success. But all things have to end.

After the band packed up and the Tiki torches doused, Howard and I pitched in and broke down the food tables. There was nothing left. Marl packed the serving dishes in his van to go back to the deli. It was time to get home.

Two o'clock in the morning in June here in Islamorada is a sultry, soul sucking ninety degrees with one-hundred percent humidity. But since I lost my soul years ago when I created Revenge-Gifts.com, I guess the heat and humidity just don't have the same effect on me that they do on a normal person. Conveniently enough, I have a normal person following me up the path to my bungalow with whom to check on this theory.

"Hot enough for you, Howard?" I turned and waited for him when I reached the front porch. Uncle Les, God bless the old dead squid, turns on every light in the bungalow just as I walk up the steps at night to creep me out, including the porch lights. So I know Howard is getting the full effect of the see-through qualities of the little linen dress I am wearing. He gave me a considering look and said nothing as he brushed past me to open the front door.

"What?" I challenged him, standing there like Superwoman with my fists on my hips and legs braced apart.

Howard pinched the bridge of his nose between his thumb and index finger and sighed. I looked down at my body from breasts to toes for anything out of place. "Are you waiting for an engraved invitation? Tara World is open." When he still didn't move from the doorway I started to worry a wee tad. "The goat's dead, Howard. Do me."

I heard him moan a quiet "Dear God" as he put both hands on his face and rubbed like he was washing. Then he ran his fingers through his hair several times which had the effect of standing it on end in a cute little surfer style kind of way. The word "agitated" came to mind.

It occurred to me that the last time I had sex, the guy was all of twenty-three years old. At twenty-three guys just need a place; sometimes they don't even need that. Howard is pushing forty. Perhaps easy access isn't the only aphrodisiac needed here.

"Damn. Don't move."

"What?"

I raced past him to the kitchen for the matches, my open bottle of Merlot with two wine glasses and a bottle of almond oil from the nearly empty pantry. I turned the lights off room by room as I made my way quickly back to Howard—Howard, who was sitting on the bedroom chair taking off his shoes instead of at the front door where I'd left him.

"Don't undress yet." He looked up from his shoes, huffed a little snort of disagreement and started to unbutton his blue silk Tommy Bahamas shirt. "Seriously!" I set everything down on the table next to his chair and grabbed a random Robin Schone romance from the bookshelf behind him.

I handed it to him figuring it would at least keep his hands occupied for a minute while I set the mood. "It's kind of a how-to manual, really good stuff, sex for the thirty-something-plus set. You know, realistic?"

He snorted, "Homework?"

I grinned. "I'm a computer engineer. There's a book for everything."

I lit the candles on the windowsill, the pillar candle next to the bed and the little heater thing for the oil. After pouring some of the almond oil into the top reservoir, I turned off the bedroom light. Howard had just started reading one of the tabbed sections of the book—yes, I tab things. I'm an Office Depot freak, so shoot me. He cleared his throat and waited patiently closing the book and setting it on the table next to him.

"You ready?" He gave me that "direct in the eye" look that said Howard was all business now.

Hell no I'm not ready, but I'm not about to tell *him* that. Even though the big secret is out that I haven't had sex in ten years, maybe more now that I think about it, I've never fessed up to anyone about how bad the sex was when I was actually getting it. Yeah. Yeah. Yeah. I was a college kid. Sex was everywhere then so there's no excuse for not finding the big "O" with someone, or even by myself—but a big plastic phallus wasn't exactly a turn on. And trust me, had I known the dry spell after college was going to be this long I would have strapped a mattress to my back and gone to class naked until the goal was reached—maybe. But here and now, I was afraid to say it, afraid to bring up the subject, terrified he'd think I'm a complete head case.

I swallowed hard, "Ready."

He smiled that wicked little smile guys do when they know they are about to get lucky. I love that smile. It does things to my inner thighs. You have *no* idea. He stood up and poured two glasses half full of Merlot and walked over to hand me one. Tapping his glass against mine he leaned in to my ear and whispered, "So am I."

Hallelujah, because really, if he had needed more than the basic prep work I was going to need time to do some review and research.

We both took a few sips of wine. He tilted his glass high and slammed back the rest of his in record time, then put the glass back down on the table. Howard was wide-awake now. He finished unbuttoning his shirt and draped it over the chair. Man-oh-man, Howard must work out. I.Q. points were flushing out of my head with every second I stared at Muffin's chest. Howard walked around me; his hands started at my waist and came around the front to brush over my breasts. My knees turned to water and the only things holding me up were Howard's hands. So warm. Then the ear and neck nibbling began. Oh, I remember the ear and neck nibbling. I missed them so. I brought my free hand up to run my fingers through his hair and give his hands better access. This is so very, very nice. This part of sex never lasts long enough for me.

He nuzzled my neck and murmured in my ear, "Tell me what you like."

I took a sip of Merlot to avoid answering. I gave a little moan of encouragement in the hope that he would just assume he was doing fine and proceed accordingly. Honestly, do women generally have an answer ready for that question? If any of you do, please send it to me, because my mind is a blank.

"Tara?" He stopped. Damn.

"Howard?" I held my breath and waited, hoping he would just take up where he'd left off. But, oh yeah, I don't have that kind of luck. I forgot.

He turned me around to face him and stepped back to arms length. I licked my suddenly dry lips and waited, afraid to meet his eyes. The bottom was dropping out of my stomach with every second of silence. Howard sighed and then he smiled.

"You don't *know* what you like. Do you?"

The ridiculousness of my position finally hit me and I looked up at him through my bangs, eyebrows raised to the hair line, eyes wide and managed to shake my head, no. He started laughing a deep, rumbling laugh and hugged me to his chest like a toy doll. God, I hope he's not quitting on me, because damn it, I can only sacrifice one goat a year and I don't think I have it in me to go another year without sex now that I've come so close to getting it again.

Our height difference puts me at heart level on his chest and I can hear it pounding.

"It doesn't have to be great, Howard."

"Uh huh. Tell you what, Tara, let's try a variety and you pick and choose your favorites for next time." He put me at arms' length again.

I set my glass down next to his and crossed my arms in front of my chest to disguise the fact that my nipples were getting hard, so embarrassing. I nervously tapped an index finger against my lips pretending to consider the smorgasboard approach. I smiled a little, picturing Howard as a buffet of love. At this point, I would agree to just about anything if it meant we could get back to the nuzzling.

"Fine."

"You sure?"

"I'm sure." I was so completely not sure. I just wanted Howard to take over again and stop asking me what I want.

"Take off your dress, Tara." Yep. Howard is back in charge. I don't like it.

I'm wearing a bra, so fear of immediate nudity isn't the problem. Hell, I've worn less on the boat fishing. What was the problem again? Oh yeah. I'm an idiot. I'm thirty-three years old and I've forgotten how to seduce a man because I am out of practice. "I need help?" I sounded pathetic. Howard raised an eyebrow.

"You got yourself dressed this evening, didn't you?"   .

"Um. Yes." Where the hell is this going? I have no idea.

"Then you can get yourself undressed for me tonight." Howard's tone brooked no refusal. It was masterful in a mean kind of way and I felt the first tingle snake down the back of my spine. I like masterful Howard. I eased my dress off and laid it over the top of Howard's chair. "Now the bra."

I pierced Howard with a hard stare and unsnapped my bra at the back. It joined the dress. Without giving him a chance to demand it, I turned to head for the bed. His arm snaked around my waist and stopped me just as my first knee bent to climb onto it.

"Not so fast," Howard whispered in my ear. His hands wandered down to my thighs, separating my legs just a little.

One finger slipped beneath my thong undies and found— mmmmm, ahem, places I'd forgotten even existed. His other hand tweaked my nipple and massaged my breast. This was going to be a very short evening if Howard kept this up.

My legs started that annoying, weak tremble thing they do. I guess once the I.Q. goes and the brain shuts down there's no automatic reflex control that keeps them steady. Howard pulled me back into his body for more support. "Relax. Just tell me to stop if I do anything you don't like."

God. If Muffin is going to insist on using his old standby lines from high school, I may have to whap him. "Stop talking."

My hand found his beneath my undies. Oh the rubbing was wet and delicious. His hands were so big and rough. I could feel him hard against my butt. He felt huge. The material of his rough silk slacks against my skin was doing wicked things to my body temperature. Friction. God I need more friction.

Mine. All mine. "I need more."

"Relax against me. Let it go, Tara."

Howard was in complete control and here I was falling apart. If I hadn't felt his hard on, I would wonder if he was even turned on at all. And then I stopped thinking as the first wave hit me. So *that's* what it's like. How hard was that? My ex-boyfriends were pigs. And, yes. I screamed. So embarrassing. God, it's that easy? Where the hell has he been all my life? I vowed at that moment to hunt down my exes and publicly humiliate them. Later.

Howard had me up in his arms before I could stop twitching. He literally threw me on the bed and started digging in his pockets for—something. Oh. Condoms. Howard threw a handful, one, two, three, whoa—a lot of them onto the bed and plucked one up as he unsnapped, unzipped and shucked his pants.

"I'm on the pill." I felt I should mention it. He was just reaching down next to my head to pick up a condom and stopped, leaned down and kissed me, hard.

"You are the most perverse woman I have ever met. You haven't had sex in ten years, told me, in fact, that you systematically put men off for your career and yet you're on the pill?" He rubbed his cheek against mine and inhaled deeply. "Do you mind if I ask for how long and why?"

"Since I was eighteen."

Muffin pulled back a bit to look at me.

"Call me a cock-eyed optimist?"

He smiled. "Good to know that at least one of us is optimistic."

I looked over at the ten condoms next to my head.

"Point taken."

He grabbed one up, ripped the foil open and smoothed it on in record time. "These are textured—" he handed me the empty packet so I could read the label—"for you."

"I don't . . ."

He shushed me. "You'll like it. I promise." His knee parted mine and as his lips claimed mine again, he grabbed my hips and plunged.

Ten condoms seem a little much.

He paused for a second and then wrapped his arm beneath my hips and pulled me up. "Wrap your legs around me," he groaned.

His arm released my hips and came between us. With each gentle caress I involuntarily squeezed my legs around his waist. He paused. I relaxed. He caressed. I squeezed. I tried counting the condoms next to my head to distract myself and slow down. Nine. The tremors were building again. Nine was probably—oh God—a good number.

Better to have too many than not enough.

Or maybe he was moving in. I . . . I kind of liked that thought. And that was when I finally broke a sweat. Howard slammed into me. After five minutes of missionary, he turned me over and pulled me back to him. He was rock hard and so big it nearly hurt in this position. I almost said something when his fingers found me again and started to rub in my new favorite spot. Magic. I came shrieking like a banshee and Howard finally joined me. We collapsed on the bed and it was several minutes before I realized that I still had on my undies.

"That was incredible." Howard's arms were wrapped around me and he was gently caressing my breasts. "You have the most beautiful breasts I have ever seen. *Playboy* breasts. Perfect."

"You say the nicest things after sex Muffin. I'll be right back." Awkward as it was, I needed to get to the bathroom to clean up. I was a mess. Howard just whipped off the condom with a Kleenex and he was good to go. I needed a little more than that.

"Don't you dare get dressed. I want you just like you are for the rest of the night. Lose the thong."

I slid back into bed with him a few minutes later. His hands slid around me. He leaned over and kissed me on the lips, softly at first and then deepened the kiss. Normally, I am not a kisser, most men slobber too much—watery lips. Yecht. But Howard—Howard applied just the right amount of pressure, of tongue, of suction. Oh man, the things his kiss was doing to me. Amazing. This reversal of fortune curse could last a lifetime for all I was concerned. I could live with Howard's fingers just there until the world ended. Howard's lips moved lower to claim a nipple and I came like a rocket. No build up—just an instant twitching mass of Tara.

He ripped open another condom, put it on.

"I have oil heating up." I decided I'd mention it just in case he wanted to slow down and play.

"Next time." He pulled me back to him and entered me from the side. My left leg draped over his hip as he rocked slowly in and out. Ahh friction. It was bliss. His hands were everywhere, pulling, kneading, tweaking. I didn't want it to end. He kissed the side of my neck and worked his way down to my shoulder. Just as we came together, I heard the fridge door open and the first egg explode against the far kitchen wall.

"What the hell was that?" Howard sat up. I pulled him back to me and started kissing my way down his chest.

"Food poltergeist. Ignore it."

"Oh." He sighed as I gently removed his condom with a tissue and proceeded to resuscitate his sorely overworked body part. Another egg hit the wall. "As long as you know what it is . . ." His voice trailed off. We had eight condoms left and I wasn't going to let the food poltergeist interrupt even one of them.

Zeke and Precious raced into the room and under the bed; so much for fierce kittens and guard cats.

Shit. Why now? A low growling started up beneath us as Zeke and Precious dug in to defend their territory. Cowards.

I only had four eggs in the fridge. Two left. One of the cats hissed at the sound of another egg splatting against the wall. Down to one. I gently played with Howard's balls as I licked up the underside of his penis like a lollypop—ten long years. I put ten years of fantasies into the best blowjob of Howard's life. His skin there was like fine satin over rigid steel.

The last egg hit the wall and Howard rolled me over onto my back, grabbed up another condom, ripped it open and put it on. He bounced me so hard on the bed that Zeke and Precious raced out from under it hissing and spitting and into the far corner of the room. I know just how they feel. Howard's shoulders were trembling as he tried to hold off his orgasm for me. He lifted my legs over his shoulder and slid in and out of me as slowly as he could, his fingers found my sweet spot and it was all over before he could touch his lips to my breast. We both came again, long and slow and I swear to god I could hear angels singing. Or was that the phone?

Shit. Who the hell would be calling me at four in the morning? And suddenly I was in a cold sweat because I knew who it was. Or rather, I didn't know who personally as in a name, but I knew who would be calling at this hour. I let the computer pick up. Unlike ordinary answering machines, you can't hear the message being left when the call talks to the computer. With any luck at all, Howard didn't even hear it ring.

"Who the hell would be calling you at four am?" He asked sleepily. He was on top of me, but that was ok, because one of my Muffin fantasies was to use him for a blanket. And besides, I was scared, more scared than I wanted to admit.

"Wrong number probably." I rolled him off of me and headed for the bathroom, again.

"Stay naked," he wheezed out tiredly. "We're not done yet."

The rooster outside began crowing.

Howard got up and used the guest bathroom and was back in bed before I came out of the master bathroom. I heard it all again in my head, the phone, the eggs, the rooster and Howard, as I rested my forehead against the cool glass of the bathroom mirror. My life was beginning to close in on me and I suddenly just wanted to crawl into Muffin's arms and cry. I only allow myself sixty seconds of self pity every day, and then I shake it off. Life is too short and people are too weird to take anything seriously for more than a minute.

I wondered if parts of me might break off if I used them too much. Nah.

I blew out the candle under the oil. I snuggled back into bed with Muffin and kissed my way down the side of his face and neck. He smelled like coconuts. I felt the stress flow out of me through my toes. Zeke settled in at the foot of the bed and Precious was purring at the top of the pillows. As I was falling asleep, I thought I heard him say, "I'm keeping you."

```
// Thought for the day on the Home Page of
Revenge-Gifts.com,
scheduled to load on Thursday.
<script language="JavaScript">
<!-- This figures out what day of the week it
is, and prints a quote. -->
<!--
  Sys_Date = new Date();
  var DayofWeek = "";
  var TaraQuote = "";

  if(Sys_Date.getDay() == 4) {
          DayofWeek = "Thursday";


TaraQuote = "
```

I have seen, heard, and read thoughts of such surpassing stupidity that they must be addressed. You've heard them too. Here [is one]: Violence only leads to more violence.

This one is so stupid you usually have to be the president of an Ivy League university to say it. Here's the truth, which you know in your heads and hearts already:

Ineffective, unfocused violence leads to more violence. Limp, panicky, half-measures lead to more violence. However, complete, fully-thought-through, professional, well-executed violence never leads to more violence because, you see, afterwards, the other guys are all dead.

That's right, dead. Not "on trial," not "reeducated," not "nurtured back into the bosom of love." Dead. D-E-Well, you get the idea.

—Lary Miller";

```
  document.write(DayofWeek + " : " +
  TaraQuote);
  // -->
</script>
```

CHAPTER THIRTEEN

The Morning After

I AM SERIOUSLY considering removing the "Contact Me" hyperlink from the website. Really, why in the hell should people have a real human being to deal with? Most websites steer the buyer through about a million pages, asking them to review the frequently asked questions, etc, so on, ad nauseam, before they give them a page where they can fire off that flame mail or get a phone number where they can call to bitch. It's cruel but hilariously funny. Until recently, I've seen no need to add the standard three hundred hoops for the user to jump through before they can email me. However, for this email alone, I have decided the time has come. Read it with me and judge.

From: KCase@SiliconMonthly.com [mailto: KCase@SiliconMonthly.com]
To: WebMaster@Revenge-Gifts.com
Subject: Promotional Request

Dear Sirs,

I am writing to inquire if your company provides free promotional samples of your products. Silicon Monthly is planning to include your website in our December issue in a spread on the wedding of the year. We were informed that your Fruit Cake will be served at the reception and that the bride and groom have purchased all of the gifts for the groomsmen and bridesmaids from Revenge-Gifts.com.

Our staff will be in the Keys this Friday and they would like to interview you and take pictures for the articles. I would like to schedule the interview tentatively for four in the afternoon. Please let us know if this time will work for your representative.

Sincerely,
Kimberly Case
Silicon Monthly Magazine
KCase@SiliconMonthly.com
(202) 555–6783

First of all, Kimmy freaking Case? It's like a cold wind blowing up my butt. Can it be the same Kimmy Case who tormented me for ten years at my old job? Second of all, I don't give away anything for free. Moochers. I have an urge to call, so I do.

"Silicon Monthly. This is Kimberly Case speaking. How may I help you?"

That voice. That voice was like nails raking down a chalkboard. I will never forget it. Hot damn. It *is* Kimmy.

"Hi Kim. This is Tara Cole. I just got your email and I decided to call rather than email you back."

Dead silence. I double clicked the time on the computer task bar so I could watch the second hand tic around the dial and keep track on how long it takes her to say something. Forty-two seconds.

"I'm sorry. Who was this again?"

The grin on my face was huge. Howard thought it was for him as he caught the blinding glow when he walked up to me from the bedroom and landed an Olympic-sized smacky-kiss on my shoulder. The sound effects of the kiss must have decided it for Kimmy that this was a prank call and she began the polite hang-up routine.

"I'm sorry. You must have the wrong number."

"You emailed *me* Kim. Revenge-Gifts.com? Remember?" *I* began the polite routine to end the conversation. Muffin had just come out of the shower. He was a slightly damp, steamy, wet and warm Muffin and he smelled really, really good. I didn't feel like talking to Kimmy anyway.

"Wait." She sounded as if she was getting her feet underneath her again. Damn. I was hoping to keep her off balance for a while longer at least. "You said your name was Tara?" Ha. She's hoping it's a coincidence.

"Yup." Howard was working his way down from my neck and I was wanting to end this conversation with Kimmy immediately. "When did you start working for *Silicon Monthly?*"

"I took the buy out, like you—" I can hear the question mark in her voice, "—did, and decided to try something a little different. So. You work for Revenge-Gifts.com? Appropriate. Who do we need to talk to for an interview with the CEO?"

"Me." I decided to let the "appropriate" barb die the ignoble death it deserved.

"Can it be arranged? Are the date and time I emailed doable? Can you give me some background information on him? A bio?" I can hear her fingers clicking on computer keys, "There's nothing online about him." Now she's sucking on her pen like a lollipop. It's one of her most repulsive habits—but kind of endearing. It made everything Kim said sound a little off, with a slight lisp.

"What time does the UPS guy get here?" Howard was back up to neck level and whispering in my non-phone ear.

"We have about two hours."

"Two hours for what?" Kimmy stopped sucking. Howard started.

"I'm talking to someone else Kim."

"Is that him? May I speak with him?"

Howard was now inching my shirt up and off and I am tired of talking to Kimberly Case. What started out as one of my perverse, boredom deviations was fast taking second place to what I'd prefer to be doing—or, more to the point, who I'd prefer to be doing. Hey. It may be my last long drink before the next dry spell. Life is too damn short to waste it playing head games with the Kimmys of the world.

I sighed heavily and then groaned as Howard's hands started inching under the waistline of my shorts to smooth across my derrière. "I am the CEO, owner and god of Revenge-Gifts.com, Kimmy. And no, the time and date you suggested are not convenient. I don't do interviews. I don't give out promos of products. And, I don't want to be featured in *Silicon Monthly*. But, thanks for thinking of me."

"Don't hang up!" I'm guessing Kimmy just realized she doesn't have my phone number listed in her caller-ID box. "We need at least one of everything for photographs."

"Then I suggest you buy one of everything."

"Tara, you are not understanding. Let me explain. This is no ordinary wedding. These are not ordinary people. When this news hits the web, everyone is going to want this for their social events. You are going to have more business than you know what to do with. The last time we featured an on-line store—not half as unique as yours—it went international in less than a year. Investors went nuts for it and the sales figures rocketed. You can name your price for your products. People will pay it."

"Then I suggest you hurry up and get your order in now before I raise my prices."

"Wait. Ok."

"Better hurry, Kim, I've got the screen up to change the prices. When I'm done and hit enter, your order had better already be processed."

"You wouldn't." I could hear her fingers clicking again on the keyboard. "Why would you do that?" She was still typing frantically. "Fucking T-1 line." This was muttered quietly but I still heard it and smiled. This is the first time I've ever heard Kimmy curse. I like it. "Tara. Give me an hour at least. We have a budget set."

"One hour then."

"Thanks. And the interview?"

"No way in hell."

"We're coming anyway. We'll find you."

"It's a small island. You might succeed."

I hung up just as Muffin was lifting me up out of the chair.

"You're sexy as hell when you're being cruel to customers."

"Kimmy isn't a customer. She's an annoying pain in the ass. Let's forget her; let's get back to bed. Being mean to people is exhausting."

"Be nice to me then, Tara. Get your second wind."

Words to live by, but honestly, I don't think I have a second wind. I sighed and turned my head away from his kiss as he set me down on my feet next to the bed. His arms wrapped around me as I turned my back to him. I covered both his arms with mine and leaned back. Just that. Just the feel of warm, strong arms around me and I can't think past this moment. Point for him that his fingers don't make an immediate beeline for my breasts and he let me hold him still for a moment.

"There's always tonight, Tara." He knows. How the hell does he know me this well?

"Is there?"

His answering laugh vibrated against my spine. "Definitely. And tomorrow night."

"Two whole nights, Howard? No wait, that would make it three." Sunlight was hitting the window slats and angles of light glance off dust motes drifting in the air. The hair on Howard's arms is nearly white blond in this light. Mine too.

"It's been a long time since I felt like this."

"I've *never* felt like this." I thought about it for a second. "What do *you* mean—like this."

His knee brushed past me as he drew us both down onto the bed. I adjusted to land on my back and he lay on his side, his body touching every inch of mine that it could. He bent one arm behind his head and rested the other across my waist. My right arm was trapped beneath his head, hand clasped in his, and my other hand held his at my hip. He snorted and didn't answer. Fair enough. We hadn't known each other long enough for the "serious feelings" discussion. It was probably better to keep it as casual as possible. After all, how many goats could there possibly be in the Keys? This could be a very temporary aberration.

"Want to tell me about the egg situation in the kitchen?"

"Are you hungry?"

"Yes. And that's not what I'm talking about."

I extricated my right hand from behind his head and rolled away from him. "Why do you want to know?"

"Oh I don't know. Maybe because it's weird as hell?"

I snorted. "Yeah, well, weird to you maybe."

"Weird. Period."

"Pick another subject. I only tell ghost stories at midnight." I got up and got dressed again. Howard rolled onto his back and stared up at the ceiling fan. As I passed through the doorway to the living room I could hear him sigh and sit up.

"Yeah, well. Did the egg ghost leave any coffee?" This, he shouted through the doorway.

"I'll make some for you." I paused at the computer to start the print of today's orders and headed into the kitchen to clean up the egg mess and start the coffee. Zeke and Precious followed me to the cupboard and starting the morning meows for food. Their dishes were only half empty, but they act as if they are starving to death. I freshened their food and gave them clean water. Sunshine was still covered and will remain so until noon. She shrieks loud enough to wake the dead if I uncover her and don't immediately let her out of the cage. Maybe tonight we can have a Sunshine B.B.Q.

I grabbed a Diet Coke out of the fridge.

Yeah. You can say it. That was one cold-blooded using night of mutual pleasure. God, I'd so forgotten what that was like. It's not like I'm high maintenance either. I don't require a ton of head games or sex toys to get off. The modern mantra says that, for women, sex is all in the head. For a man, sex is just physical. Women think too much. Where did *that* come from? It probably roots back to the fifties where men were supposed to do all the thinking for the women, when in fact, all men were thinking is that they needed to get laid.

One of the guys I used to work with used to say, "Nothing wrong with him/her that a good roll in the sack wouldn't cure." Derrick's line I think. I was pretty sure at the time that he was a virgin. This made it all the more ironic because there was so much wrong with Derrick that I was convinced mere sex could not have cured him. I kind of miss Derrick.

Now that the challenge bloom was off Howard's rose, I expected him to run for the hills. But still, he loitered about the bungalow like the myriad of ghosts who come and refuse to depart no matter how much I starve them of the attention they so crave. Curioser and curioser. I am beginning to worry.

I got the orders packed and stacked and Howard was on his second cup of coffee. I was now on my third Diet Coke and Nick is late. I have instructed Howard to keep a proper distance from me. It's bad enough the entire island knows we did it last night. They do not need an eyewitness account from Nick. If there were a polite way to scoot Howard out the door, I would do it. As it is, I'm having a bitch of a time keeping my hands off him. I have an uncontrollable urge to grab him and drag him into my bedroom, tie him up and keep him forever.

It's official. I'm losing it.

He hasn't even complained yet about not getting fed. I checked my watch. It's been well over and hour since the Kimmy call and time to raise prices. What? You thought I was kidding?

CHAPTER FOURTEEN

Revenge Weeds

PEOPLE ARE WEIRD here in the Keys. But, I do believe Kathy was taking weird to an entirely new level. She drove up just as Nick departed and was even now unloading— something. It looked like shrubs.

"Those look like shrubs."

"They are. There were work crews with those big circular blade things trimming the trees and bushes along the eighteen-mile stretch. I asked the guys working if I could snag a few of the cuttings. They said, sure and loaded me up." She hefted out bundle after bundle of cuttings as she talked. I'm not sure but I think a few lizards just disappeared back into her trunk.

"And you did this because . . ." Usually the work crews down here are prison labor. Kathy has no sense of self-preservation. She is living proof that God protects fools and innocents.

"Brazilian peppers."

I took a closer look at the shrubbery and damn if she wasn't correct. The branches were loaded with tons of red

Brazilian pepper berries. She was dumping branch after branch of one of the ten most hated nuisance non-native plants in South Florida onto Sherry's beautifully, expensively maintained grounds.

"Why are you unloading weeds onto Sherry's expensively manicured landscaping?"

"Red peppers will break the curse."

I thought about this for a minute. I weighed the bliss of the past twenty-four hours against the dead zone of the previous ten or so years and decided to protest.

"I don't want to break the curse." And really, I don't. If being cursed means mindless sex with Muffin, then curse me ten ways to Sunday.

Like she didn't even hear a word I just said, Kathy proceeded to shake the berries out, following the circular path around my bungalow. Howard dove into the thick of the madness and actually started to help. After pondering the situation for a moment, I decided to inquire about the limits of Kathy's cure.

"If I am standing outside this circle, is the curse still broken?"

Kathy and Howard paused and stared at me.

"What?"

"How does this break the curse? I mean, the goat met its untimely demise at Crusty's. Now I'm here. As far as I can tell, I would probably need to wear a sarcophagus of red berries around me at all times to really break the curse."

"And your point would be?"

Kathy isn't liking my logic. I can tell. Not that curse-breaking is an exact science anyway, but this particular idea is so loaded with holes even I can see through it.

"I'm just saying."

Another thought occurred to me, "You know Brazilian peppers are in the same family as poison oak, right?"

"Nice try, Tara. Don't you have emails to answer?"

Kathy and Howard got back to work on the berries. I decided to go back inside and finish sifting through my emails. Obviously, I was not wanted here. I wasn't sure about the poison oak thing anyway. I wondered, briefly, if it would be good filler for the allergy pillows. I remember thinking when I read it that it was just tree hugger propaganda to keep people from cultivating the plant. I guess we'll find out one way or another in a few hours. Maybe less.

My desktop icon for phone messages was flashing and I suddenly remembered the phone ringing at four this morning. Do I play it? My heart is racing out of my chest. I closed the dialog and stopped the phone answering service. Maybe I'll play it later . . . like next spring.

I stared out the window to gauge Kathy and Howard's progress. Sherry's gardeners are going to be pissed. I can just picture Kathy stopping on the Stretch, the most infamous road in the Florida Keys, to ask the convicted felons working there for weed cuttings. She loves me. I'm going to have nightmares for months. The woman has no freaking sense of self-preservation.

"Tara?" Kathy's at the screen door calling me.

Sigh.

"Yeah, Kathy. Coming out."

"Howard says you guys haven't eaten yet. Let's go to Gus's."

I am suddenly very hungry. "Good idea. Hang on a second while I get my shoes on."

"Howard's going to drive."

"Great." This means Kathy and I will be sharing the front passenger side seat. Ahh, high school, I do remember it fondly. And college. Ironically enough, college was the last time I got laid. Here I am sharing a front passenger seat again, right after I got laid. It's all one big circle, life. I hurry because I can hear the property manager dialing the grounds crew all the way over here. I uncovered Sunshine as I walked past her to leave and she started making kissy sounds. When she realized I wasn't going to take her out of the cage she spun up for a loud squawking session. Sunshine is louder and more obnoxious than a Canadian goose when she gets pissed.

I hate that damn bird.

I feel some sympathy for Precious and Zeke, but I know from past experience that Sunshine will shut up as soon as she thinks I'm really gone. A strong smell of turpentine hit me as I stepped outside.

"What smells?"

"The pepper leaves." Kathy had the grace to look slightly chagrined.

"You've surrounded my entire dwelling in a plant that smells like turpentine?"

"It only releases that smell when you step on the leaves. Just step over it."

I stepped over the line of shrub branches while shaking my head in disgust. Since I am fairly certain she is capable of coming up with something even more repulsive if I reject her Brazilian pepper plan, I keep my mouth shut. I can live with the smell for a day or two. With any luck, the peppers are poisonous to eat and my rooster problem will be solved. I seldom have that kind of luck; so don't get all excited at the thought.

We never made it to lunch.

The rest of the day was spent at Mariners Hospital getting Kathy and Howard treated for plant poisoning. Sadly, I was right about Brazilian peppers being related to the poison oak family of plants. I made a brief call to the property manager to warn him and apologize. He said we had been punished enough. I hadn't been punished, except for the fact that I was seriously starving. He didn't need to know that I hadn't touched the plants. He said the grounds crew were used to poison wood and such and wore protective clothes in any case. Not to worry. So I didn't. By the time Howard dropped

Kathy and I off, it was time for work. I am now exhausted and starving. I think Kathy's pepper berries must have worked, because I was bordering on miserable.

I showered again and dressed in record time. I barely had time to scarf down a scoop of ceviche before the first of the dinner crowd arrived. A poker run had finished up in Key West a day ago and the bikers were slowly working their way back north. What looked like acres of Harleys started pulling into the parking lot. I have a bad feeling. I am beginning to suspect that my Australian customers from a few days back talked up Crusty's to their fellow poker runners and now all of them are stopping in to see for themselves.

Kathy's curse cure has killed me. Shit.

For the next three hours Riqué and I were run off our feet. The local customers just wrote up their own orders and Sam even went in the back, put on an apron and started cooking with Riqué. Kerry came in, again looking for Sherry, took one look at the sea of wealthy foreign men and started bartending like the pro she is. I owe her now. Shit.

By the time Kay and crew arrived for the closing shift, I was sweating buckets and dripping tips all over the main wait. Kerry was sloshed but working her ass off and Sam had retreated to a dark corner of the bar with Sunshine. All the activity was making her squawk and stamp her feet. She needed calming.

The Koala crew and extended gang settled in for a night of hard drinking with their American, French, German, and what-the-hell-ever compatriots.

What looked like a gris-gris bag was hanging from the side of Kay's shorts tonight.

"Ok, Kay. I finally have to ask."

"What?"

"Is that a gris-gris bag hanging from your shorts?"

"Sort of. I went to Kathy's and got her to mix me a totem with white sage ash for luck."

"Why?"

"It seemed prudent."

"Again, why?"

"Everyone knows about the curse, Tara. I just don't want any overflow spattering me." She headed off to take over a table by Sam and Sunshine. Sam flicked her gris-gris bag as she went by and the smile she turned on him dazzled even me.

"Curses aren't real," I said, when she came back with a drink order.

"Maybe not, but better safe than sorry." She put the food order up for Riqué. "And anyway, if you didn't believe it, why all the weirdness lately?"

"What weirdness?"

Kay stopped in mid-stride and turned around to stare at me, hard.

I tried to stare her down but ended up looking away first. "Yeah, well, who's normal around here anyway?"

"True." She took off again to her next table. I closed out my number and retreated to the office off the kitchen to total the deposit and finish the week's paperwork. Tomorrow is payday. I wrote up gift certificates and added two crisp one-hundred-dollar bills in the envelopes for Kerry and Sam and took them back out to them. It's not the first time they've jumped in and lent a hand. Well, Kerry has never actually done more than self-serve when I was too busy to get her drink. Still, I appreciate the help. Maybe I shouldn't paint her with Dennis's taint so harshly. I make a note to myself to do better. Because Kerry is sloshed, I offered her a ride home. Sam offered too. She accepted Sam's over mine, naturally, but not before stuffing a wad of napkins with phone numbers and names into her purse. Kerry is trolling for the next Mr. Kerry. Dennis is an ass. He deserves it. I'm glad to have helped.

It was going to be a long night. I decided to stay and bartend until the extended Koala crew departed. They didn't depart until closing time at one in the morning. By the time I got home, I smelled like smoke and fried food. My hair feels greasy and there is no way I can sleep with myself until I take another shower.

Two in the morning and I am exhausted but wide-awake. I did not drink my usual glass of Drambuie at the bar so I feel no guilt about pouring a snort for myself now. The wind is kicking up and I've opened all of the windows and doors. We don't get the huge crashing wave sounds that most of the east coast of Florida gets. I love that sound. Damn. But, we get the wind through the palm trees and boats clinking against the dock. We get the soft sound of small waves lapping against the hulls of the boats and the shore. And, we have the sound of wind chimes spread across the strange and varied sea of Keys dwellings, mine included.

I have all night to sit and wonder how Kathy and Muffin are doing. Kathy's skin was forming blisters when we arrived at the emergency room. They wanted to keep her but she insisted on leaving. She hadn't wanted to go in the first place, preferring to try herbs and creams from her shop first. Howard insisted. His rash amounted to a few itchy blotches. No big deal.

I feel for them both. Except, maybe, Kathy a little less— and a little more, for breaking my reversal of fortune curse and causing me to spend a very long night waiting on squids instead of snuggling with Muffin. She's definitely paid for her good deed in spades though. Maybe she'll think twice before good deeding me again. Nah.

Gotta love someone like that.

I'd take her breakfast first thing in the morning. In a perfect life, I'd spend the rest of the night with Howard and we'd both bring Kathy breakfast in bed in the morning. Sometimes I wish I lived an ordinary life; A normal life. I squelched the urge to walk up the beach to Howard's house and sneak into bed with him. It's time for all bad little girls to be in bed. It's been a long, weird day.

```
// Thought for the day on the Home Page of
Revenge-Gifts.com,
scheduled to load on Friday.
<script language="JavaScript">
<!-- This figures out what day of the week it
is, and prints a quote. -->
<!--
  Sys_Date = new Date();
  var DayofWeek = "";
  var TaraQuote = "";

  if (Sys_Date.getDay() == 5) {
          DayofWeek = "Friday";
TaraQuote = ""I think we're gonna need a bigger boat."—
Chief Brody, Jaws";

  document.write(DayofWeek + " : " +
  TaraQuote);
  // -->
  </script>
```

CHAPTER FIFTEEN

An Ordinary Ghost

ZEKE IS BOUNCING off the walls again; but I don't need him to tell me my newest addition to haunted bungalow number three has returned for an early morning visit. Nope. I know all the signs now. I can hear the blood roaring in my ears. My stomach just dropped two miles in under a second. And, I am cold and sweating all at the same time.

I was facing the alarm clock as I opened my eyes. Four o'clock a.m. I'm beginning to hate this ghost. Doesn't she know I need more than an hour and a half of sleep?

Zeke settled down to a purring pace at the foot of the bed. It took every nerve in my body to turn and focus on the bottom right bedpost where Zeke was now doing his happy cat dance.

"What is . . ." The ghost paused for what seemed like forever, "a normal life?"

I gave the question as much thought as my freaked-out brain cells could muster and managed to produce a small, helpless shrug. Her eyes seemed to sadden at this and she stopped petting Zeke to give me her full attention.

"But you wished for it tonight. I heard you."

That got my full attention. Any part of me that wasn't already focused on the ghost before this statement was now completely riveted to her.

"You were thinking it. You can't deny it." Now she looked amused, but her expression seemed the same. Odd. I am trying hard not to be afraid, but fear wins out every time.

She stilled completely and said, "How is it, then. That you can want a thing—about which you know nothing?"

I shrugged, again. I felt her annoyance rolling toward me in waves. I decided it would be prudent to answer with more than a shrug. My body is frozen stiff to the bed but, with luck, my mouth still works.

"I want it because I don't have it?"

Her eyes snapped to focus high and right on the wall behind me. A popping sound preceded every light in the bungalow turning on at once. The phone started ringing. She was gone.

I rolled back to my side to glare at the phone and the clock and decided to let the computer pick up. When it hadn't answered by the fifth ring I remembered that I'd turned the service off on the computer—damn it.

The rooster started crowing.

I caved and answered the phone.

"Someone had better fucking be dead." That's just my way of expressing to the caller that four a.m. is an inappropriate time to be calling someone unless there is an emergency.

"Someone *is* dead. We killed her, you and me." Click. Dial tone.

Wacko. As if I don't have enough to deal with, now I have nut jobs fantasizing about murder and me. I laid my head down after I returned the receiver to its cradle.

Why the hell can't Uncle Lester turn *off* the lights for a

change? That would at least be useful. I dragged my body out of bed and walked through each room turning off lights. There is little to no chance that I will be getting back to sleep anytime soon, so I decided to check email.

There's just no excuse for the first email I open. The writer is complaining that Revenge-Gifts.com incites people to "do evil." Yeah, and?

I used to answer these flame mails. I paid real lawyers to cover my butt from everything but God; maybe even from God. Still, I am watching the lawsuits brought against the gun manufacturers with a keen eye. I don't believe my products can be held responsible for killing people, especially in their shipped form. Hell, even the pillows are separated from the fillers the customer orders. They have to unzip and stuff for the final effect. While you could equate that with loading a bullet in a gun, let's just say, it's a stretch. I ponder a possible patent for safety zippers for a brief moment. Make them only work for users who can answer a few relevant I.Q. questions. If the person is too stupid to work the zipper, I could give them a refund on return. This might prevent someone from doing something stupid. My head could trip down this lane for days if I'm not careful. Fortunately, I remember that if stupidity were a deal-breaker for purchasing and using American goods, nothing would ever get sold on the market in this country.

I've learned that answering emails like this one is a colossal waste of time. Apparently, some people are just looking for a reason to bitch. Shift. Delete.

There is a new email from Kimmy, informing me that *Silicon Monthly*'s writer and camera crew will be staying at The Moorings and will be in contact with me shortly after they check in; I care. Shift. Delete.

There are twenty-three penis enlargement SPAM mails. I live for these. There are almost as many Viagra SPAM mails. I have six offers to refinance my mortgage and two messages letting me know that my computer is spying on me, promising to explain how. I kind of like this flavor of SPAM, because the paranoia to which they play means the market for my business is alive and well. In fact, all of these pander to a population so well fed and comfy, people have nothing but time on their hands. Time to go looking for trouble. It's *Dangerous Liaisons* brought down to the middle class. I call that the epitome of societal success.

The fact of the matter is my computer probably *is* spying on me. Evil bastard. For all I know, microchips and kilowatts are the miasma breeding a super race of miniature beings watching my every keystroke for clues as to how to take over the known universe, which they call Tara. What possible difference does this make to me? Shift. Delete.

The last email I open is a joke from my one and only sister. She uses carbon copy rather than blind carbon copy so that every recipient's email address is available to everyone else on the list. In this list of emails is everyone she has ever met or whose address has ever passed through her email in a carbon copy section of a joke mail message. She also leaves the forwarding information from the past sixty incarnations of this joke mail and the indent darts. I literally have to wade through a mountain of crap to get to the ten lines that make up the actual joke. I estimate that she is ten email addresses away from being shut down and TOS'ed by AOL for Spamming. I contemplated warning sis of her impending TOS. I weighed it against the possibility of an actual phone call from her when AOL TOS's her. I replied that I loved this joke and thank her for sending it.

My sister is a complete computer squid, but I love her anyway. Hey, at least she emails me once in awhile. I take what I can get. The rest of you can die waiting for a personally written letter. I'll be over here happy that I'm at least on her joke email list, still.

Wading through all that crap has exhausted me. Some people do crosswords to fall asleep, I read SPAM. Whatever works!

CHAPTER SIXTEEN

A Reversal of Fortune

ORDERS HAVE TAPERED back to manageable levels. Is it because of Kathy's red peppers? Or could it be because I doubled my prices. You decide. I put my money on Kathy. Very few people are thinking hard enough to bargain shop when seeking avenues of revenge. Now big-ticket items like murder, people get thrifty and clip coupons for murder at a reasonable cost. Revenge? Not so much. I believe there is the perception that murder, for the most part, is a little too extreme to justify under all but the most heinous circumstances. But we can justify revenge on the slightest whim. It's harder than you think to execute ending a life. It's much easier to find justification for making someone we hate miserable, maybe because so many of us are miserable ourselves. Some say that revenge opens the gates to hell. I say, when you're on the wrong side of them, you do whatever it takes to open those gates. Of course, there are the ones who closed the gates on you in the first place. They tend to disagree with my philosophy, until they decide they want a little payback themselves.

I've received two irate and abusive phone messages from recipients of revenge gifts on the computer answering service. The computer is now set to fax mode. I also called in another request for a number change. Someone has obviously posted my phone number somewhere else on the web. It's time to change it. The cell phone will tide me over until the number change gets processed.

I've got everything boxed and stacked at the door for Nick. Time to shower and get dressed for the day.

Flowers arrived via Chanté of Chanté Creations. You get that. Right. Like enchanté? Exactly. I think she had her name legally changed to Chanté when she moved to the Keys. Getting the whole name scoop is on my "to do" list in any case, as in asking around on the history of Chanté. For a fact she knows *my* complete life history. Bitch.

Chanté in person is a sight to behold. I'm not completely certain Chanté is, in fact, a she.

Today Chanté is wearing a cute little strapless number that I recognize as an altered Roxy sundress from last year's Surf Shop sale. In its original form, I seem to recall that dress as having substantially more material than it appears to have now. She's wearing matching flip-flops and her toes screamed professional pedicure with little sun decals laminated on each big toe. She has a few really cute toe rings and an ankle bracelet made of gold conch shells leashed together.

I know Chanté, not because I frequent her shop, but because she frequents Crusty's. Chanté comes in every other week and milks a single glass of Merlot for hours. She never leaves with the same guy twice. She has never left with Sam. The fact that Sam, a man with almost no standards or hangups, avoids her is a telling fact. I have no idea what it means, but I guarantee you it means something interesting.

This is the first bouquet of flowers I have ever received in my entire life. I am stunned.

"God, Tara, this is—like—the first time I've ever made a

delivery to you, ever. How cool is that?" Chanté stepped inside the bungalow like she's home, swept the room in one long glance and headed for the dining room. The bouquet in her arms covered up the entire diameter of my four-person table when she set it down.

Women over a certain age should never, ever say phrases like, "How cool is that?" unless they are goofing. It's just wrong. I pulled five dollars for a tip out of the seasonal urn on the coffee table. Uncle Lester is on the windowsill. Chanté does not see the tip as a hint to shut up and leave. Sadly, she looks like she wants to chitchat. I may have to direct her to the door.

"UPS!"

I see no good coming of this. Glad I showered first.

"Whoa." Nick just noticed the arboreal offering to Yukiyu: Hard not to. "You got any flowers left in the shop, Chanté?

"Nope, but this work of art paid the rent for the month. Look at this." She guided him closer to the table. "There are four orchid plants making up the base of the bouquet. I had to make a special trip to Homestead yesterday for those. The customer specified vanilla orchids. Very expensive."

I moved in closer too. I'd never seen vanilla orchids.

"Kind of ugly, aren't they?"

"Tara!" Nick tsk'ed me. I hate being tsk'ed. "That man must be crazy in love with you to spend this kind of cash."

"Vanilla is an aphrodisiac, or rather, the smell is." Chanté supplied helpfully. "There are chocolate orchids and ylang ylang, too. Those smell great even after they are dead but they die really fast."

I sniffed in the general direction of the ylang ylang. It was overpowering, sort of like night-blooming jasmine. Damn. This thing was going to have to go outside. The bungalow was already beginning to reek.

"Weird." Chanté chewed the inside of her lip and appeared to be contemplating something important.

"How so?" Nick beat me to the inevitable question. "Where is the card?"

You know, it's *my* bouquet. If anyone should be hunting for the card it should be me. I would have thought to look eventually, once the shock wore off.

"That's the thing," Chanté said. "There wasn't one. There was no card and no name on the order. The shop in Miami that took the order said it was paid for in cash and the customer said it was a surprise."

"A surprise huh?" Howard had outdone himself on this gift but yeesh. The sex was awesome, true. But, being that he was the only guy in my life at the moment, I didn't see the point in all the secrecy. Worse, it's so ostentatious it bordered on tacky. Dead rock stars don't merit flower arrangements this huge. I began to worry that Howard had issues I'm not aware of. I mean really, it's just enormous.

"That guy must like you a whole bunch, Tara." Nick's expression kind of had that watching-a-triple-X-rated-movie hue as he handed me his electronic slate thing to sign.

"Uh, Nick?"

"Huh?"

"You're picking up, not dropping off." He nearly dropped the slate in his embarrassment. I know what he's thinking. He wondering how hot the sex must have been to rate the raping of Borneo's entire crop of flowers for the year. He smiled at me and shook his head in bemusement.

"I guess ya just never know about a person until . . ."

"Take a brain detour, Nick. That head trip is going to get you hurt." I hustled both Nick and Chanté to the front door—nearly made it too—when Muffin arrived. Perfect timing. Nick let him in with a huge grin. The bouquet immediately mesmerized Howard.

"That's some work of art." He stared down at me for a second and then walked over to have a closer look. I heard a low whistle escape his lips. "Someone must think you're pretty special." He said it with such a serious tone and look. I felt compelled to say something nice: An unnatural state of being for me.

"I love it, Howard. It's beautiful. But really, you shouldn't have."

His head whipped around in surprise, "I didn't." And now I understood the expression on his face. Howard was jealous.

You could have heard a pin drop, it was that quiet all of a sudden. It felt like all the air was sucked out of the room and everyone was holding their breath. Since there were no pins dropping, it was easy to hear Miss Good Voodoo shouting like a fishwife in front of the bungalow.

"Bring your sorry self out here and face me like a woman. I know you in there. Come out!"

I pierced Chanté and Nick each with a hard glare, "Don't you two have businesses and mail routes to run?"

Nick just laughed at that. "You're joking, right?" He pushed open the screen door and stepped out of the way of Chanté, who barreled out past him with a quick, "excuse me."

"I don't have any flowers left to work with anyway. I'm expecting a delivery at two." She was sizing Miss Good Voodoo up with interest. "And anyway, this kind of day is like a gift that just keeps on giving. I mean, I've always wanted to get to know you better and here I am—how cool is that?" She finally cast a sideways glance at me, but she wasn't smiling. In fact, I was noticing that her face had literally no expression at all. Botox? Probably.

Howard hung back a bit and leaned against the doorframe. I had to squeeze around him to get out to the porch. Miss Good Voodoo was a sight to behold in red. Her braids were wrapped peek-a-boo style with a blood-red cotton scarf. Her dress was an island wrap that left the shoulders bare, made from the same material as the scarf. It was wrapped around and around her breasts for support, leaving the thin single layers exposing her waist down to her hips where a second layer of wrap clung precariously angled. The skirt was made up of hundreds of gauze strips. Her dagger-sharp fingernails were so long they curved under and were painted with a matching red polish. She was stunningly beautiful and she appeared to be pissed.

Her ensemble matched the ring of Brazilian peppers that lay around the bungalow in a foot-wide band in front of her. The branches were long gone, but the berries remained. She swept her arm around at the circle of berries.

"You think this will stop Miss Good Voodoo?"

"Stop Miss Good Voodoo from what?" I sensed immediately that this was the wrong thing to say. I backed up a step. She unleashed a torrent of rage.

"He say, you *eat* that goat." She jabbed a finger in the general area of my face. "You feed it to your friends. He say, 'See that? She one hell of a woman.' An' I say, she got nothing on Miss Good Voodoo." Her right open palm smacked her chest with all five daggered fingernails splayed out for emphasis.

"Who would 'he' be?" This was from Muffin. Me. I know enough to keep my mouth shut when a voodoo queen is pissed and bitching.

"Darius." That was it, just Darius. I wanted to ask her to spell it for me. I just knew I was going to spend the rest of the day Google'ing every possible spelling. "He say, he love me, sure. But he say, he want the vengeance queen too. Well I say, I eat revenge for breakfast—" She stomped her foot— I kid you not—stomped it just like Sunshine does when she's squawking up a good mad—"and shit vengeance for lunch. You are nothing. This?" She swept her arm around again to indicate the pepper berries. "This no barrier to Miss Good Voodoo."

On another arm sweep, hundreds of black and brown Grackles descended from the trees and started eating the berries. I mean, hundreds. I had no idea we even had that many in the Keys. Ordinarily, if one wanted to swim through a sea of Grackles, they'd head up to Fast Food Row on Highway U.S.-1 in Florida City. My ring of protection was disappearing. I looked over at Muffin. And considered the curse return possibilities. I can't say I was all that disappointed. God, the man has thighs that just don't quit.

With one final glare, Miss Good Voodoo turned and walked toward the beach and out of sight.

"I see where this day is going and I think I'm going back to bed. Bye, ya'll." I grabbed Howard's arm and dragged him inside, closing the door firmly behind me on Nick and Chanté.

I let go of his arm and headed into the bedroom, collapsing across the bed on my side, pausing only to hug my favorite pillow and Precious to my chest. She was already on the pillow; where she knows she's not supposed to be, so don't feel sorry for her getting squeezed. She's purring like mad anyway, one of the reasons I love her so much, her instant purr reflex. I looked up to see Muffin standing in the doorway to the bedroom. Zeke was pacing around his feet, rubbing his face along the rough seam of Howard's Sebagos.

"Do you want to explain that little scene outside just now?" He was jealous, but now I could see that he was worried. It was a weird feeling, having a guy worry about me. I wasn't too sure I liked it.

"Nope."

"Do you have any idea who sent you those flowers?"

I considered lying, but after Miss Good Voodoo's shriek fest I was pretty sure I knew. "Probably Miss Good Voodoo's boyfriend, Darius—whoever he is."

"You've never met him?"

"Never met him. I don't want to talk about this right now."

"Can I ask you one more question?"

"Can I stop you from asking one more question?" I was slightly scared and getting annoyed. Miss Good Voodoo when she was calm was scary. Miss Good Voodoo in a frothing rage was blood chilling. I wanted to pretend it never happened and get on with my day. There was no way Howard would want to stick around after that bit of weirdness. Hell, *I* didn't want to stick around after that bit of weirdness.

"No you can't. Is this—" he paused. "Is this normal for you? Are all your days like this?"

I considered lying. I wanted Howard to stay for a little longer at least. But it wouldn't be fair to him and I couldn't even begin to pretend to be anything but what I am. This is my life. Now that Howard has really had a chance to see it in all it's glory there is no way he will want anything more to do with me, except maybe buy my urns.

"This is fairly normal for me."

He smiled. "You're like an 'E' ride at Disney, Tara. The wait is long but it's a thrill you keep wanting to get back to again and again."

"Well, Howard. If I were a theme park ride the park would more closely resemble Hellacious Acres than Disney, but hey . . . you've got the only fast-pass."

"I'm going to laminate that fast-pass. I don't think I'll ever get bored with this ride."

"Park security may have something to say about that," Damn, Howard could get me hot with the dumbest damn conversations. I'm going to have to hire Miss Good Voodoo to exercise the Disney ghost out of him if he's going to stick around much longer. We'd need to do a little wardrobe work as well.

"Some risks are worth the reward."

He looked like he really meant it. I was good with the "thrill ride" part, but I'm hell-and-gone from being anyone's "reward." A reward is a wee tad too permanent for me. For one pathetic moment I contemplated what "permanent" would be like with Howard. Howard putting the moves on me here and now was a wet dream for most women. He's beautiful to look at, successful, kind and clean cut . . . a man any trophy wife would die for. He probably fended them off on an hourly basis after the first trophy wife gave up the ghost. I wanted to believe he had genuine feelings for me. Hell, doesn't every woman kind of wish love was real? But . . . I've never lied to myself about my marriageable assets. I would be attractive to any one of the myriad of bums and critters that roam freely up and down U.S.-1 from Key Largo to Key West. I have a habitable dwelling, a job and unlimited access to booze. For a guy like Howard, I couldn't be much more than quick bit of strange. I'm good with that. Who knows if I'll ever get this close to something like Howard Payne ever again? I might as well enjoy it while it lasts.

"What do you want to do?"

"I thought we could pick up breakfast and take it over to Kathy's." He bent and picked up Zeke, cradled him in one hand with his fingers entwined between Zeke's front paws and chest, and rubbed behind Zeke's ears with his other hand.

Aside from the great sex and his apparent love of cats, I am beginning to understand that one of Muffin's finest qualities is his ability to focus on what's important. I gave Precious a kiss and set her back down on the pillow.

"Good idea. Let's go."

As it turned out, Kathy was practically cured. When we arrived she was dressing for work. Her assistant opened the shop for her at nine so she didn't have to race in; which meant she could sit and scarf up a few spoonfuls of the cut fruit Howard picked up at the Islamorada Deli and a couple of bites of a muffin. I saw the muffins in the box when he opened it and I swear I had a horrible suspicion that he knew my pet name for him. He seemed oblivious to the significance so I let the thought slither into oblivion.

"It was only on my wrists and forearms in any case."
Kathy took a serene nibble of pineapple. "I coated my arms
with my special cream, covered up with elbow length gloves
and this morning the rash was nearly gone. See?" She held
out both wrists for our inspection. Howard took her hand in
his and turned it palm up. By comparison, his wrists were a
real mess and he had actually been in better shape yesterday
than Kathy. She took back her hand, opened her jar of salve
and slowly coated Howard's wrists with a thick layer of it.
"Keep it on for as long as you can. You'll see a real improve-
ment by this afternoon."

The salve soaked into Howard's skin almost immediately
and disappeared. It smelled kind of minty to me. Sigh. Anyway, it was a short breakfast since I'd forbidden Howard
from telling Kathy about my morning. That little jaunt to the
hospital for them convinced me that no curse was worth
fighting if it left friends debilitated. Howard's hands are important to me and Kathy's well being . . . well, let's just say I
can count on two or three toes how many people actually
care whether I live or die and I can't afford to lose even one
of them. My karma was already black as hell. I didn't want
to see Kathy's shiny clean karma dinged. Sherry was planted
physically in one of Arizona's famous Harmonic Resonance
Centers for a good cleansing, so I figure she's safe as long as
she stays where she is, away from me, and Dennis. Howard?
I have no idea about Howard. It's not as if he's been around
long enough for me to grow really attached to, but he's growing on me day by day. He seems to exude a natural insula-
tion in any case. But, just to be safe, we'll be sleeping at his
house for any future overnights.

Since I kind of expected Miss Good Voodoo to make her
move within the next twenty-four hours, Howard was getting
dropped off at his place like a hot potato. It burns my ass to
have to take any precautions at all, but the Power of Three
principle gives me real hope that Miss Good Voodoo was,

even now, covered in a mountain of bird poop. One really good curse on me should take her out for the rest of the century. After that, things will be back to normal. Life is good.

A thought occurred to me. If her reversal of fortune curse was what got me laid, somewhere out there, someone who *was* getting sex on a more regular basis, just had the spigot turned off with interest. I pondered the sadness of that for a moment and wondered who the unlucky nympho was.

CHAPTER SEVENTEEN

Dry Spell

"I SWEAR TO God, Tara. If I don't get laid tonight I'm going to have to head up to Miami to troll South Beach. I've never seen it so dead in this town." Sam was scratching Sunshine's head just under her crest, her favorite spot. She was trembling all over and about to go into her mating convulsions. Sunshine was at the end of her six-month cycle for egg production. Every six months she lays one egg. Don't ask me why, I have no idea. Just before she lays the egg, she gets all quivery every time someone pets her. All I know is that as Sam's attentions reduce Sunshine to a weird parody of a squawking chicken, Sam himself is squawking about his lame love life.

"Thanks for sharing that, Sam. I can't tell you how much I sympathize with your plight." I do, in fact, feel a little guilty. His drought probably has nothing to do with my little two-person hurricane the night before last, but I don't rule anything out. I gave him a drink on the house and settled in to listen to his bitching. It's the least I can do.

He flipped his Costa Del Mars back up to cover his eyes,

the poster boy for dejection. While it's possible Sam is playing the sympathy card on me, I kind of doubt it. It's also possible that he's hoping my recent, personal, private screening means that I'll be announcing a public premier sometime in the near future. Could Sam be camping out at my door? I squint a glare at the top of his head. He's bent over Sunshine, bringing her back down off her little inner bird of happiness session all over the mahogany bar. I'm getting delusional. I know this, and yet I can't help pondering the myriad of possibilities. There's nothing more refreshing than a good dose of paranoia after sex. I gently pushed a few bar napkins and another bag of sunflower seeds over to Sam. What if Sam and I were to—you know? Would that balance out the elements again and put the world back on an even keel? It's something to think about, so I do.

Riqué, not so gently, slammed Sam's order down on the pass-through between the bar and the kitchen and rang the "order-up" bell. Instead of moving away from the window like he usually does, Riqué waited for me to walk over and get the plate of food.

"What?" I tried not to sound accusatory, but after all, he did send Miss Good Voodoo to my bungalow in the first place. I hold him kind of responsible for this morning's little drama.

"You pissed off Miss Good Voodoo."

"And?"

"She burn my ear for three hours last night. I get no sleep." He sniffed as if I owed him something and waited.

"Did she say why she was pissed?" It's a fair question. Not that I'm expecting anything close to an answer.

"Darius."

"Spell that for me?" I have the pen and order pad ready just in case he actually tells me.

"All you need to know is what it means to you." He turned away and headed back into the kitchen. Squid.

"And what does Darius mean?" I hate shouting at his back, but really, I have to know.

He turned briefly to answer, "God is coming."

"And that means *what* to me?"

But Riqué was done talking. Deep down I feel that Riqué could kill me in the parking lot at midnight and feel no remorse. He's just cute that way, damn it: I have no idea why.

I set Sam's plate in front of him on the bar with silverware and a bottle of catsup. Sunshine stole a fry off his plate and raced over to her perch at the other end. I left them both to it and waited on the evening's patrons who were beginning to trickle in for dinner. All in all, things look pretty normal for a Friday night at Crusty's.

Two a.m. found me safe and sound in my pink bunny boxer shorts and matching spaghetti strap tank top reading emails in the dark. I'd showered the smell of Crusty's off of me when I got home, poured a glass of Drambuie and decided to unwind. I would read you a few of these but they're just the same old shit. Oh. And the Little Shop of Horrors bouquet is now sitting outside on the back porch. I have all of the front windows and the door open and the back door open with the screen door closed to blow the smell out of the rooms. It was sickly sweet and pungent by the time I got home tonight.

The wind was blowing at a steady ten knots. Sucks for fishing but it's exhilarating on shore. I could hear the waves lapping at the hull of *Till Death* and the lines were creaking as it strained against the dock. The palm trees are rustling and the wind chimes are doing what they do best. I love nights like this. We just had a full moon so it's in waxing mode. I wish I could bottle up nights like these for winter. Cozy.

There was a faint clicking sound all of a sudden from the back porch and suddenly the battery back-up for the computer started to chime. It took me a full minute and a half to register the fact that the power to the bungalow had just cut out. Since none of the lights were on, nothing else shut off.

This is an island. Sometimes the power cuts out for no reason. Still, as I finished shutting down the computer and shutting off the UPS, I can't help muttering under my breath, "Gee. Thanks Uncle Lester. Good to know you are perfecting the art of turning things *off* for a change."

The only light in the bungalow now is coming from the dock lights and the nearly full moon, which was my first indication that, perhaps, only my bungalow was affected by the power outage. My second clue was the sound of a deep, low chuckle coming from the doorway to the kitchen. I froze in place. "Uncle Les?" God I hope it's Uncle Lester. I promise my next year's bar tips to charity if it will just turn out to be Uncle Lester. But the soft sigh that followed it and the tsking sound just didn't remind me in any way of my not so dearly departed relative. Someone is leaning against the doorframe leading in to the kitchen, there in the darker shadows of the room I can just make him out.

"Not Uncle Les, no." He moved into the room and made his way over to the open front door, never taking his eyes off me, his head turned in opposition to his body, with each measured step. "Darius."

"Darius?" My eyes were starting to adjust to the darkness and I could see that he wasn't much taller than me. His skin was ebony, the kind of black that shines at the slightest hint of light at night, and his hair was a mass of ringlets draping down past his waist. He was wearing a simple pair of hip hugging jeans, black and no shirt. Barefoot. Glinting in the half-light was a dagger pendant hanging from his left nipple. Waves of muscles hugged his bare chest flowing out to well defined arms, tapering down to manicured, overly long fingernails. "*The* Darius?"

Probably not the best of my possible choices for response, but my heart is racing and I'm trying to gauge if I can make it to the back door before he can catch me. He just laughed, again. For a few moments, all I can hear are the ordinary sounds of night as both of us stood stock still, waiting. I'd played this game with Howard. I can wait all night if he wants. At least, that's what I tell myself. I searched for that Zen gene Kathy is always assuring me everyone has inside them. All I find is cold sweat. Unlike Muffin, I don't sense that Darius has *any* kind of thoughts racing through his mind. He seemed content to just stare at me through the darkness, saying nothing.

He chuckled again and turned to look outside.

Adrenaline should be zinging me into an overdrive search for escape, a weapon or help. Adrenaline is kicking my ass at the moment and all I can do is stand there, watching him. Slowly, I focused on unclenching. While his eyes were off me, I forced myself to take a few deep breaths and relax, one muscle at a time. As I took a tentative step toward the kitchen, I felt his eyes on me again. I got all the way to the door, ten whole steps, before he reminded me, "You threw out all the knives yesterday, Tara. Scissors too."

My hand stopped inches from the wall phone just inside the kitchen. He tanked this plan as well. "You unplugged all the phones, beloved. You have no defenses, but you do not need them. I would not harm a single inch of that beautiful body."

"No?" It's not that I'm suspicious and distrustful by nature—wait, I *am* suspicious and distrustful by nature. It's just that, I don't remember inviting this man over for an evening of terror and fun. And, I'm a little concerned he's psychotic.

A slight jingling sound preceded Zeke's arrival from the bedroom. His gold collar glinted through tufts of black fur as the chain shifted around his little neck. I can hear him purring even from here as he headed straight for Darius. Precious padded out and sat in the doorway to the bedroom cleaning her front paw and face. Zeke made a cake of himself rubbing back and forth against Darius's bare feet. I'd like to think a dog would be better protection from a house intruder than this but the fact that it would be *my* dog kind of negates that possibility.

Darius picked up Zeke and snuggled the kitten up to his chest. Zeke immediately twisted his body around in Darius's hand to swat at the dagger pendant, claws out, naturally. I was silently urging Zeke to go for blood and when it looked like he struck home, Darius chuckled that low spine itching laugh of his that I am starting to really despise.

"You kept all of my gifts." He indicated Zeke and pointed in the general direction of the gris-gris I'd left hanging next to the front door, de-fanged of course.

"Gifts?" I couldn't hide my skepticism.

"Oh, the first one was a curse—definitely. But the rest . . ." he paused to shift Zeke onto his back and rub his tummy. "The rest were only meant to scare you—give you a small thrill."

"Why?"

"I received your metallic underwear, five pair."

"Not from me you didn't."

"Oh, not from you, true." He conceded quickly. "But nonetheless, they were from your mind, your evil."

At this I couldn't help keeping a snort from escaping. He pursed his lips and smiled.

"Yes. I know all about your disclaimer, still, I wanted to hurt everyone who had a part in my detention by Federal Agents at the Miami International Airport for five excruciating hours." He dragged out the word "excruciating" until it almost hurt me to hear it. "My status in this country is . . ." he paused again for effect. "Precarious."

"I'll bet."

He laughed again and strolled a few steps closer to where I am standing. I backed up to the computer desk again. He followed. When the only thing separating us was Zeke, Darius stopped. Zeke's purring climbed up a few decibel levels. Darius leaned in and sniffed the air around me.

"The heat of your skin puts off a most unique scent. I was here earlier tonight, searching for a hint of that smell. Without your heat, it's just empty."

Darius smelled of vanilla and cinnamon. I wasn't going to mention that to him.

a. Because I wasn't in the mood for polite chitchat and

b. Because I didn't want him to think I gave a shit how he smelled.

He was scaring me and I hate being scared. This is how I smell when I'm scared and it's turning him on. Sick.

His jeans were tight enough that I was reasonably sure he wasn't armed with anything large or dangerous, but then again, what do I know about weapons? Zilch, that's what. He didn't need them. He looked strong enough to damage me any time he chose with his bare hands.

"There are laws against this." I decided to pretend I was confident and act all intimidating—turn the tables on him. Of course, that only works in the movies. Darius wasn't buying it. He handed me Zeke and took my arm, very politely, and drew me over to the open front door.

"I want to show you something." He stepped to the side and gently placed me slightly behind the door. "Look over there by the palm tree on its side. What do you see?" He pointed to a spot just outside my bedroom window.

"Nothing. I'm practically night blind." Really, I am night blind. It takes forever for my eyes to adjust to the darkness, because they are so big that they let in too much light.

"Wait a second and look again."

I'm thinking, I am at the door and he's behind me. I should make a break for it and run. I tense to do the minute dash and suddenly a movement by the tree caught my eye. Someone is standing there, looking at my bedroom window. I can't make out if it's a man or a woman. But he, she, or it was definitely watching my window.

"He's there every night." Darius said. I made a noise of

protest and Darius shushed me. "He was there the night before last when you and your friend celebrated the sacrifice of
the goat. I know, because I was watching him, watching you."

"Please say you are kidding."

"I would never joke about a night like that."

"Why are you telling me this?" Sick bastard. If he hadn't
cut off my electricity, I think I would be looking for a way to
zap him.

"Because you have become something of an obsession for
me, because your indifference challenges me, because you
are only half alive and I want to bring you the rest of the
way. You asked for a goat. I gave it to you. If he were worthy
of you, he would have butchered it himself, taken some of
that fine control away from you. But you ran the show. You
never lost yourself, even a little."

I yawned. I swear I couldn't help it. You know how stress
affects me. I get sleepy. I guess I just realized that the only
way he was going to kill me was to talk me to death. Instant
stress release, sleepiness wins. Shoot me.

He laughed again. God I hate the sound of his laugh.
And then he began to pet Zeke, only Zeke was snuggled
just below my breasts at tummy level and the knuckles of
Darius's fingers brushed back and forth over my left breast.
Zeke's purring intensified at the extra attention and my
nerves shot through the roof. Sleepiness gone, just like that.
His other hand brushed against my waist and held me still
as I tried to back up. I was suddenly cornered between the
wall and the door,

I took one shuddering breath and found my voice, "Please
leave."

Did I just beg? Shit, I hate how weak that sounded, but his
hand was sending a wave of heat down to my knees and I
was, honest to God, terrified I would just jump him for the
thrill of it. Was sex like revenge? Once you give yourself
permission to do it, do you become an addict?

Zeke struggled to find space between us and sent the strap of my top down my shoulder. Darius bent to kiss me there and when he did, I could see past him to the tree. Our watcher had taken notice of us at the door. I could see that he had turned in our direction. For a moment, I thought we had locked eyes and then he turned and looked away. Darius's lips moved lower.

"Miss Good Voodoo's going to have your balls for breakfast if you go one inch lower, Darius."

That stopped him. Good to know that fear works both ways.

"Thanks for the reminder." He laughed again and stepped away. "Torn between the queen of vengeance and the empress of evil. I am a happy, happy man. I'll let you know when I decide. Of course, one of you must go."

"I'll make it easy for you. Keep her."

He laughed again. "But the loser dies, Tara." He walked off laughing at his little joke. I heard him flip the main circuit breaker to the bungalow on as he passed through the kitchen and out the back door. I looked outside at the bent tree. The watcher was gone. I stood there for a minute, my heart racing, trying to think what to do when a faint clicking sound preceded every light in the bungalow turning on.

Fucking Uncle Lester. "Where the hell were you when I needed you?"

```
// Thought for the day on the Home Page of
Revenge-Gifts.com,
scheduled to load on Saturday.
<script language="JavaScript">
<!-- This figures out what day of the week it
is, and prints a quote. -->
<!--
  Sys_Date = new Date();
  var DayofWeek = "";
  var TaraQuote = "";

  if (Sys_Date.getDay() == 6) {
          DayofWeek = "Saturday";
```

TaraQuote = " "... my hair has that I-am-not-going-to-work-
today, ponytail of pathos look." —Miss Alli" ";

```
  document.write(DayofWeek + " : " +
  TaraQuote);
  // -->
  </script>
```

CHAPTER EIGHTEEN

The Internet Wave Is Flushing Down the Toilet

OF COURSE I called the police. It was a complete waste of time. Three in the morning does not bring out the best in anyone, and our local finest are no exception. I had almost fallen asleep when the rooster began crowing at four a.m. Some days just suck. This was going to be one of them.

I was still in my bunny jammies when Kimmy "yoo-hoo"d at the door. Does she have even the slightest clue how annoying that type of greeting is? Probably. Bitch. I decided to answer, dressed as I am.

"I told you I'd find you." And there she stood, dressed in early Jackie-O, complete with hat and clutch purse, only Jackie wouldn't have been caught dead in that shade of Day-Glo yellow. Seriously, it was blinding. It did terrible things to her complexion and hair color. Her shoes looked a little worse for the wear after trekking over pea gravel. I'm starting to feel better; weird how that works.

I smiled. "So you did."

She backed up from the door a few steps.

"It's nine a.m. Tara." She was wagging her finger in admonishment. "You should be dressed and ready for the day."

"It's Saturday morning in the Keys," I countered. "I should still be in bed."

I'd stacked the orders for the day outside the door because I was planning on going back to bed and didn't want Nick to have to come inside. Kimmy's cameraman knocked the stack of boxes over in his effort to gawk at me in my jammies. The day was starting to suck again.

"Give me a minute. I'll get dressed." I closed the door in her face and made my way to the bathroom for a long hot shower.

By the time I came back out, Kimmy had managed to get breakfast delivered and was setting up a little buffet on the back porch.

"We always have shoots catered. I hope you like crêpes."

The word crêpe was all the warning I got before Jack walked around the corner of the bungalow, directing an employee on where to set up the circular griddles.

"Do you have an outside power outlet? If not we're going to need to run a line from inside." Jack was dressed in Palm Beach casual. Loose linen slacks with an oversized white Oxford shirt. Only the middle three buttons were done up, leaving most of his chest and stomach bare. His long black hair was braided and shackled in an interesting B & D style. I'm guessing it's made of brass and copper from the look of it. I'm jealous. Jack has nicer hair accessories than me. Add ten to the day's suck factor.

Petty? Hell yes.

"Now, Tara, we've shot the products in the studio and we'd like to get a few shots of them with you. Our stylist Jan has several possible wardrobe selections set up and once that's decided she'll take care of your hair and makeup."

I've decided that Kimberly Case must die.

"Ladies, let's hurry, the light is perfect and we don't want to lose it."

The photographer dies next.

"Miss Cole? This way if you please?" Jan, the stylist was an elderly woman dressed in tan chinos and a short-sleeved button down periwinkle shirt. Her hair is cut in that tasteful, boyish bob fashion dictates women of a certain age must adopt. I'm guessing she's in her mid seventies. She is all of five feet tall, if that, and ninety pounds soaking wet. I'm thinking I can take her. I refuse to budge. She took my arm and pinched me hard on the fleshy upper back part.

"Ow!"

"Come along, Miss Cole." She smiled at me with all the innocence of a seven-year-old in church.

"I have things to do," I protested.

"What? Run your business?" She pursed her lips. "This *is* your business. Dozens of women and men depend on the success of your business for their livelihood."

I must have looked brain dead, because she smiled and continued, as if lecturing a little child.

"I've read up on your little enterprise and I've read between the lines. Our research department did a very thorough job of it, interviewing the Keys Crafting Society. We are meeting with them tomorrow for photographs and copy. They are a lovely group of ladies and sing your praises for giving them the ability to semi-retire here in paradise with some comfort. You provide local artisans with much needed income during what is the traditional slow season. The farmers up in Homestead supplement their income, providing you with blooms that cost them nothing to grow. People *depend* on you, Miss Cole, and whether you like it or not, I am going to see that you shine in this article for their sakes."

I looked at Kimmy. She shrugged. I shrugged.

"She's a talker, huh?"

"You have no idea." She tilted her head slightly to one side, smiled and indicated the direction in which I was expected to walk. The stylist lady was already heading that way, confident that I would follow. For reasons known only to my feet, I did. Jack would have to find his own power outlet. I'm guessing he's handy that way.

When it was all over, the photographer had photographs of me, Precious, Zeke, and even the rooster and hen. They managed to get a really good pose out of Precious on one of the allergy pillows and the rooster, hackles risen, was shot as the hen nested next to a basket of chocolates. Me they dressed in metallic boxers rolled down to the hips, a custom made matching, shiny chainmail bra lined with satin, and a belly chain. They posed me on the bow of *Till Death* and arranged my hair in a riot of blond curls. A pair of Ray Ban Aviator Sun Glasses and I was good to go.

The title of the piece is going to be, and excuse me while I laugh hysterically at the irony here, "Living Well is the Finest Revenge." I recommended "Tara Bytes," but they failed to see the humor—and they call themselves a magazine for the geek social elite. Frauds.

What? Yeah. I was stunned that a seventy-year-old woman had a belly chain and metal bra on hand as well. They let me keep them as a gift. Wanna know the most disturbing part? Kimmy had given them my measurements for the bra. Let's back away from that thought real slow.

Jack's lunch was surprisingly tasty. He did some of the cooking himself and directed the rest. Our future dead clients will eat well on Howard's boats. Tables and chairs were placed at casual intervals in and around the palm trees for everyone. Jack, Kimmy, and the scary stylist sat with me.

"You were absolutely correct, darling. She looked perfect in that shoot. I can't wait to see the galleys." Scary stylist was cutting up a chunk of pineapple. I believe that with one more slice and she will be splitting atoms, her pieces are that small.

"Thanks, Mom. You did amazing things with her hair. I didn't think anything could be done with it. Tara always wore it in a braid at the office so I wasn't sure . . ."

Wait one. Mom? Aww man! It figures.

"You let your own daughter dress in that color?" I snorted. "Some stylist." And then I remembered that I put my own appearance in her hands and stopped smiling. The suck factor was rising again.

"She never listens to me. I told her it was too hot for raw silk, but it's like talking to air."

I agreed with her there.

"As to the color . . ." She pretended to consider Kimmy's dress for a moment. "It's not all bad. She's really a brunette you know. So her skin coloring can tolerate that palette better than most. But, in all fairness to the designer, that color would look bad on anything but a yield sign."

"Maybe not even a yield sign."

"Ladies." Jack interceded in Kimmy's behalf. "Be nice." He dished a few forkfuls of star fruit onto my plate. "Put something sweet in your mouth for a change."

I let it pass. Jack has a line on really nice hair accessories. I figure I can insult him after he reveals his source. Squid.

"By the way, loved you in the bondage bra. You could wear it to swim in too."

"Yes. I could." I smiled. Kimmy scooted over a few inches. "If I wanted a mastectomy by a barracuda."

"Didn't they use that material to *protect* divers from attacks? That's what we're saying in the magazine piece anyway." Kimmy was now jumping to Jack's defense from big bad Tara wolf.

"They didn't use the shiny kind."

"Oh."

"Yes. Oh."

"What the hell difference does it make if it's shiny?" said Kim at her snittiest.

"Kimberly Case, please watch your tone." Scary stylist wins a few brownie points.

"I'm just asking."

"A lot of things in the ocean are attracted to shiny objects. Most of those things have sharp, sharp teeth with which they bite first and decide if it's tasty after."

"Oh."

"Yes. Oh."

"Well *I* didn't know. Shoot me." She struggled out of her chair; which had settled into the soft sand and huffed off to issue orders to the crew. Yep. That's the Kimmy I remember. Scary stylist hastily excused herself and left as well.

"I have a feeling you could wear whatever you liked in the ocean. Even the fiercest predator would think twice before biting." Jack blew me a kiss and departed as well.

Yep. Fish fear me.

I could have been nicer, true. But you have no idea what that woman put me through when she had me at a corporate disadvantage. I never forget torture on that scale and I never forgive. And some day, I'll get even.

CHAPTER NINETEEN

Puddin's Chase

BY THE TIME Kimmy's crew had packed up and scrammed, the day was shot and it was time to head in to Crusty's. Unfortunately, they'd used my kitchen and stuffed the leftovers in my fridge. Three hundred and sixty five chocolates were sitting in resplendent state in a basket at the dead center of the freezer. A mountain of cut fruit, leftover crêpes and assorted salads and side dishes were Saran-wrapped within an inch of their shelf lives and geometrically stacked in the fridge.

I know. I'm screwed, but I just can't bring myself to throw it out. Worse, I don't have time to deal with it, so I duct taped both doors closed and hoped the ghost couldn't manage to get them open before I figured out what to do. Maybe I'll invite a few friends over for a leftover feast fest.

Sam was at the door waiting for me as Sunshine and I arrived at the bar.

"Why didn't you just go in, Sam? The lunch crew hasn't left and Riqué is always here by now." He put his hand up against the door, barring me from opening it. Sunshine climbed off my arm and up his to his shoulder.

"Doesn't a gentleman usually *open* the door for a lady?" It was a stupid thing to say, but Sam was making me a little nervous. When people change their patterns I get nervous.

"I talked to Sheriff Jim." The usual boyish gleam was absent from his eyes and Sam looked as serious as I have ever seen him. In fact, I've never seen him this serious. He looked positively grim. He was even ignoring Sunshine's gentle nudges to his neck.

"Yeah, and?"

"And I talked to the Muffin man this afternoon on his cell. Did you know he's in Orlando?"

"Actually, I didn't. Thanks for the update. And how long have you known my nickname for Howard?"

"Everyone knows, Tara. Don't be silly." He shifted his stance to replace his left hand with his right and leaned down to whisper in my ear. "You have a new roommate as of tonight, two when Howard gets back—he's not sure when, but as soon as he can. I'll take the sofa."

I can't help it. I have to laugh. "Thanks for the offer, Sam, but it's not necessary. I'm fine."

"No. Tara. You are definitely *not* fine. And, I'm not asking you for an invite, I'm inviting myself." He stood back and jerked open the door for me. "Besides, it's not like I have any plans for getting laid. My sex life has dried up and blown the hell away. Now get to work and make me some grub, babe."

He smacked my ass as I walked past him. I stopped, turned and glared. "You better sleep with one eye open, Sam. Because that smack is going to cost you."

He grinned and that boyish gleam I loved was back in his eyes. "Looking forward to the pleasure." He laughed. "Punish me, master. I've been a very bad boy."

"God." Why? Why? Why?

Sunshine started making her kissy sounds and Sam finally rewarded her with a neck scratch.

My impenetrable shield of unpleasantness was beginning to crumble and I have no idea how to rebuild it. I'm not sure if people are seeing past it and deciding it's a front or if they see it as a challenge, a wall that must be climbed. I mentally began to sort my friends and acquaintances into one of these two categories. Kathy has always seen through me and proceeded as if my surly tangle of thorns didn't really exist. Sam, I suspect—hell, I know—has always viewed me as a challenge. I think Howard is just the type of person for whom there are no obstacles to the things he wants. Patient is our Howard, patient and persistent. Kimberly saw the tower of Tara and called in her mom to deal with it. At seventy plus years, Jan Case apparently doesn't feel limited by other people's boundaries. There's no good defense against that kind of entry, except maybe death. I considered Uncle Les and revised. Perhaps not even death.

I may have to move.

By nine p.m. Crusty's was stuffed to the gills with locals. I guess the rumors had been flying around long enough that people just needed to get a look at the object of all the gossip. I couldn't leave. I hadn't scheduled enough staff to cover the shift with this many customers. Statistically, with no holiday on Friday or Monday and the heat being a stifling hundred in the shade with one hundred percent humidity, business was generally slow but steady this time of year, with Europeans and other foreign tourists and a few locals.

The Canadians are gone until next winter. I love their accent, eh? They drive down in any case. Europeans fly. Airfare is cheap; relatively speaking, and room rates are low. But this crowd, this was ninety-nine percent local. One of the yachts docked close to the bar set up loud speakers and was blasting Jimmy Buffet and Bob Marley. I decided to set up the hurricane fans and propped open the doors for airflow. The AC was still blasting and older patrons were guarding their spots under the vents with grim determination.

People shamelessly grilled me for details on my home invasion. One man offered me an obscene amount of cash if I would relay all the salacious details of my night with Howard. I considered it for a moment. I really did. I haven't said no yet.

As the night wore on, I began to pray for some shocking scandal to occur. I wanted something so huge it would divert everyone from my love life. It was a long freaking night.

I managed to move the stragglers out to the docks to party around one a.m. Kay and crew stayed to the bitter end even though one or two of them were scheduled to get off at ten.

The kitchen at Crusty's was nearly restored to order when Puddin came racing through in hot pursuit of a lizard. I had no idea Puddin could move that fast.

The lizard jumped to the far wall of the main wait and made its way, upside down on the ceiling tiles back toward the door leading outside. Puddin leapt up onto the counter and then the shelves above the food service counter and then did something I'll never forget as long as I live. Twenty-six odd pounds of Puddin jumped straight up and grabbed the ceiling tile with as many claws as she could sink into them and almost got the lizard. Instead, she pulled the tile down on top of herself as she hit the floor. The lizard got away. The suck factor of my night saw my bet and raised me double. It wasn't the ceiling tile that bothered me so much as the bricks of cocaine that came tumbling down with it. There, half hanging from the roof of Crusty's kitchen ceiling was a shit load of trouble. I dialed the sheriff.

"You got a shit load of trouble here, Tara." Jim Walker, or, rather, Sheriff Jim as most people call him, is a native Florida Cracker. His daddy and granddaddy had been sheriff here in South Florida for decades past. Jim was the black sheep, kind of. He felt the town his daddy was still sheriff in was too small for the both of them and settled for heading south. He was a fine officer of the law. God knows he'd arrested almost all of my neighbors, but they didn't hold it against him; it was just business. "Who do you know that's storing stuff in your store, gal?"

"Nobody." I thought about it a minute. "Dennis has been acting weird lately. You might want to ask him about it.

"Dennis is always acting weird. But I'll ask him." Monroe County's finest had all of the ceiling tiles of Crusty's down and were busily stacking blocks of cocaine in a truck pulled up snug to the back door. I'm no expert, but it looked like a lot to me. "Anyone else you can think of?"

"Not off the top of my head, no."

"Sorry it had to happen tonight, what with last night's trouble and all." Jim had been just down the street when I called, pulling over the drunks leaving Crusty's—rich pickings on a weeknight. The man knows his business.

"You know what they say. It's not a party if the police don't show up."

Jim laughed a deep belly laugh and tucked away his pad and pencil. "Now that's a fact, gal. That is a fact."

"When do you suppose I can lock up for the night?" Sam was wilting on a barstool and Sunshine was tucked up in her wing for the night on her perch.

"We're just about done here. I can lock up for you if you want to take off. I'll bring the keys over when I come to talk to you tomorrow."

"Thanks, Sheriff. I owe you one." I handed him the keys and picked Sunshine up in a football hold.

"Sam!"

He lifted his head up from the bar and gave me a bleary eyed look. "What?"

"Time to go."

"He's going home with you?" Sheriff Jim's grin nearly split his face. "Don't that beat all. I thought you was hooked up with that northerner fellow—bought the Sells place?"

"I did. I am. Sam is just standing guard tonight until Howard gets back." Not that it's any of Jim's business.

He sucked his teeth for a minute. "You could do way worse, gal. This boy's one of the few locals I haven't arrested yet."

"Come close a few times," Sam mumbled as he passed us to go out to the car.

"That I have. That I have. Years back. Never thought he'd come back here after college. Not many do, once they get away."

"I'll bet." It seemed to me that no one ever leaves the Keys, even for college. Well not for the educational kind of college. The local joke is that, every time someone gets arrested for running drugs, they tell his kids he went to college. Mom is in a sorority and they do road trips to visit Dad in college. Sad, but it works for them. Maybe their kids will go to real college. Maybe. Not my kids. Not my problem. It's time to pack it up, so I hand off Crusty's keys to Sheriff Jim and head home.

Did I really wish for a scandal to take everyone's attention off my love life? This is the kind of shit that happens when you aren't more specific when you wish.

```
// Thought for the day on the Home Page of
Revenge-Gifts.com,
scheduled to load on Sunday.
<script language="JavaScript">
<!-- This figures out what day of the week it
is, and prints a quote. -->
<!--
  Sys_Date = new Date();
  var DayofWeek = "";
  var TaraQuote = "";
  if(Sys_Date.getDay() == 7) {
DayofWeek = "Sunday";
```

TaraQuote = "I can only please one person per day.

         Today is not your day.

         Tomorrow isn't looking too good either.
         —Tara Cole";

```
  document.write(DayofWeek + " : " +
  TaraQuote);
  // -->
  </script>
```

CHAPTER TWENTY

New Roommates

"WHY IS YOUR fridge duct taped shut?" Sam was standing in the dark kitchen staring at my fridge. Sam pulled the tape off the fridge and opened it. He stared at the mountain of food and then turned his head to stare at me.

"You must have the metabolism of a Hummingbird."

I sighed. There, standing in front of my fridge was a feast for the eyes. For a moment, I wanted to give him a flirty response and begin the dance of eyes, looks and sighs that lead to guiltless ecstasy. Just for a moment. I'm not exactly saving myself for Howard. But my life is a little complicated right now and I am having trouble focusing on what to do next as it is. Distractions like Sam I do not need. Even so, I looked my fill of him for a moment. My eyes walked down the muscled edges of his arms, revealed in the half-light of the open fridge, down the collar of his shirt to the pulse beating at the base of his neck and lower to the inch or so of rock hard abs revealed by gaping shirt buttons. I stopped there, fascinated by the fantasy of opening the rest of his buttons and running my fingers over all that beautiful tan skin.

He flicked his hair back and my concentration broke. Our eyes met and I realized just how far out of the box I had just traveled by the considering look Sam gave me, like he knew exactly what thoughts had just gone through my head. He liked it. He smiled.

"Just make yourself at home." It had been a long fucking night. I left him to his food expedition to pull out the sofa bed. By the time I had the sheets on it and the pillows fluffed, Sam emerged from the kitchen with a plate full of crêpes and pasta salad. He sat down at the head of the sofa bed and looked around the room.

"Tara."

"Sam."

"Where's the TV?"

"There isn't one."

"For real?"

"Fact."

"Babe. You've got some serious issues." He looked a bit lost until his gaze fixed on the computer. "You got chat software installed?"

"Nope."

"Jesus. That's just unnatural." He inhaled his food and took the plate back to the kitchen.

I sat down at the computer and downloaded ICQ for Sam. I left him happily cybering and went to bed. He's a big boy. He can tuck himself in.

I got a grand total of two hours sleep.

I woke up to the sensation of falling. Zeke was rubbing back and forth against the bedpost at the bottom of the bed. My ghost had returned. At some point, my little bungalow is going to reach critical mass and explode.

"Not exactly a ghost," she protested.

"So you say."

She smiled.

"If you aren't a ghost, what are you?" Either I was punch

drunk tired, stupid or just getting brave, but I was starting to like her.

"Miss Good VooDoo would call me your Loa. Kathy would call me your spirit guide. You probably think I'm a bit of undigested beef." She laughed and Precious hissed. I'm back to being creeped out.

"Why are you here?" Might as well go whole hog since she was in a talking mood.

"I'm here for you."

"Ok." Whatever the hell that means. Here for me? "Me" needs sleep. "Me" needs some normalness. "Me" needs to not have Sam sleeping on the sofa in the other room and Darius waiting outside in the bushes with stalker-man deciding whether or not he wants to kill me.

She remained silent. Good response. And then—a thought hit me. Don't the Irish believe these kinds of visitations are harbingers of death?

"That's not exactly true," she said. "I have always been here. It's just that now you can see me because death is near. It lifts the veil between."

At first I thought she was fading, but then I realized that when I tried to look at her directly, she was harder to see. She came into better focus in my peripheral vision. Weird. She was dressed a lot like I dress, beige Capri pants and a v-neck T-shirt. Her hair was shoulder length, mine's longer, and she had that Mariel Hemingway look.

"Loas possess people."

"Only if asked in."

"What kind of death is near?"

She didn't answer. I swallowed hard and searched for the courage to ask the question more directly.

"My death?"

She looked up and right and paused in her petting of Zeke. A popping sound preceded every light in the bungalow turning on and her disappearance.

"Damn it, Uncle Les! You are such a complete shit sometimes."

I heard Sam groan in the living room. "Aw, mom. I was in under curfew. Turn the lights out and let me sleep."

There was a light knock at the front door and I heard it open.

"Hey, man. Where ya been?" Sam's sleepy voice bled through my door.

"Driving." It was Howard's deep voice answering.

"Is there some master switch outside you turned on? What's up with the lights in this place?"

"I have no idea." Howard's voice sounded closer to the bedroom door and I heard a knock just before he opened it.

"Why do you knock if you are just going to come in any-way?" A huge weight lifted from my chest and I was able to sit up. I scooched over and sat at the edge of the bed as Howard closed the door behind him, removing his tie and unbuttoning his shirt. I started to stand up as he hit the light switch next to the door and plunged the room in darkness. I hesitated between sitting and standing and decided to sit back down until my night vision kicked back in. Sounds of Howard undressing, the rustling of clothes, shoes being kicked off, all served to distract me from scary thoughts of death and ghosts. I heard something heavier than clothes and shoes being placed on the night stand as Howard sat down next to me to remove his socks.

"What was that?"

"Gun."

"Loaded?"

"Yes." He rolled me onto my back and started kissing me just beneath the ear.

"Oh." I contemplated what the food poltergeist would do with a gun in the house. "Don't leave it in the kitchen, Ok?"

"Shhh." He kissed his way down my neck to the tops of my breasts and tugged the spaghetti straps off to pull the ma-terial lower. He licked and nibbled his way down to a nipple and gently took it between his teeth, flicking it with his tongue. Each flick stimulated nerves in lower parts of my body. Intolerable. I am not this easy. Am I? God.

His right hand smoothed a light caress down my shoulder to the other breast and brushed the tip with his palm. Once. Twice. Before traveling down the curve of my waist and tunneling beneath the edge of my silk pajama pants. His head followed his hand down and both hands lifted my hips to draw down my pajama bottoms and spread my legs wide enough to accommodate his shoulders as he rolled off the bed onto his knees. He pulled me closer to the edge of the bed and ran his hands up from my knees to my inner thighs. His thumbs parted my outer lips and I clenched my knees to his shoulders, trying to close them. I started to sit up but he slid one hand up to my tummy and held me firmly in place. A finger slid inside me as his teeth gently latched onto my sweet spot and his tongue began the same flicking motion he'd started at my breast.

My hands grabbed his at my stomach and pushed, writhing and squirming like a mad thing. This was torture at its finest and at its worst. I groaned a protest and lifted a foot to his shoulder, then wrapped my knee behind his head to pull him in closer. My breathing was reduced to guppy gulps of air as I tried my best not to scream. The walls were thin enough. I knew Sam could hear everything anyway. I was losing control by inches. It was embarrassing and thrilling all at the same time.

Howard released me with his teeth and sucked as much of me there into his mouth as he could, spreading me even wider by inserting a second finger. And that was all she wrote. On a shuddering last breath I felt every nerve in my body begin pulsing to a new rhythm and I buried my face in a pillow to scream.

Before I'd finished, Howard flipped me over to my stomach as if I weighed nothing and adjusted the tip of his penis to slide just barely inside me. The twitching there intensified and he groaned a little, bent down to my ear and whispered, "Mine."

"Yours," I agreed. And, I meant it, God help me I meant it.

He pushed in a little farther and brought his hands up my sides and under to hold each of my breasts. "So perfect." He whispered as he tweaked each nipple. "This was all I could think about on the long drive back." He pushed in a little farther, just a little more, but I was still twitching and I think he was waiting for me to stop. Afraid he would come too fast with too much stimulation there. "I concentrated on fucking you to keep my mind off of you damn near getting killed." He was all the way in and now his cheek was resting between my shoulder blades. "When Sam called me I nearly went mad with fear. I can't lose you now that I've just found you. It would kill me."

He lifted up and eased himself in and out in a progressively faster pattern of short and long thrusts. One hand moved to my clit and stroked. The other hand held my breast in maddening stillness. I needed him to tweak there, pinch and pull. I lifted up a few inches to put my hand over his and show him what I needed. But it was too late. The pulsing started at my groin and traveled up to my breasts until I came again in ragged breaths of air, my head thrashing back and forth.

"God!" Howard came a close second, unable to hold it off after I lost control. He collapsed next to me and pulled my back to his chest, one hand holding a breast with the other over my stomach. He didn't allow even an inch of air between us and I could feel his heart pounding out of his chest against my back. I'm not sure I heard everything he said but it kind of sounded like Howard was falling in love with me. I considered that little fantasy for a moment with interest. Nah.

"Howard?" He was nuzzling my neck. I love having my neck nuzzled.

"Tara?" My hand covered his at my breast and moved his fingers to brush over my nipple.

"I missed you." He pulled the covers over both of us and eased me to the center of the bed, tucking pillows beneath my cheek and adjusting things here and there.

"I missed you, too, Tara." He sighed and kissed my neck. "Now go to sleep."

And I did.

CHAPTER TWENTY-ONE

Ozzie, Harriet and Ozzie

THE SUN SLANTING through the window slats and the sound of the guest bathroom toilet flushing woke me up. My eyes opened and fell on the gun Howard had set on my nightstand. While I appreciate the cavalry riding to my rescue, I don't feel any safer knowing the cavalry is armed. Call it a hunch, but I have a feeling Darius is far more comfortable using a gun than Howard. I'm guessing Darius is handy with a multitude of weapons Howard has never even heard of, but I decide to leave him his illusion of confidence. There's nothing like telling someone you think they'll lose to make them actually lose.

I just need one trauma-free day to think things through and plan. Howard's arm tightened around me and he kissed my shoulder. Hard to think at the moment, obviously, but it's Sunday and I can let any orders for Revenge Gifts slide until tomorrow. The sounds and smells of breakfast cooking wafted over us and I nudged Howard to get up. It's been a while since I've had houseguests but I'm pretty sure I should be the one feeding them, not the reverse.

I cleaned up in the master bathroom and slipped out to the living room. I smelled eggs and bacon. I know for a fact I do not have eggs and bacon in my fridge.

"Good morning?" I stood in the doorway to the kitchen and watched Sam scramble what looked like a full dozen eggs around in my cast iron skillet. He'd found the bacon press and had it sitting on top of about ten strips of bacon on the flat square griddle. "You shopped?"

He didn't turn to look at me but grinned and kept scrambling. "Yep. You had nothing for breakfast and no paper delivered outside so I shopped. Coffee?" He pointed to a coffeemaker on the far counter filled with dark liquid.

"You bought a coffeemaker?"

He snorted. "I don't know how to make coffee without one and I hate instant. Besides, every civilized person on the planet should have a coffeemaker. What kind of savage are you anyway? Oh wait; I heard the jungle monkey love screams last night. I almost couldn't sleep with all the noise in there."

I blushed beet red. I swear to God the man is a pig.

"She's a screamer." Howard brushed past me into the kitchen smiling and made himself a cup of coffee.

"If only I'd known." Sam was just asking for damage . . . Howard, too.

A toaster popped up two halves of a bagel and Sam turned the heat off under the eggs. He added the bagel to a plate already stacked with three more, already toasted.

"You bought a toaster?"

"Had to."

"You know, when I told you to make yourself at home, I was speaking in terms of . . ." I thought about it for a moment and realized that Sam had really made himself at home. "Never mind. Thanks for making breakfast. I can't remember the last time I had a full Sunday breakfast at home."

Howard found the paper and started reading it as he

stepped outside the back door. I heard him sit down on one of the porch chairs and set his cup on the glass table. Howard seemed pretty good at making himself at home as well.

"You really shouldn't have," I said. "I could have gotten the bakery to deliver whatever you wanted. That's what I usually do on Sundays."

He turned the heat off under the bacon and forked it onto a plate covered with paper towels. A batch was already draining there on one side of the plate.

"You need a little normalness in your world, Tara. You need a coffeemaker and a toaster and a refrigerator without duct tape. You need to let your friends in closer than the Continental Divide and you need to relax and eat breakfast. Come. Fix yourself a plate. Howard!" He shouted that last bit out the back door. Zeke jumped up on the counter and tried to steal a bacon strip. Sam picked Zeke up and handed him half a strip as he put him on the floor. He gave Precious the other half.

"We've known each other—what? A year? Two? I see you every night at the bar. You know my whole life story and thanks to local gossip hounds I know yours, or at least the interesting bits. This whole time I'm figuring you're gay, what with your friend Kathy and all. And now I find out you're not. Worse, I find out you're a screamer in bed—my favorite by the way—and all this time, all I needed was a goat to get you hot. It's tragic." He said all of this as he was fixing a plate of food and pouring a cup of coffee. "Lucky for you, I like the Muffin man here—" he waved his cup in Howard's direction as he walked in to fix a plate. "Or I would be completely crushed."

He opened the silverware drawer and pulled out a fork. "Why the hell don't you have any knives in this place?"

I walked past both of them to get a room temperature can of Diet Coke out of the pantry, opened it and took a long swallow.

"That is so wrong." Sam shook his head and walked out.

Howard stopped and looked over at what I was doing and snorted.

"Everything about her is just right as far as I'm concerned." He took his plate and his freshened cup of coffee outside again and left me looking at the closed back door. I grabbed a piece of bacon and tucked the rest in the microwave out of reach of Zeke and followed them outside with my soda.

They were shamelessly talking about me. Anyone who thinks men don't gossip either doesn't know men or isn't from this planet. Men gossip a thousand times worse than women. It just seems like less because their focus is so very narrow. For the most part, men only discuss subjects related to sex.

"I'm serious, man. I thought she was strictly of lesbian origins. How did you spot the available signs?"

"She checked me out so hard the day I met her my pants caught fire."

"Ewww. I didn't check you out and I'm not—argh. Men."

"Oh and Nana told me not to pay any attention to the 'Alternative Lifestyle' rumors. She said Tara was one hundred percent into men, she'd just forgotten how to get one."

"Gee thanks, Nana." I took another swig of Diet Coke. I'd gotten the end chair next to the tower of flowers. A cute little green iguana was perched on the side munching away happily on various blossoms. Next time Darius shows up I will have to remember to thank him for the lizard feeder. Ha!

"Pants were on fire, eh? She never checked me out like that, at least, not when I was looking." Sam didn't seem all that disappointed, probably because Sam doesn't believe anyone is in an exclusive relationship. If they are human and have a pulse they are probably available. The human part might even be optional for all I know. Sam's weird—cute, but weird.

"Well her reputation is surely made after last night."

I looked at Sam in mid sip of my soda.

"What?"

"Both of us spending the night? You know how people talk."

"How the hell do people find this stuff out?"

"You know the guy who rents out and manages the other bungalows?" Sam asked.

"Yeah."

"Him."

"No shit." Maybe he's the one watching my bedroom window at night. Damn. Maybe he's the one calling. "How do you know?"

"Nick told me, said he gives a run down over at the Lorelei every night and gets the gossip from the other hotels and rentals. They have a whole club thing these guys."

"That little shit. I am going to kill him. First I'm going to fire his ass and then I'm going to kill him."

"As your lawyer I have to advise you against it. As your friend I strongly urge you to find his replacement before you fire his ass because, as you well know, good help is very hard to come by here, especially honest help. And, he provides a much needed service here on the Keys coconut telegraph. Many people would be very upset with you for firing one of their best coconuts."

"Many people starting with you, you mean."

"I would be in that line, yes."

"Well what would *you* do, if you were me?"

"Cultivate his friendship and bribe him to keep his mouth shut on the juicier details. Do you even know his full name?"

"No."

"I rest my case. How can you fire someone when you don't even know his full name? What loyalty does he have to you if you never say hi and chat with him once in awhile? Tara, my love, you need to get out more. Mingle."

"You're starting to annoy me, Sam."

"I'll shut up." He flashed me an innocent smile.

"Thanks." I chugged the last of my Diet Coke and headed back into the bungalow.

"Hot sex doesn't sweeten her temper one bit, apparently."

"Apparently not," was Howard's non-committal reply.

I picked up Precious on my way through the kitchen and headed back to bed. It's Sunday. There's no need to get out of bed until four p.m. I snuggled back into bed and under the covers. Somewhere in the bungalow I heard a cell phone ringing. I know it's not mine because mine is turned off.

"Hello?" It's Sam's voice answering. He paused for a minute to listen to the other person. "Yeah man, bring bait and ice. And we're good to go. I got my rods and tackle." He paused a minute more. "Ok. See you then."

Good. They're going fishing. I never realized how much I like my solitude. Now that my personal space is fully invaded, I want it back. I need peace and quiet. I have abuse pop-ups to program into Revenge-Gifts.com. I have quotes to add for the days of the week. I have sleep to catch up on. Precious and I need our rest or we get cranky. I snuggled deep into my pillows and scratched Precious behind her ears. The bed smelled of coconuts and I sort of wanted Howard back in bed with me.

I must have fallen asleep again, because when I opened my eyes, Howard was in bed with me and Sam was knocking on the bedroom door.

"Wake up, guys. Time to go fishing."

"Be there in a sec." Howard said over my head. He leaned in to kiss my shoulder and then whapped my butt. "Hop up. We're going fishing."

I rolled onto my back and looked at Howard in confusion. "I'm not going fishing."

"Yes you are."

"Why?"

"Because Kathy's going." He smiled. I wasn't buying it.

"That's not a great reason."

"I'm not leaving you here alone. I can't protect you here as well as I can out on the water. And, more important than anything else, Sam and I are in the mood to fish. Let's get moving."

"Bossy." I rolled out of bed and looked for my shoes.

"Yup."

The truth is I like fishing and I love getting out on the water. Howard doesn't have to push me too hard to go with him on this little jaunt. By the time I came out of the bathroom, changed into a bathing suit, shorts and white leather Keds (fish blood washes off of leather better than cloth), Kathy was on the porch waiting for me and Sam and Howard had the boat loaded up with drinks, food bait and fishing gear. Guys are good about that sort of thing.

"You ready?" Kathy gave me a once over and smoothed back my bangs to look at my eyes. She does that when she's worried. I hate it, but I let her.

"Ready. You?"

"Ready and willing."

I followed her down the path to *Till Death* and stepped on board first. Carlos had the engines warming up and he was checking his electronics. I'm guessing Sam called Carlos but I have no idea how he knew Carlos was the one to call.

"Your estate manager's name is Jerry Cameron. He's sixty-two years old and a widower from New York. He has no criminal record, which is a miracle in this town, as you well know, and he gave me Carlos's number when I walked down to his bungalow to ask. Nice guy, but he has no idea when the hell to shut up. He thinks you're a good girl and I assured him you and I did not do the nasty last night." Sam flipped his Costa Del Mars back up his nose and grabbed a beer out of the cooler. "You have a very expressive face. Never try to lie, you don't have it in you."

"She doesn't." Kathy agreed.

I gave them both withering looks and grabbed a beer from the cooler too. I dug my Ray Bans out of my bag and settled onto the fighting chair in the middle of the deck. Kathy grabbed a cold bottle of water and sat on the deck chair.

"Why didn't you tell me someone broke into your bungalow the other night? And why do I have to find out about the drugs falling out of the ceiling at Crusty's from a customer today?"

"I didn't want to worry you."

"I'm your friend. It's my job to worry about you."

"I don't want you to get hurt."

"I'm not going to get hurt." She set her water down on the deck and twisted her hair up into a Scrunchi leaving it tucked up rather than let it fall into a ponytail. That's one of my second favorite ways to do my hair on bad hair days. I can still see the blotchy red spots on her arms from the Brazilian pepper tree sap. She followed my line of sight and shrugged. "That could have happened anyway."

"But it happened because you were trying to help me."

"Doesn't count."

We pulled away from the dock and headed out to the drop off, the deep blue water where the continental shelf falls away. The ledge runs from about sixty feet to two hundred feet deep and the fish love it there. The guys are up top on the fly bridge with Carlos gossiping and looking for birds. There are a few boats heading out in the same direction we are but, in all honesty, serious fishermen got out there at the crack of dawn. This is a bunny trip. We'll be lucky if we catch anything at this hour of the day.

"You don't have to tell me everything. I'm not your mother," she continued.

Speaking of shit. I forgot to call my mom again and it was Sunday. Shit.

"Can I use your cell phone?"

Kathy gave me a look that said she knew I was delaying and dug it out of her bag. "Here."

I dialed my mom's number, hit send and waited.

"Hello?"

"Hi, Mom."

"Tara?" Jesus, is it too much to ask that just once she recognize the voice on the other end of the phone calling her "mom" as her daughter's?

"Yeah, it's me. I'm just calling to see how you are doing."

"I'm doing fine dear. Miss Wendy tells me you and her grandson are hitting it off really well. I was so relieved to hear that, Tara. I was beginning to worry that you would never find someone and settle down."

I could feel my eyes start to water and my head start to ache. "Actually, I just called to find out how you are, Mom."

"Oh you know, same as always. Your sister checks on me every day. She's closer you know. She took me to the doctor last week and he says I'm in great health for a woman my age. I do yoga every week, you know. You should do that. Your friend Kathy, she teaches Yoga right? You should take her classes. You'll get out of shape if you don't exercise and sitting in front of that computer all day every day is going to ruin your eyes."

I covered the receiver for second as Mom lectured me on diet and exercise. "How many minutes do you have on your plan?" I asked Kathy.

"Don't worry about it. I have unlimited on the weekends. Talk to your mother."

I have no idea what she just said, but I made sounds of agreement and tried to catch up on the lecture.

"And when will you be bringing Howard over for dinner?"

"It would have to be a Tuesday or Wednesday, Mom. How 'bout we take you out somewhere?" I covered the receiver again. "Howard!" I shout up to the fly bridge.

"Yeah?" He leaned over the rail to hear me better.

"What are you doing next Wednesday?

"Nothing. Why?"

"I'll tell you later."

"Is next Wednesday good for you, Mom?"

"That's fine dear. Call me next week and let me know what time."

"Bye, Mom."

"Good-bye, honey."

"Man. She's taking you to meet her mother." I could hear Sam all the way down on the deck. "That's serious."

I didn't hear Howard's answer and in all fairness I didn't really care what he had to say in response. He'll either go or not go. I'm going regardless.

"She says I should start taking your Yoga classes."

"Couldn't hurt you." Kathy responded.

"True, but then I'd have to start eating healthy and it's a long slow slide into the light. I'm just not ready for that yet."

"Suit yourself. You haven't sidetracked me. I still want answers."

"This isn't metaphysical shit anymore, Kathy. It's out of your realm of experience. The drugs I'm not worried about. It's the police's problem now. The night break in, I refuse to worry about until I can think of what to do. The peeping tom is probably just Jerry, the manager guy."

"It isn't," this from Sam at the rail. He is leaning over and blatantly listening to our conversation.

"Don't you need to be looking out for birds hitting the water?" Birds hitting the water mean a school of fish is feeding below.

"Howard and Carlos are looking."

"How do you know it's not him?" I asked Sam.

"Because I asked him."

"And he said no?"

"Yup."

"Well of course he said no. What did you expect him to say?"

"I can spot a liar a mile away, Tara. He wasn't lying. He hits the sack at nine p.m. and doesn't get up until six a.m. He had no idea Howard showed up last night at your bungalow until he saw the cars out front and us on the porch eating breakfast. He mostly just keeps track of the cars coming and going."

"You have a peeping tom?" Kathy sat straight up in her chair.

"Yeah. I have a peeping tom."

"You can come stay at my place. The sofa folds out and we have plenty of room. It's time for you to move out and buy a house anyway. You have more money than God. You can afford something nice."

"I'm not moving out."

"She has more money than God?" Sam was coming down the stairs, tired I guess of not being able to hear the entire conversation very well.

"I do not have more money than God. I don't even know what that means."

"She can afford to buy a decent house, trust me." Kathy sniffed.

"Christ, woman, you tend bar for a living and work your ass off when you don't even have too? The more I find out about you the more I think you need therapy. I have a very good therapist. I'll give you her number when we get back."

I decided to join Howard up on the fly bridge and leave Kathy and Sam below to gossip about me. We'd better catch a shit load of fish is all I can say.

CHAPTER TWENTY-TWO

Swimming with the fishes

WE CAUGHT A shit load of fish. Carlos put us on a weed line that I swear didn't end until Georgia and we caught dozens of schoolie-sized dolphin, half of which we released. It was a good day on the water.

Sherry was waiting for us when we arrived back at the dock.

"Dennis is dead," she said with no preliminaries. I stepped off the boat and hugged her hard. "I am so glad you are back."

"What happened?" Kathy asked.

"When Sheriff Jim finished up at Crusty's last night, he did a sweep of the docks. He found Dennis jammed under a piling at the end of C dock."

"No shit." Sam said. "I wondered where he was last night. Everyone in town was at Crusty's but him, even Kerry. Accident?"

"They don't know yet. I got a call at about two in the morning and caught a flight back."

"You should have called me; I would have picked you up at the airport." I said.

She looked at me funny and said, "I did call. I got a fax machine and your answering service on the cell phone. What the hell is going on around here? Did you get Sunshine out of hock or did you buy your own bird, because when I knocked on your door I swear I heard a cockatoo."

"It's Sunshine."

"Something really must be wrong for you to have her in your bungalow."

"It's a long story."

"I have time." Sherry cocked her head to one side and looked up behind me. She offered her hand to Howard. I did the introductions.

"Sherry, this is Howard. Howard, Sherry."

"I've heard all about you. Glad to finally meet you, Howard." She offered her hand to shake. He took it and looked over at me.

"Not from me." I said.

"From Jerry. He keeps an eye on the place you know? I'm thinking of selling it. I can feel all of the badness swamp over me the minute I step off the plane in Miami."

The fact that no one is shedding a tear over Dennis's demise doesn't surprise me. Sherry thinking of selling the place does surprise me. I know she's not really happy here, but she seemed rooted in the community. Her family has been here for generations. I guess now that Dennis is gone, her last reason for being here got buried along with her parents. I kind of like to think that I'm a pretty good reason for her to stay but it's not like I have really deep roots here either. The ground is just too damn hard here for planting the kind of life that lasts. It's great for tourists to *ohh* and *ahh* over. But, for year round living, it's hard on the soul. If I had a soul, I mean.

Too bad; now I couldn't tell Dennis that Sherry really was here.

The general organized chaos ensued over cleaning fish

and unloading the boat. I used Kathy's cell one more time to call the bar and check on the day crew. Business is hopping and the day line cook is threatening to quit. Damn. I need to get cleaned up and in early. Sam, Kathy and Sherry head back to their respective domiciles and Howard is sticking to my side like freaking glue.

When I came out of the shower he was already cleaned up, changed and running a load of laundry. What kind of person is it that just moves in and gets homey in less than a week? I have to be in a place for months before I feel comfortable. Baffling.

"You don't have to come in with me tonight. There'll be tons of people around. Nothing could possibly happen to me there." I was perched on the edge of one of the dinning room chairs braiding my hair as Howard passed back and forth between the kitchen and the bedroom. I do love watching him walk. He has a natural grace you don't see in most guys.

"Tell that to Dennis." He said quietly as he headed back to the bedroom. "And if you keep watching my ass like that you won't be going in to work tonight, period."

"I am *so* not watching your ass." Actually, I was watching his ass. Sue me.

He came back out, paused at the door to the bedroom and smiled a knowing little smile.

"Are too."

"Am not." I secured the braid with a small plastic band and twisted it up in a barrette at the back of my head, looking at my feet the entire time as if that's what I was doing when he walked through for the tenth time.

"You know, I could let this slide like I do most everything else where you're concerned, but I do believe it's time to pick up this gauntlet." He stalked over to my chair with deliberate steps, the kind of steps you try to take when you don't want to spook what you are stalking into running. I froze. "You are going to admit that you were watching my ass as I walked by or you are not leaving this bungalow for the next twenty-four hours."

He placed one hand on each arm of my chair, caging me in and bent down to one knee in front of me. "Admit it, or suffer the consequences."

I stared at him stubbornly through my bangs and contemplated the consequences. I decided to try a diversionary tactic because, honestly, I would rather die right now than admit I was checking out Howard's ass. Don't ask me why. Most of the time I have no idea why myself.

"Have you considered the fact that Dennis could be one of our first customers?"

He didn't miss a beat. "Don't change the subject. You were checking out my ass. Admit it."

"I'm pretty sure he went to church even though he was the antichrist, I'm thinking we should suggest the religious holiday line of urns. I'll even call Kerry and see if she's given it any thought."

"I'm going to take that as an admission that you were checking out my ass and let it go at that." He stood up, turned and gave me a close up view.

"How the hell do you make that connection?"

"You didn't deny it after I asked you to admit it for the third or fourth time. Guilty as charged." He smiled as he walked back into the bedroom.

"It is a really nice ass!" I shouted after him.

"Thanks," he said as he emerged back into the living room. "Let's get going. People are waiting for you."

Crusty's was packed to the gills, again. I called Kay and gave her a list of supplies to pick up at Winn Dixie before she came in and told her to have them put it on our account. I called the manager at Winn Dixie and told them what to have ready for Kay when she arrived. Kay drives a cute little F-150 truck. She should be able to haul it all. I called Riqué and asked him if he knew any other cooks who might want to come in for a day wage rate, hundred dollars. He said he would bring in his cousin from Homestead.

Sherry arrived about an hour after I did and announced that the drinks were on the house for the next hour but that it was a self serve bar. Several locals jumped behind the bar to take over the duty. The same boat that had set up the loud speakers last night was set up again today and playing the same set of songs. Nick, Howard and Sam went to the storage unit out back and unearthed the resin tables and chairs we had used for the goat roast and the hurricane fans and set them up outside. When Kay arrived, they helped her unload as the day shift, Sherry and I waited tables and lent a hand cooking the food.

Everyone wanted to know about the drugs Puddin had found. They wanted details on what happened to Dennis. A few suicidal locals even had the guts to ask Sam if I was any good in a three way or if I was so rusty I squeaked. I didn't stop to listen to his answers. I didn't want to know.

When Kerry showed up, all hell broke loose. Everyone started talking at once and Kerry answered questions like a trouper. No they hadn't completed the autopsy so they didn't know how he died. They suspected drowning. Yes. Dennis could swim. He had brought the boat around to C dock yesterday afternoon and that was the last time she saw him. She was devastated, just devastated.

All eyes turned to Sherry across the room waiting on tables.

"Oh, she's been an absolute rock." Kerry went on. "I don't know what I would have done if she hadn't arrived this afternoon. I didn't know what to do, what arrangements to make. She's already got a lawyer handling everything, absolutely everything."

Someone snorted. "You trust her?"

"She hated Dennis."

"Maybe so, but when I called her at four in the morning hysterical, she took the first plane home."

Wait one minute. Sherry answered a call from Kerry at two a.m. her time in Arizona? I knew for a fact she'd been avoiding their calls for weeks. What made her decide to pick up? I stored that away in the back of my head for later. Kerry, I might add, looks sunshine perfect in a peach shorts set with matching toenail polish and sandals. Her thin blond hair is fluffed to perfection and her eyes have just the right amount of purple shading to appear tired. I'm not sure if it's makeup or natural but I'm betting on cosmetics. Cynical? Hell yes. But why am I the only one who notices these things?

Riqué's cousin, it turns out, is just as unpleasant as Riqué and just as hard a worker. They spent the evening talking back and forth to each other in Creole and ignoring everyone else while they prepared the orders. It's a beautiful language, very easy on the ears, kind of like French spoken with a Jamaican accent. I let them be.

By eight p.m. Sherry and Kerry were working behind the bar together like sisters and I marveled at how much they resembled real sisters. Sherry's hair is cut very short. It's almost silver white against her deep tan. She has that same thin but athletic build as Kerry but without the breast enhancements. They are deep in discussion on what to do with Dennis and how to handle the funeral arrangement when I decide to interrupt.

"You know, he wanted to be cremated. Why don't you let Howard handle it?"

They both thought that over for a minute and nodded. "A funeral at sea?" Kerry asked?

"We could sink him in his boat!" Sherry smiled.

"Oh hush. You know you can't do that." Kerry chided her.

"How many people do you suppose we'll have to plan for?" Sherry asked doubtfully. "I mean the boat would have to be pretty big."

I looked around the room. "It depends on if you are going

to provide food and booze I would imagine. If yes, then plan on a crowd about this size."

"Does Howard have a boat lined up that can handle a crowd this size?" Kerry asked looking skeptical.

"I'll ask him."

"Let us know." They finished making the drinks for my order and I put them on the tray and left to make another round of the dining room area. I was thinking about stepping outside for a break when Kimmy and crew stepped in the door and paused to look around for a table. Ha! There were none. Makes my day, I swear. They turned, headed back out to the dock area, and managed to grab a resin table and chairs.

Here and there I also caught sight of a few local detectives. Interesting.

I headed out through the back kitchen door and walked as far away from the building as possible and still stay in the marina. Sherry's back and I can take a break again. Sherry's back and Dennis is dead. In my world this counts as a good day. I wandered up and down the docks looking at boats and the lights on the water.

On C dock I paused at the end and stared into the blank windows of the *'Till Death.* It was Dennis's boat and even as I thought the name, I felt—something. It wasn't the chill of evil; it was more like a warm sigh of despair. Dennis had been found just below my feet, pinned between the dock and *'Till Death.* Was it an accident? Sometimes fate has a sense of humor that way.

I shrugged it off and wandered back to the main cross-dock and on to the end and up the length of the last dock in the marina. The moon was waning but still bright enough to glisten across the ripples of dark satin and suddenly I was reminded of Darius. The warmth of the night air chilled a little. I looked around and realized that this section of the docks were empty. There were no lights inside any of the boat cabins indicating that live-aboards were in residence. All the lights were over on A to C docks. I was on F.

"Just realizing you're in danger, beloved?" Darius's voice came out of the darkness, but because water carries sound, I couldn't pinpoint from where. I froze. "I love that you sensed me here. I wasn't going to say anything. I would have just let you pass me by, just as you do every night when you go to the arms of your lover—or is it *lovers* now?"

There was no anger in his question but, since I was pretty sure he was insane, that told me nothing at all about his mood or what he would do.

"Oh, don't worry. I am not a possessive man. Women exist to be loved." His voice sounded closer but was he behind me? I turned around and there he was, standing on the dock, blocking my retreat to safety. He was dressed the same as he was the night before, black jeans, barefoot, gold stiletto pendant piercing his nipple. His hair flowed down his back in luxurious waves of black curls. If he were a woman he would still be beautiful—scary, but beautiful.

He smiled and the moonlight caressed his teeth in a pearl white shine. "Why are you so scared of me?"

I shrugged. "Call me crazy, but last time we chatted you said you might kill me."

"So I might. So I might indeed." He laughed.

That pissed me off and I had a perverse desire to hurt him. "Thanks for the iguana feeder."

He just smiled wider. "I saw that. It's good that you didn't just let the flowers all die. I like that you care about even the reptiles of the world."

Christ, he's as perverse as me. I'm screwed. I could be in love, too, except Howard got to me first.

No, I did not just admit to being in love with Howard.

"The hen has been laying eggs already," he said. That got my attention.

"Where?"

"On your roof."

"Shit. I knew that would happened." I was pissed again.

"They'll come down in about twenty days, then you can hose it off. I'll have a coup made for you by then."

"Am I going to live that long?"

He shrugged. "Who knows how long any of us will live?"

"Did you kill Dennis?" His smile dimmed and he turned away from me. He was walking away. "Did you?"

He paused and turned back around just a little. "Why would you think that?"

"I have a feeling."

"You've got *some* feelings there, beloved. Scares me how close your feelings come to me, especially in the darkest part of the night." He turned again and disappeared, swallowed up by the darkness.

I stood there, staring at everything and nothing until the humid, warm night air blanketed me again and the chill slipped away. I made my way warily back to the bar, trying not to jump at every shadow. Not even Howard had noticed I was gone. I eased my way back into the ebb and flow of life swirling in and around Crusty's and paused once in awhile to appreciate the beauty of it all. There's nothing like death and near death to bring the world into full focus.

I have always accepted the fact that we can't control much in this life. I was just now learning that the list of things over which I have control is growing smaller and smaller by the minute. It's kind of liberating, living in the moment.

```
// Thought for the day on the Home Page of
Revenge-Gifts.com,
scheduled to load on Monday.
<script language="JavaScript">
<!-- This figures out what day of the week it
is, and prints a quote. ->
<!--
  Sys_Date = new Date();
  var DayofWeek = "";
  var TaraQuote = "";

  if(Sys_Date.getDay() == 1) {
          DayofWeek = "Monday";
```

TaraQuote = "U.S. Sen. Bill Nelson said, "The net that we
have around the country—in this case Coast Guard patrolling—
is not 100 percent foolproof. That's the lesson.""";

```
  document.write(DayofWeek  +  " : "  +
  TaraQuote);
  // -->
  </script>
```

CHAPTER TWENTY-THREE

Chocolate Bomb

HOWARD SLEEPS LIKE the dead.

I heard the refrigerator door open and I was wide awake at three freaking a.m. But, instead of eggs hitting the wall I heard what sounded like sighs and moans, like someone in pain. I know from past experience that walking into the kitchen when the food poltergeist is busy doesn't stop it. It just puts me in the line of fire, so I waited in silence. Wondering what it was doing this time. Maybe the Saran wrap mountain was thwarting it.

The bedroom door opened and Sam crept in to my side of the bed.

He leaned down to whisper in my ear. "Are you fucking hearing this?"

I heard another sigh with a groan erupted from the kitchen.

"It's into the chocolates," he hissed. "How the hell do you live with this shit going on every night?"

"Last night you didn't believe me," I finally whispered back. I sat up and Sam made a strangling sound in his throat.

I grabbed the sheet back up to cover me. "Could you get out so I can get dressed?"

"I'm scared."

"Well I'm not. Now get the hell out." But I spoke too soon, because just as he moved I saw the face in the window. "Sam!" He turned in the direction I was looking and saw it too. Sam was out like a shot chasing after him in his bare feet over pea gravel. I was up and throwing on clothes and following. Sam had him up against a palm tree but it was a struggle. I ran back to the bungalow and grabbed a flashlight. When I got back Sam had the man pinned to the ground, face down, with his hands tie wrapped behind his back.

"Where the hell did you get tie wrap handcuffs?"

"I always have them." He stood up and jerked the man to his feet. He barely strained his muscles, making me wonder if Sam was just that strong, or if the other guy weighed less than he looked. He was more hair than human from what I could see, kind of like Cousin It on the Adam's Family.

"You go to bed with them?"

He shrugged, "It's a habit."

"Uh-huh. You were hoping to nail me." The man's an incorrigible leech. I can't believe I just let him sleep one room away from me.

"I have few goals in this life. Nailing you is one of them." He turned his new prisoner around to face us. Right. We'd discuss Sam's "to do" list later. I turned the flashlight on the man's face.

"Derrick?" He wouldn't look me in the eye but I knew it was Derrick. Standing there, under a year's worth of beard and uncut hair it was Derrick, my Candy-A-Day ex co-worker. "What are you doing here?"

He started to cry.

"Oh, for God's sake." Sam raised his hands in a "What the F?" gesture and started to pace. "You *know* this guy?"

"I used to work with him." I decided to ignore Sam and

concentrate on Derrick. "Why didn't you just call or knock, man? Peeking through my curtains does *not* put you in charity with me."

He stopped crying for a minute and sniffled. "I did call. You turned off your phones."

"That was you? Son of a bitch! You scared the shit out of me calling like that." He started crying again, harder. "Aw, man. Stop crying. Please?"

"I wanted to talk to you." He was sniffling again and he sat down Indian style on the ground so that Sam and I had to look down at him.

"Then why didn't you?"

"Because I couldn't." He still wouldn't look me in the eye. Yeah, I remember that: Derrick can't take direct confrontations. I know I'm not going to get any good answers out of him until I get at least one drink in him and calm the situation down about ten decibels.

"Let's go inside."

Sam helped Derrick back to his feet and held his arm as he walked Derrick inside my bungalow and into the kitchen. Bad things had been happening in the kitchen while we were outside playing cops and bad guys.

The freezer door was open and chocolates were scattered all over the kitchen. Three hundred and sixty-five chocolates and it looked like half of them were no longer in the basket. As soon as Derrick stepped into the kitchen a barrage of chocolates hit us like a hurricane. The sighs and groans had turned to shrieks and screams. It wasn't shrieks and screams that a human voice would make. It sounded like it was coming through an intercom system, all around us in stereo.

"Bad idea," yelled Sam as he dragged Derrick outside again and I dove into the bedroom to get Howard. But the deluge stopped as soon as Derrick's feet hit the front porch. I turned around at the bedroom door. It was breathing heavily all around me. And then the crying started and it wasn't Derrick this time.

"What is it?" I asked the air around me. "What do you want?"

The crying stopped and then it was just gone.

"I want *you*, baby doll. Come back to bed," Howard answered sleepily. "What's the matter?"

"Sam's up and we have company. Get dressed." I watched him get up and let my eyes linger over all the good parts before closing the door on him.

I cut the tie wraps off of Derrick's wrists and gave him a glass of wine. Derrick never drinks anything stronger, and never more than one glass. He took a sip, tucking his beard under. He smelled clean enough, but I swear he looked like one of the swamp critter people that live out in the Everglades off of U.S.-1. Revolting.

"No offense, man, but you look like hell."

Derrick turned puppy brown eyes up at me and I felt like I just hit him.

"What are you doing down here? I thought you took a job up in the great North West?"

"I lost it."

"It happens. That still doesn't explain why you are camping out under my window rather than coming up to the front door like a normal person." Howard emerged with a glass of Drambuie for me, and two beers, one for himself and one for Sam. Sam was draped casually across the railing along the porch. He had his back braced against a post that goes all the way to the roof and one leg gracefully trailing the wooden slats of the porch. He had on jeans and no shirt. Howard, dressed in loose khaki shorts and a polo shirt, took his usual stance by the door. The light from the bungalow spilled out over both of them, casting their eyes and half their faces in shadow. I wouldn't let anyone turn the porch light on. I didn't want to spook Derrick any further.

"Not to me it doesn't. But I deserved it. I deserve whatever bad things happen to me. I'm a rotten person, Tara."

"Just for peeking in my windows?"

He looked at me then, confusion written all over his face. "No. Not for that." He took a long swallow of the wine and set it down, closed his eyes and let his head fall back to the chair. "I killed Aileen."

I almost laughed, but managed to stop myself. "You did what?" The idea of Derrick killing anything was ludicrous; of course I wouldn't have thought he was capable of stalking anyone until today either. "Aileen's dead? Why didn't you email me or call me for crying out loud?"

He sighed and rolled his head around, keeping contact with the chair back. "We killed her, Tara; you and me."

Sam snorted and started to laugh. "I knew you were a scary bitch, Tara, but murder?" He paused and looked me up and down in that suggestive way of his. "Strangely enough, I'd still do you."

"I did not kill anyone. Now shut up, please, or go away."

Derrick pressed his hands on the seat of his chair and started rocking back and forth. Howard adjusted his stance at the door just slightly and I realized, at that moment, that Howard had his gun tucked at his waist and he was positioning his hands toward it.

"I know him, Howard. He's harmless." Howard didn't say a word. He also didn't relax his stance. He was letting me handle it but he wasn't taking any chances.

"I hated her. I hated her so bad. Every single day, day in and day out, she tortured me. She never let up. Not once." He was rocking faster and faster in rhythm to his words. His hands were under his thighs now lifting him up with each pass back and forth. "I kept sending her the chocolates. I kept sending and sending. She was frantic, Tara. You would have loved it. She saw a therapist. She did everything she could to lose the weight. She tried to find out who was sending them but I kept changing the company I used, and then I found your website and I ordered them from you."

He stopped rocking back and forth. "You were my god then. I knew you hadn't forgotten about me. I knew you still cared." He stopped talking.

"What happened, Derrick?" I ran a nervous hand over my face. My breathing was growing shallow with dread but I needed to know the answer. He just stared at me like he was seeing something else, somewhere else. It's four in the morning and I remembered the Loa. Her favorite time to visit was now. "What happened to Aileen, Derrick?"

"She had her stomach stapled. She got an infection, starved herself and died." He brought his hands up in front of him and started twisting them inside each other. "She's dead." He nodded his head up and down. "She's very, very dead."

I made a mental note to myself to limit the candy-a-day orders for one address to three months total. It will piss off Sheila, but once I explain the circumstances, I think she'll agree.

"Man that's some cold shit." Sam sat up from lounging against the post and took a swig of his beer.

"Tell me about it." Derrick seemed to be coming out of himself finally. I could see the color returning to his face.

"It wasn't your fault, Derrick." In actual fact, it kind of *was* Derrick's fault, indirectly. But now was not the time to split hairs. I have a bad feeling that Aileen is my food poltergeist and I'm thinking I may have to have the bungalow exorcised. I wondered, briefly, if Kathy might know anyone who could handle it. For a fact I'm not sleeping another night with her in the house, crazy vindictive bitch, even in death. "Where have you been living, Derrick?"

"Here and there." He waved a hand aimlessly around.

"Come on. You need to shower, shave and change into some clean clothes." I took his hand, pulled him up from the chair and guided him into the bungalow. There was no screaming or crying—maybe my Loa was keeping Aileen away. "I'm burning that outfit you're wearing right now so toss it outside the bathroom door when you get it off."

I keep extra toothbrushes, toothpaste; throw away razors and soap, in the guest bathroom. I pull out one of each and wait outside the door for his clothes. The door cracked open and he peeked out around the corner of it, handed me his clothes and hurriedly closed the door. "You better look like a human being when you come out of there!" I shouted at the closed door. "And don't think I've forgiven you for spying on me."

Derrick is about my size so I pull out some drawstring sweats and a T-shirt and leave them by the closed door, after tossing his clothes in the outside trash bin. By the time I got the chocolate disaster in the kitchen cleaned up it was five a.m. and Derrick was looking almost human again—almost.

"Got any scissors?" He held up a dripping wet lock of honey brown hair.

"I threw them away. Sit down." I grabbed a brush out of my bathroom and some leave-in conditioner and brushed out his hair. I braided it in one long plait down the back. He almost looked like I remembered. If not for the haunted look in his eyes, I'd say he was doing all right.

"I'm not broke, Tara." Derrick looked up at me sadly.

"Glad to hear it." I went and got us each a Diet Coke and sat down across from him. "But you can't keep living outside, Derrick. You need to get another job and find a place to live."

Sam grabbed another beer and sat down next to Derrick. "What's he do?"

"Computer god." I answered for Derrick.

"No shit. Not much call for that down here. Miami maybe."

"Is your resume still online, Derrick?"

He nodded.

"After I get done with packing orders I'll print it up and we'll get it pretty." I thought about it for a moment. "Do you have any family?" Sad that after ten years of working with him I didn't know the answer to that myself, but there you have it.

"Yes." He swallowed about half the can of soda, burped and continued. "I have a huge family."

"Do they know where you are?"

"Yes." That surprised me.

"Do they know what you've been doing?"

"No." No. Of course they don't know. Stupid question. "It's really nice here outside." He looked me full in the eye. "You slept outside."

Christ, who the hell doesn't know about that night?

"Until it started getting warm, it was nearly perfect weather. Sometimes it rained and I found a boat or a porch to sleep on. There's always plenty of food at Crusty's after you guys clean up at night."

"Oh, eww."

"Hey, don't knock it till you try it. That Riqué is one fine cook. You've got a pretty sweet setup here, Tara. I missed you." His voice took on a plaintive tone that nearly broke my heart. I'd missed him too and I'm not the kind of person who misses much of anything—least of all other people. But the words were hard to say in front of an audience, especially since I was still completely pissed with him for watching me having sex with Howard.

"Don't push your luck, Derrick."

Sam grinned so widely I thought it would split his face. "That means she missed you too, man."

"I'm not sitting here and taking this shit. I have work to do." I got up and headed over to the computer to print out all of the day's orders and headed into the bedroom with

Howard. He was reading and answering his email on his
Palm Pilot. He looked so darn cute sitting there on the bed,
being all high tech. As I was closing the bedroom door I
heard Sam comment.

"Jesus, they're like minks those two."

"I noticed." Derrick agreed. "She doesn't have a TV in
here, does she?"

I ignored them both and locked the door. Howard looked
up and I put a finger to my lips to shush him. He smiled and
set the PDA on the bedside table. He patted the mattress
and waited for me to come over to him. What can I say?
I'm smitten.

"Sadly, no." Sam said outside the door.

"I miss TV." Derrick's voice was deeper than Sam's.

"There's one on the boat." Sam said.

"Yeah?"

"Grab a drink and let's go."

I heard the front door open. "Or, we can watch them do it
at the window if you want?" Sam said.

"Tempting, but I think she'd kill me if she caught me a
second time."

"Wise decision." The door closed behind them and I
watched them walk down the path to the dock.

I turned back to Howard and smiled a knowing, I plan to
eat you for breakfast, smile. "The kids are gone for awhile,
honey. Want to do it?"

"Always," he said on a sigh as I jumped him and rolled
him over from his side to his back. I kissed the living day-
lights out of him on every part of him I could reach.

I started with his feet and worked my way up. I keep waiting for the other shoe to drop and it felt like time was running out. I wanted to ask Kathy how this works, how long the
effects of the curse will keep Howard looking at me the way
he does, but I'm afraid of her answer. So I bounced him
harder than Tigger and had my wicked way with him. He's

bound to come to his senses sooner or later, hopefully later.

It's like Christmas, Easter and New Year's all rolled into one, and suddenly, I have an idea for a single seasonal urn for the seasonally challenged. I hopped off the bed and grabbed a sketchpad and drew. I sketched out a quick Christmas tree, exploding at the top in fireworks with and Easter bunny underneath and little skeletons hanging interspersed with ordinary Christmas tree ornaments. Should I have and exploding Jack-O-Lantern on top with the fireworks? Nah. Two minutes later I was back in bed with Muffin, starting at his toes again. I looked up the long length of his body and caught him grinning at me.

"That attitude will not get you a blowjob," I admonished him.

"Yes. But it might get you one." And with that comment, tickle sex was on. We spent the next twenty minutes giggling like fiends and torturing each other until I think I passed out.

"I WANT TO SHOW you something." The Loa was back but not really. Half of me knew I was dreaming. Not dreaming in the traditional sense, dreaming as in half awake but drifting, sort of daydreaming.

"What?" She was like a real person now, no peripheral vision required to bring her in and out of focus. For a second, I thought it was Kathy, but her hair was lighter and longer.

"Ask me to help you." There was a sense of urgency in her voice, compelling me to just do as she asked.

"Help?" It's a dream. What difference could it possibly make?

"Done." And suddenly I wasn't in my bedroom and the Loa was nowhere to be seen. My back was to a wall in a dark bedroom and a couple was hard at it on the bed, half covered by blood red satin sheets. My eyes adjusted to the gloom almost immediately and I knew I was in a very bad place when I saw who was on the bed.

"I gave you four days to kill her, love." Darius was on his back in all his magnificent splendor, hands behind his head, completely relaxed. His eyes were closed. "Two days are already gone."

"I killed the other for you. That extended the deadline." Miss Good Voodoo was riding him in a slow, sensuous dance. She raked her long red nails down his chest as if she were stroking a cat. They were having sex, obviously, but the sex was an afterthought. Maybe that's how they always do it. All I know is I am not a voyeur and the Loa is in big trouble for this, because I can smell the incense and sweat. I pull back farther into the shadows against the wall. It's solid and warm against my back. Where the hell is the door?

"Dennis was less than nothing for a woman of your talents. I would be insulting you if I extended the deadline for such an incidental chore."

"You should have shot him." She leaned down and licked his chest right about where his heart would be if he had one. "It sets an example for everyone else." He pink tongue circled his nipple around the stiletto pendant. "It tells them that to fail Darius is death."

You know, I always knew Dennis was stupid, but it never occurred to me that he was suicidal. I'm guessing the drugs in the ceiling at Crusty's belonged to Darius. Dennis had wanted to buy the place—scratch that—was desperate to buy the place because he was storing them for Darius. I kind of feel bad for putting him off now. Oh wait, no I don't. Squid.

Darius brought the palm of his hand tenderly to her face and sighed. His fingers twined into her hair and delicately combed through the braids. "I should have shot your brother for giving me the metallic boxers for a birthday present."

"Ma'amba would have killed you—slow. Riqué is her favorite."

Miss Good Voodoo's mother has a mean streak? Shocks the shit out of me.

"Fuck both of them."

"You should not have laughed at him. Had he gone to Ma'amba, She could have done much worse to you and I would be powerless to help you against a curse from my mother."

"Your mother needs to get a sense of humor." He brought her head up from his chest and kissed her. I felt like a bird, fascinated by watching snakes mate. Fascinating as Darius and Miss Good Voodoo were, I was too close for comfort. I pulled as far back into the shadows as I could and took another look around the room for a door.

The floor beneath my bare feet was wood. It was not the wood-over-concrete quiet kind of wood; it was wood as in "This is a shack on the beach" noisy kind of wood. I could see daylight between the slats. The windows were also slats, angled to keep the sun out and let the ocean breeze in. Floor length curtains, made of shells and wooden beads, covered every wall, making it impossible to tell in the demi-light what was a window and what might be a door. Fortunately, they made a pulsing clacking sound with the breeze that covered any sounds I might be making fairly well.

The bed was a four-poster mahogany plantation throwback. It was so elaborate and so ornate that it screamed wealth. A matching chest of drawers took up what little space the room had left. It sat at an angle, wedged in the corner between walls. The bed sat at an angle in the opposite corner, putting me a little behind the bed. If Darius looked up, he would see me. I prayed that he wouldn't look up and sank slowly and quietly to a crouching stance, making myself as small as possible. If I was lucky, I could crawl my way out of here and no one would be the wiser.

"The drifter's anger was too weak. I couldn't build it on a waning moon." She leaned down and kissed his chest.

Wha??? Damn I missed something.

"Maybe, but I am beginning to wonder if she is stronger than you." He gently bit her lip as she pulled back. She bit back, harder. Darius reared up and slapped her away, rolling her off him and the bed in one smooth motion. Unfortunately, she fell on the side where I was crouching.

She wiped her mouth and started to stand, paused and looked right at me.

"She's here." I froze like a deer in the headlights. I could see the door, finally, half covered by a beaded curtain. If I could get past her, I could make it.

"Where?" Darius rolled over the bed to sit on the edge next to her. "Where?"

"That fucking bitch is here, watching us." She jumped to her feet, breasts swaying, glared at me, and headed for the chest of drawers by the door. She wrenched open the top drawer and riffled the contents, pulling out bottles and small packets randomly. She ripped the herb packets open and threw them in front of me, sprinkled them in oils and lit a match.

"I don't see anything!" Darius shouted. His voice was panicked, chest heaving in fear. "Where?"

Miss Good Voodoo started chanting. I was in seriously deep shit. I heard the word "Bind" and ran for the door. As I pushed past her I felt an electric shock and she flew back away from me into the chest of drawers. When I passed through the door I passed into another place completely.

I was standing on a wooden deck in the mountains. I didn't need to look behind me to know that I had been here before, in dreams. This was a cabin in the woods. The deck was a platform perched on the side of a mountain. The platform was bigger than the cabin itself and I could see forever.

Sounds of a stream far below reached my ears as hummingbirds buzzed past like oversized bees. Precious was winding around and around my feet in her happy little cat dance. I walked to the edge of the platform and sat down, letting my feet hang into space, brushing treetops with my toes. Kathy was wrong. I wasn't creating a shit hole for myself with bad karma. This was my real home, the place where I live away from the madness of the world. My heart was settling down and in this part of the dream, Howard was there, but it wasn't really Howard.

"As help goes, Loa, that left a lot to be desired." Warm arms wrapped around me as Howard sat down behind me and adjusted his legs on either side of mine. His chin rested on my shoulder and he spoke.

"You needed to see."

"So I hide a few days and my problem is solved? Fine. I'll call in sick." I took a deep breath and inhaled Howard's scent. His forearm is resting on my chest over my breasts and his hand is caressing my face.

"It won't be enough."

"Well I'm tired and I'm fresh out of plans. I have no defenses against someone like her." I'm not whining and I'm not giving up, but I know my limits and I'm only human. I think it through a little more. "She seemed afraid of me."

"Yes, and?"

"She was terrified of Uncle Les before." I took another deep breath. Too bad Uncle Les can't be convinced to scare her to death for me.

"Focus."

"He wouldn't do it. All he can do is turn on lights in the bungalow. Now if I gave Aileen a few knives, she might be able to do something, but she'd be more likely to aim them at me."

"There is another who hates her. He has reason to want revenge, but no means. Give him the means."

"Who?" I turned my face into the palm of his hand and kissed it, so warm, so alive.

"You felt him on the docks last night."

"Darius?" I mentally recoiled at the thought.

"No, the other." He nuzzled my ear, the way I love. It sent a shiver down my spine and I tilted my head to encourage him to nuzzle more.

"Dennis?"

"Yes." This was said on a kiss to my neck.

"I have no control over Dennis." I pondered that, the implications of that. Dennis was a ghost now? Does everyone who dies become a ghost?

"No. But strong emotions hold them here until they release them. Talk to him."

I pictured myself standing on C dock talking to air and decided I'd feel stupid. I don't talk to the ghosts I have already, if I can help it.

"When you talk to him, it focuses your energy to give him life. Your talent is in drawing people in pain to you. Bring him into your circle. With him, the others will follow and his anger is so new and so hot, it will turn on her completely. It is what she fears most of all and your only defense. Use it."

"I could just shoot her."

"Bad idea."

"Why?"

"Think on it for a moment. It'll come to you."

Howard moved and I was awake, staring at his gun on the nightstand. If I kill Miss Good Voodoo and she becomes a ghost, I will never freaking get rid of her. I had a half-assed plan forming in my head. Insane, but it just might work.

What time is it?

"UPS!"

"Oh *man*. How could you let me fall asleep like that?" I smacked Howard's shoulder. "Just a second, Nick!" I shouted through the door.

"I just had the weirdest dream." Howard sat up next to me

and kissed my cheek. "We were at a cabin in the woods, on a mountain. Beautiful. We should take a vacation there."

I stared at him with my mouth agape for about a minute thinking, not possible. Was it?

He grinned. "You were gloriously naked and fucking my brains out on a huge wooden deck. I have splinters in my ass to prove it."

"That's a crying shame. I love your ass." Situation normal. Howard is teasing. "I didn't pack the orders."

"I did." A voice said at the closed bedroom door.

"Who the hell is 'I'?" I said as I found my clothes and pulled them back on. I opened the door, once Howard was dressed, and there were Derrick and Nick.

"Do you guys do anything else anymore?" This was from Nick, like it's any of his business.

"Where's Sam?" I looked around the room and out the window for him.

"He had to go to work." Derrick and Nick were stacking a mountain of boxes on the dolly. It looked like there were at least two trips worth.

"How many orders were there?"

"Forty. You are out of metallic boxers and cat hair for the pillow inserts, and you have two orders for the fruit cakes that I didn't know what to do with since it's out of season."

"There are more boxers in storage and it's delivery day from the pet groomer. She always has at least two lion cuts a week in the summer. I'll take care of the fruit cake orders."

Howard followed Nick out to his truck to help him load it. I smiled at Derrick. "How did you know?"

"I've been watching you work for weeks. It was easy. And you were sleeping. I didn't want to wake you up."

"Thank you, Derrick."

"You're welcome, Tara." He smiled the first genuine smile I've seen on him since our last day at work.

Nick loaded up the rest of the packages and we waved him off. Word would be out that Sam was no longer part of our little threesome. By tonight, it would be all over the island that I had captured a swamp critter as a house pet and I was holding him prisoner to do all my work while I had crazy sex with Howard, the nice northerner who bought the Sells place up the beach, in the next room.

It's a perfect day.

"Let's go shopping."

CHAPTER TWENTY-FOUR

Voodoo Dog

SHERRY GAVE DERRICK the bungalow next to mine for a month in exchange for playing handy man around the house and at Crusty's for four weeks. The way she looked him up and down in his new surf shop wardrobe, I feared, ever so briefly, for his virtue. He did look pretty damn hot. Living rough gave him muscles in interesting places and the long hair was trés chic. His first job was carting Sunshine back to Sherry's house. She made kissy sounds all the way up the path. Good riddance. Sam will be crushed. He can visit.

I bought Derrick one of those cheap Lindows computers at Walmart just to get him online. He's in alpha geek heaven. The rest is all up to him. He's promised to pay me back for everything as soon as his mom FedExes his wallet and stuff to him.

I told him he could come over and pack the orders for Revenge Gifts to work off his tab with me. A month of not having to deal with it is worth whatever it cost. I even gave him the cell phone to fend off hate calls for me. Whatever it costs, seriously.

In a way, I am ruining his life. And not just with the cell phone call duties. He has no bills, no obligations, nothing to worry about right now. Soon he will have a car, a phone bill to pay and a life to maintain. He was better off as a swamp critter.

The first call he took was from Howard.

"Hello." Derrick answered the cell phone and I held my breath. I was outside combing out Precious for emergency cat hair filler because the pet groomer said she was going to be a day late with her delivery due to an illness in the family. Uh huh. I saw her at the bar last night. She was completely shit faced. The illness is most likely a hangover. I forgive her. I just hope I don't get any orders for cat hair or I may have to shave Zeke. If she shows up at Crusty's tonight, she'd better be toting two Hefty bags full of flea-less fur.

"It's Derrick." He paused to listen. "She's out on the porch combing out one of her filthy diseased rodents." Did I mention that Derrick hates cats? Zeke has been tormenting him all day. Instinct? Stupidity? You decide.

"Howard's going to charter one of the party boats that take people out day fishing and he wants to know if that's ok with you, Tara?"

"Tell him, yes!" I shouted back.

None of the boats he'd contracted originally was big enough and I heard him making phone calls earlier as far away as Tampa looking for a deal on a bigger boat for the fleet for future charters.

"I'll tell her." Derrick said. "I'll tell her," he said again. "Ok." And he hung up. "Howard says you have to wait for him to pick you up to take you to Crusty's tonight. He says he already talked to Sherry and she will handle the first hour or so. He says you really ought to consider taking the next night or two off."

"Give me the phone." Derrick came out and handed me

the phone. I must have given him a look because he scooted back a step.

"What?" He asked.

"It's not you." I hit the call back button on the cell phone and waited.

"Darling?"

"I'll be taking myself into Crusty's tonight. Sherry doesn't need to be working. She has funeral arrangements to make."

"Sherry doesn't want to have to make funeral arrangements for someone she actually likes in addition to Dennis's funeral."

I didn't pretend not to understand what he was talking about. And he had a point. But I need some space to get out to the dock to talk to Dennis and I can't have the A-Team tagging along for whatever show Dennis may put on, if any.

"I'll be fine. What can happen in a crowded bar?"

"Don't ask me questions like that, Tara. I have nightmares as it is." Suddenly I had a sinking feeling that he was remembering his wife and I just knew he was feeling the helplessness of wondering if he had done everything he could. I felt his emotional baggage all the way through the phone.

"Nothing's going to happen, Howard." I should have left the death threat out of the police report, but I was so damned rattled by it, I wasn't thinking straight. Well, I'm paying for that mistake in spades now. "Sam will be there, and I'll drag Derrick."

There was silence on the other end of the phone. I'm guessing that he's wondering if he really is overreacting and if Derrick and Sam are any kind of protection against someone like Darius. The fact of the matter is no one is any kind of protection against a man like Darius. He's a force of nature until nature reins him in, if she ever does. Knowing this is not a comfort, but the inevitability of fate keeps me from worrying much about anything, ever. This is no different.

"I'll meet you at Crusty's," he said, finally.

"Ok." For some reason I feel like crying. "I'll see you in a few hours."

"Bye, Baby Doll." I hate being called Baby Doll, so I respond in kind.

"Bye, Muffin."

He laughed. I hung up. Derrick was watching me intently.

"I never ever thought I would see the day." He said smugly.

"What day is that?"

"The day Tara Cole fell in love." He grinned.

"It's not love, Derrick. It's just really great sex. You, more than anyone else should know; you had a front row seat after all."

He had the grace to blush and dropped the subject. Squid.

I finished combing out Precious and contemplated my options. I discarded the idea of calling Sheriff Jim and relaying what I thought I saw in the Shack between Darius and Miss Good Voodoo. There are people in the Keys who would take that kind of report seriously, but they all live on a special island we like to call Key West. I haven't moved that far south just yet, so I decided to keep my dreams all to myself.

I couldn't bring myself to talk to Aileen with Derrick in the bungalow. God knows what she would do. I'll save that scene for later tonight maybe. Uncle Les can wait too. That leaves the little experiment with Dennis on the docks, not that I think it will work, but nothing ventured, nothing gained.

It's Monday. The day I make lace at Miss Wendy's house. I explained this to Derrick.

"Want to come?"

"Not really, no. But I'm coming anyway."

Good enough.

I was late and all the good rocking chairs were taken. I sat on the cement rail and rested my back against a post. My piece was nearly finished. I'd experimented with colors and threads and tried using a nylon thread used to wrap fishing rods. It was a disaster to work with but it looked beautiful. I had also experimented with the pattern a bit, turning a basic flower weave into a sunflower. Getting the center done with brown threads was the worst part, but I am nearly at the end and it's basic back and forth from here on out.

"I spoke to your mother this morning." Miss Wendy was well into prying mode. She'd no doubt heard all the gossip and wanted to pin down a few salient facts.

"Did you? I just spoke to her yesterday. Howard and I are going to go over there next week some time and take her out to lunch. Would you like to come with us?"

She beamed a megawatt smile at me. "I was just going to ask you if I could tag along. I see her so seldom. She's a lovely woman, your mother."

"Yep. She's the best." I am a liar. We knew this.

"Howard seems completely taken with you. I knew you two would hit it off."

I smiled and squinted into the sun. It wasn't a question so I let it go. I definitely owe her a lunch for shoving Howard in my direction. The conversation around us began to pick up again and the afternoon idyll was over far too soon for me.

It was time to get ready for work.

Business at Crusty's was a nice steady slow when Derrick and I arrived. Sam wasn't in yet; neither was Howard. I'd called Sherry and told her to stay home and meditate. She argued a bit but finally said Ok, only after I assured her I would call her if business picked up to unmanageable levels.

Riqué damn near went into shock when he realized Derrick was the same bum he'd been feeding at the back door every night. He was even more shocked when he found out Derrick and I go way back.

"That explains it," he said enigmatically and refused to

elaborate. He made Derrick dinner and then put him to work prepping food. They had a lot to talk about, or so it seemed. I left them to it and went out front to take care of the bar.

"You know what I want, babe."

Sam leaned toward me to look down my shirt. I still hate being called babe.

"Kir Royale?" I realize that I like Sam more and more every day, lecherous to-do list and all.

"I knew you loved me." He flipped his sunglasses back up to cover his sky blue eyes.

"How was work today?" I figured that was a nice Ozzie and Harriet question.

"Oh. You know, the same old same old. Bad guys getting off free as birds because I am an amazing lawyer." He took a sip of his drink.

"Don't you ever want to throw a case? Like, when the guy is just a pestilence on the planet and he smells really bad?"

"Clients who lose tend not to pay me so there's always that incentive not to throw a case."

"Is the money worth it though?" I'm waiting for him to call me on the conscience lecture, but that's not Sam's style. He knows I'm being a hypocrite.

"Hell yes. Chicks dig it. I'd never get laid if I were broke."

I nodded my head up and down in a knowledgeable way. "Yup. A man with money gets us every time."

Two women walked in and sat at a table on the other side of the room. I turned on CNN and handed Sam the remote. It was time to get to work.

I spent the next two hours bartending, waiting tables and trying to find a good time to go out onto dock C and commune with Dennis. Just when the time looked ripe I realized that Howard was standing next to Sam at the bar. I debated coming around and hugging him hello but since I can't ever recall hugging anyone hello voluntarily in my entire life, I decided against it.

I pondered the implications of this for a full minute. I have no reservations about jumping his bones on a whim, but a hug requires serious thought and meditation. I'm screwed up. On the other hand, you don't see guys hugging casual hellos, so I probably settled into this phobia back at my old job. If the other guys didn't do it, neither did I.

"The boat is arranged and I saw the autopsy report. He drowned. I checked with the sheriff to see if they were ok with releasing the body for cremation and he said yes. They are ruling it an accident."

"It wasn't an accident," I said automatically.

"What makes you think that?" Sam asked.

"I just . . . have a feeling," I said. I need to shut up now. Key West is getting closer by the minute.

"Everything is arranged for Wednesday," Howard said solemnly.

"That's nice." I can tell already that I don't want to have anything to do with the actual burial at sea side of this business. I do not know the politically correct noises to make in response to sentences like, "Everything is arranged for Wednesday."

"Did you buy a dog?" Kay was here and putting her purse under the bar.

"Why do you ask?" Kay never asks conversational questions, so I am pretty sure I am not going to like any answer she gives me.

"Because there is a huge black Doberman snoozing on the back seat of your cruiser."

"Seriously?"

"Seriously." She handed me a copy of the local tabloid, rolled up. "If you don't get the paper, you might want to see today's issue."

I left it rolled up. It seemed perfect for shooing a dog out of the back seat of my car. Howard, Sam and Derrick all followed me out back. Kay could care less. Once she delivers news, she's done.

At first I didn't see it, because it was, as she had said, laying down in the back seat, napping. I looked down at it and nudged it with the rolled up paper. I am not a dog person. If I were, I would have taken the old adage to let sleeping dogs lie as gospel and left it alone.

It growled a low, deep threatening growl. I backed up a few steps, but the damage was done. Car-jacking Cujo was pissed. It leapt up to all four paws and bared its teeth in a truly chilling display of territorial aggression. I heard a click behind me and I glance back to see what it was. Howard had his gun out and was taking aim.

"I took off the safety. Move slowly out of the way, Tara."

As I backed up further, she settled a bit, but she didn't relax her stance. It almost felt like her hostility was completely focused on me, but Howard had her undivided attention. She had the markings of a Warlock Doberman, but she had pale blue eyes like a Siberian husky. Zombie dog? Maybe.

"Is that a real dog?" I asked no one in particular. I got some funny looks, but hey, it's good to be thorough and check these things. It drooled a little on the seat of the car. Shit.

"I'm going to say, yes. It's a real dog." Sam said.

"Why in the hell would it be in the back seat of my car?" Everyone shrugged.

"You need to move further back, Tara."

"Why?"

"Blood spatter. Back up. Sam? A little help please." Howard was moving up as I was moving back and the dog was making sounds like a Tasmanian Devil rending flesh.

Blood spatter? Oh no, no, no. Not in my cruiser.

"Do not shoot that dog, Howard."

"Why not? She's hostile, aggressive and obviously dangerous."

Jesus, Muffin has some seriously screwed up priorities. "That—" I paused for dramatic effect "is a 1984 Cadillac convertible. It has the original cream leather seats and banana yellow paint job. I coat those seats with UV protective cream twice a week. She only has forty thousand or so miles on her and the insurance company will not pay me one tenth of what it is worth if you scum it up with dog guts. Now put the safety back on the gun and put it away."

Howard looked to Sam for a translation. Sam shrugged. "She has a point."

The dog whined in agreement and started wagging her butt where her tail used to be.

"Derrick? Could you go ask Riqué for a hamburger, or some piece of meat, and a pair of extra long tongs?"

"Sure," he said. He headed inside.

"You think it's too late to call Animal Control?" Howard asked.

"They close around five," Sam answered.

"You know, stray dogs are usually not a problem here in the Keys." I was pacing now, and every time I turned a one-eighty, Bowser Baskerville growled. Bitch. I have suspicions about who deposited her in my car, but I'm not going to say it out loud.

"It better not poop or pee in my car or someone is going to die." As soon as I said it, the demon dog lifted her leg and peed all over the back of the front seat. I watched in horrified fascination. Does the dog understand me? Impossible.

"Anyone have a can of mace?" I asked.

They shrugged. Of course not, why would they have a can of mace? The dog growled again and I hadn't turned the corner yet.

Derrick came out with a tray of hamburgers and set them

at intervals leading away from the car and Crusty's. He used the tongs to set one on the trunk of the car. I thought for some reason that setting a burger on the back of my car was a bad idea but couldn't pinpoint why. Voodoo dog scrabbled both front paws onto the trunk and grabbed the burger, scratching the hell out of my original, pale banana yellow paint job.

Oh. That's why.

We backed up a little more and watched. The dog didn't take the bait of the remaining burgers. She just stared at us. I didn't want to know what those claws were doing to my cream leather seats.

I went back in to Crusty's, rolled up paper still in my hand, and poured myself a huge snifter of Drambuie. Hey, it's not like I'm going to be driving anywhere anytime soon.

"Did you see the picture?" Kay was ringing up an order.

"What picture?"

"In the paper," she answered, and walked away to take an order from another table.

I unrolled it.

There, on the front page, was a picture of me in the metallic bra and boxers. It was the pose I had done on the front of *'Till Death* with the Ray Ban sunglasses and the waist of the shorts rolled down. I was wearing a matching thong and you could see it at my hips. The boxers were rolled below it. Because I actually have breasts, I look like I'm posing for *Playboy*. Aw, man. In small print it said, "Courtesy of *Silicon Monthly*" and the caption read, "Local girl hits the big time."

"Well that sucks."

"Will you autograph it for me?" Kay was putting an order up for Riqué.

I stared at her for a minute. "Are you making fun of me?"

She smiled. "Nope. Sign it?" I grabbed a pen off the register and signed it.

"Hide it. I don't want anyone else to see it." She dutifully stuffed it under the bar next to her purse and smiled.

"You're blushing," she teased.

"I don't blush." Admit nothing. Deny everything. Blame something or someone else. "I just drank a full glass of Drambuie. It makes my skin flush a little."

"Uh huh." And she went back to waiting tables.

I headed back outside, hoping to slip past the guys and get some alone time on dock C.

"Where're you headed?" Howard caught me as he and Sam were coming in.

"I'm just going to walk the docks for a little while to catch some fresh air, relax. Meditate on what that dog is doing to my car."

"I'll go with you," he said, and stepped closer to me.

"I don't really want company, Howard, thanks all the same. I'll be right back."

"I'm coming with you anyway." He followed me out on to the main dock. The wind was kicking up and it was whistling through the rigging of nearby sailboats. Waves were lapping at the pilings and I could hear the dock line creaking on most of the bigger boats.

"Nothing's going to happen in the five minutes I'm out here, Howard. I'll be fine."

"As fine as you were last night when you came in from the docks looking like death was chasing you?"

"I did not look like death was chasing me."

"You looked spooked," he maintained. "And, while I'm not going to pry details out of you if you don't want to volunteer them, I am not going to make the same mistake and let you take a stroll out here alone tonight."

I sighed and decided to try the truth. "I am going to C dock to have a talk with Dennis."

His eyes searched mine for a moment and he gave me a sad little smile. "You're really broken up about his death, aren't you?" He said it like it was fact. "I never know how to read you. I would have thought you hated his guts, but you cared about him. Didn't you?

I may throw up, but if it will get me shed of Howard for five minutes while I do this, then I can live with him thinking I have a compassionate side to me.

"Yeah. I feel just awful about what happened to him." And I would feel *really* awful if the same thing happened to me.

"I still can't let you go out there alone."

"Fine." The Loa hadn't said I needed to have a conversation with Dennis, just that I needed to address him as if I could see him, or something like that. I think I can do that. It'll humiliate me, but I've done way worse in my life. I'm thinking the picture in the paper tops this small humiliation by an order of magnitude of ten. I marched to dock C without waiting to see if Howard is following. A warm sigh of wind hit me, the same as last night, and my chest tightened. I suddenly felt like I wanted to cry, and the hair on the back of my neck was standing on end. It was electric. I turned around to see Howard. He was at the base of the dock, leaning against a piling. I sighed again. Good enough.

"Hi, Dennis." The wind settled, briefly, and then picked up a bit, like a sail lofting as the breeze shifted. "I'm sorry about the bug bomb." I waited to see if anything else happened. The urge to cry grew stronger. "Sherry and Kerry have planned a beautiful send off for you. Open bar, lots of food. Everyone is coming to say good-bye."

I got a feeling like a hand was brushing my hair away from my face and tried not to flinch; if he was here, and this close, maybe he could hear a whisper.

"I know it wasn't an accident. I know who did this." I whispered it into my hair, which the wind was wrapping, around my face. "I need you to help me get even for you."

I waited for some sign of a response and realized that the urge to cry had passed. There's nothing like talk of revenge to lift depression.

"Come home with me."

I heard Howard's footsteps coming up the dock and impulsively blew a kiss to the *Till Death*.

Howard wrapped an arm around my waist and led me back to Crusty's. I looked back over our shoulders, hoping I hadn't just imagined it, hoping I'm not an idiot.

All of the hamburgers Derrick had set out to bait my newest pet out of my car were gone. I looked over at the car, and the dog was still there in the back seat. Great. All we'd managed to accomplish was to fuel it up for its next bathroom break. Suck factor rising exponentially. What are the odds, I wonder, of me being able to find a white male dog of adequate size, at this hour? I'm guessing slim to none.

I went back inside to close out my tables and finish up my shift. I let Howard drive me home. Derrick said he would walk it later. He wasn't ready to call it a night.

I wasn't really in the mood to go inside. It's funny how, when there's no television in a house, the draw to be indoors is less compelling. Howard and I strolled hand in hand down the path to the dock and the site of our first semi-date. You remember, the night I told him I hadn't had sex in ten years. Next to the dock, Sherry had cleared a small beach area. There are no natural sandy beaches in the upper Keys—at least, not any that last with out constant maintenance. If humans didn't constantly interfere, mangroves would take over every shoreline, sending out traveler roots, spreading over the ocean, building more and more little islands. Good thing we put a stop to that.

Sherry's beach is more of a rocky oasis among palm trees and orchids. Quaint wooden benches and hammocks were interspersed with Adirondack chairs and lounge chairs. It was cool and cozy during the day. By night, it was a rat-infested hell. As long as you don't stop and sit for too long, you won't see the little rodents. At least they aren't the huge sugar cane rats they get up in Miami. Nope. Everything in the Keys is on a decidedly smaller scale. We have cute little Key deer, adorable marsh rabbits, burrowing owls that will fit in the palm of your hand, and the endangered wood rat. I'm not sure why they qualify as endangered, or maybe they are just threatened; anyway, I see them everywhere at night. It drives Precious nuts because they run the rain gutters. She hates that.

We made a complete circuit of the path.

Bad things had been happening while Muffin and I strolled down lovers' lane. My Hell Hound was now curled up in front of my door, snoring. I seriously thought I was screwed, but as we approached to slide around to the back door, a really weird thing happened. The nice doggy woke up. That's the bad part. She started to growl, also bad, and stopped, cocked her head, put her tail between her legs and scurried off the porch and out of the way. I heard a scuffling sound brush past me on the opposite side of Howard and the lightest brush of a ghostly hand through my hair. I do believe that Dennis has followed me home.

I stood there for a moment, weighing the implications of this as Howard approached the dog with his palm down to let her sniff his scent. She growled for a second and then slinked even farther out of the way. I went to the side of the bungalow and filled a bucket up with water for her and hustled Howard inside before he got his hand bit off. Sillyhead.

Men. Gotta love them.

```javascript
// Thought for the day on the Home Page of
Revenge-Gifts.com,
scheduled to load on Tuesday.
<script language="JavaScript">
<!-- This figures out what day of the week it
is, and prints a quote. -->
<!--
  Sys_Date = new Date();
  var DayofWeek = "";
  var TaraQuote = "";

  if(Sys_Date.getDay() == 2) {
          DayofWeek = "Tuesday";
TaraQuote = "My cat can beat up your cat";

  document.write(DayofWeek  +  " : " +
  TaraQuote);
  // -->
  </script>
```

CHAPTER TWENTY-FIVE

The New Ghost Just Isn't Fitting In

TUESDAY. JUST AFTER five in the morning and Howard is fast asleep next to me, Zeke is definitely not doing his happy dance at the end of the bed. Nevertheless, there is someone besides us in this room. I opened my eyes and saw a shadow rapidly backing away from my face. It hovered just a few feet away and then dissipated. Since this is neither the MO of Aileen nor Uncle Les, I have to assume it is Dennis. He's going to be as annoying in death as he was in life. When things settle down, I'm going to have to figure out a way to get rid of him. Kathy says it's as easy as just asking them to leave, but I somehow doubt that Dennis is the polite kind of ghost that will just mosey off to the netherworld because I say please.

The icky thing is, I was having the most erotic dream and now I wondered if some of the caresses and things I thought I was dreaming were really happening. Sick. Just sick.

I rolled over and snuggled on Muffin. On my other side, the bed gave just a little.

"Get the hell out of my room," I hissed over my shoulder.

"No," a voice whispered.

I froze. This was new. I mean, Aileen had moaned over the chocolates, and the Loa talked but, technically, she's not a ghost. I had no idea ordinary ghosts could talk.

"Go away?" I whispered back.

"You don't know what it's like." His voice was growing stronger and damn if he didn't sound just like his whiny live self.

I was afraid of waking Howard, so I rolled quietly out of bed and went into the living room. I sat in front of the computer and brought it up, opened an email and scanned it. After a minute or two, I looked up at nothing. Oh, Dennis was there, though I still couldn't see him. But I knew that Miss Good Voodoo would be able to and it would scare the shit out of her. He scared her dog into submission and for that alone I could be patient with him.

I sighed. "I'm hoping it's a long time before I do know what it's like, Dennis, but if you want to tell me about it, I'll listen."

"Thanks. But I can't describe it." He paused for a few seconds and then continued. "Until you showed up there on the docks I thought I was in hell." He paused again. "Oh man. This could be hell."

I didn't disagree.

"When you spoke to me, it was like you were breathing life back into my veins. I started to focus, to remember, to hear. When you offered me a chance for revenge, I almost felt like myself again."

For awhile, all I heard was the silence of the night. And then I could make out the sound of Dennis breathing.

"I wondered if I could touch you. So I did. You look like a sunset to me. There's like a constant glow surrounding you in peachy pinks, deep blue, and aqua green. And Howard is the same only more blue."

"You know, Dennis, there are two other ghosts living here

in the bungalow. Why don't you entertain yourself by getting acquainted with them?"

"I haven't seen anyone," he said diffidently.

"You haven't?"

"No one, just you and Howard. Oh, and the cats." His voice was growing clearer the longer I spoke with him. And, I wondered.

"Uncle Les?"

Nothing.

"Aileen?"

Still nothing. Hmmm. Maybe they left? Could I have that kind of luck? Just as I thought it, I heard the refrigerator door open and a popping sound preceded all of the bungalow lights turning on. Howard came out of the bedroom all cute and sleepy-eyed, and the rooster started crowing. If there's a God, the dog will eat that freaking rooster before another sunrise plagues me.

"Come back to bed, baby." He held out his hand and I went to him, shutting off the lights and finally, shutting the bedroom door behind me, hoping Dennis would get the hint. I would have to ask someone about the ghosts seeing other ghosts thing. Weird.

Howard woke up before I did and made breakfast. Sam had Saran wrapped the egg carton and tie wrapped it to the shelf. Why hadn't I thought of that? I marvel. Voodoo dog got leftover crêpes. She growled and snarled at me when I came out with the bowl of food, but quickly backed off, whimpering. Good doggy.

The stack of orders for today is almost as tall as yesterdays and if Derrick hadn't showed up to help pack them, I'm not sure I would have finished them before Nick arrived.

"UPS!" Nick was at the door stacking boxes on the dolly. "Hey, Tara. Can I get your autograph?"

He held up several copies of the local paper and a pen. He handed Howard and Derrick a copy. Howard whistled.

"Wow," said Derrick. "My fantasy."

"Mine too," snorted Howard.

"Luscious huh?" Nick agreed. "It mentions you as her boyfriend, so could you sign it too?

Uh huh. I should have read the article last night. I scanned it for a few seconds to see if there was anything interesting in it and discovered that I am, in fact, a local eccentric. Hmmm. Given that the Keys are nothing short of a lunatic asylum, being considered eccentric here is a major accomplishment.

I read further and discovered that, yes, everyone knew the goat roast at Crusty's was a "carefully planned pagan ritual for the summer solstice, heralding in the end of a ten-year self-imposed celibacy." Huh. I can't argue with that. "And who," it continued, "was the lucky man of choice for the Queen of Revenge, but our newest year 'round resident and successful entrepreneur, Howard Payne." Also true, I thought. "The Keys are full of color and colorful people, our hidden treasures." Aww, that is so nice. I can just see the stalkers coming here from all over the globe, because this paper is online and boasts of getting emails and subscribers from as far away as Australia.

It's a perfect day.

I signed all of Nick's papers and shoo'd him off to finish his route, then I headed inside for a beer. Today feels like a beer day. Anyone want to say something about that? No? Good.

With orders taken care of, Derrick off to work for Sherry and Howard gone to make final arrangements for Dennis's funeral, I considered my options. My car is at Crusty's covered in dog pee and God only knows what else. This means I am on foot at least as far as Crusty's. I am going to have to walk there and get my car if I want to go anywhere today.

"Tara?" Kathy called from outside. I opened the front door and looked around for the dog. She was standing on alert at the edge of the porch, blocking Kathy from coming any closer. I opened the screen door and walked out. The dog spun a one eighty and bared her teeth at me.

"I fed you crêpes, you ungrateful bitch."

I got a bark and a growl in response. I glared back.

"That's not a normal dog." Kathy said. "And you have a new ghost standing next to you." Her voice was shaking just a little. She slowly eased her backpack off her shoulder and hunched down to unzip it and rifle around for—something. Salt?

"You said salt doesn't work." At least she'd said it didn't work on gris-gris bags.

"This isn't the same thing. This is possession." She stood and started pouring a circle around the bungalow.

"Excuse me. But I am *inside* this circle."

"You'll be ok. Do you have any more salt? This isn't going to be enough." I left her with the dog following her every move on the porch around to the back. I met them both at the back door and handed her a new container of margarita salt. Hey, it's all I have. Sue me.

She took it and worked her way around to the front of the house, closing the circle. A shuddering breath escaped her chest and she gave me a very frightened look.

"Go inside, Tara. Close the screen door and leave the other door open so I can talk to you."

"What?"

"Just do it! For once, don't argue." She sounded really, really scared. I backed my way into the bungalow and shut the screen door. Kathy gave a sigh of relief. "Do you have any basil?"

"Nope."

"Cumin?"

"Again, no."

"Rosemary?" I could tell she was getting frustrated with me.

"You've known me for how long? Do I look like the spice rack type?"

Kathy bit at her upper lip in consternation. "Garlic?" she asked hopefully.

Sam had shopped. Garlic was a possibility, knowing him. "I'll check." I went into the kitchen and looked in the fridge and there, nestled in with chives and horseradish, was a single head of garlic. I grabbed it and went back to the screened door. "Got one." I smiled at her triumphantly.

She huffed out a breath of relief. "Ok. Go get a piece of paper and a pen." I did. No point in arguing when Kathy was acting all witchy.

"Got it." I held it up for her to see.

"Write on the paper that you will the dog free of the demon possessing it."

I started to write and paused, "How do you spell possession?"

"Wing it," she said. Obviously time was of the essence so I winged it.

Kathy gathered up a few sticks and leaves and piled them inside the circle of salt. She sprinkled some sort of oil over it and lit a little bonfire.

"I want you to do two things very quickly. I want you to take a bite out of the garlic and then throw it and the note onto the fire."

"Oh *ew*. Raw garlic?"

"Just do it!" She shouted.

I braced my self for the pungent bite of garlic and chomped down.

"Now move!"

I opened the front door and tossed the note and garlic onto the fire, spitting out the garlic from my mouth. God. Out of the corner of my eye I just caught sight of Voodoo dog coming at me. Kathy reached across the salt line and yanked me across.

"You need to take certain things a little more seriously, Tara."

The dog stopped at the line and stared at us with those eerie blue eyes. As the fire consumed the garlic and the note, the dogs eyes changed slowly to brown and the fire swirled out its last dying embers in a miniature funnel cloud of smoke. Kathy crossed over the line and held her hand out, palm down for the dog to sniff.

"Good doggy. Friend." It sniffed and then licked her hand and she patted her on the head.

"Safe now?"

"Safe."

"Good. I need a bottle of mouthwash. I'll be right back."

Kathy was waiting on the back porch for me feeding the dog crêpes one by one. "Sheba's a really good doggie. Aren't you Sheba? Yes you are." She was petting and hugging the dog like a teddy bear. "Did you see her collar? It gorgeous."

I hadn't noticed the collar, because to get a good look at the collar I would have had to get close to her and until now getting close had seemed like a bad idea. Now that I looked at it, I could see that it was made of a silver type of metal with blue stones set in a pattern spelling out the name "Sheba".

"Those are Larimar stones. They are only mined in the Dominican Republic. It's what happens to copper under pressure for thirty million years. They bring you good health."

"Good to know."

"Can I have her?"

"If you want her."

"I do."

She looked up at me a frowned. "You've stopped calling me when bad things happen. Why?"

I glanced at her bare arms, nearly healed now and sighed.

"Of everyone you know, I am the only one who will believe you if you'll just tell me what's happening. You've added another ghost to the bungalow and he says you invited him. Only a natural disaster could have possessed you to invite a man like that into your home. Now, you either tell me what is going on or I am going to get very angry with you. And you don't want me angry."

Good Lord. Kathy was kind of scary when she lectured me like this, but not scarier than Darius and Miss Good Voodoo. I debated what I could and could not tell her and told her all about finding the dog in the back seat of my car and the peeing and the hamburgers and just generally bullshitted the hell out of her. She made all of the right noises and looked up past me at the kitchen screen door as if someone were standing there and frowned.

"Are you people getting all of this?"

I turned to look and still saw nothing there. I stared off at the trees, my eyes focused on nothing. I had no confidence, in spite of her little ritual, that she was any match for a seriously pissed off Voodoo Priestess. I was also afraid the ghosts would book rather than stay and help me.

"None of us are leaving, Tara." A voice whispered in my ear. It was Dennis.

Kathy grabbed the dog's collar, stood up and moved away from me by about eight feet. "They are trapped here by revenge. He's right. They won't leave. Until each of them gets the vengeance that they seek, they will remain with you."

"Joy." I am the poster girl for depression right now. I remembered my manners, finally. "Thank you for helping with the dog."

"He told me you offered him a chance for revenge. He said he was murdered."

"He was."

"You can't play with these people, Tara. You're in over your head." She stepped off the porch and over the salt line.

"Does that work?" I had to ask.

"What?"

"The salt line? Can Dennis not cross it? Is he trapped until it's broken?"

"I think so, yes." She backed up a few more steps.

"Test it, Dennis." I said.

Kathy moved well back as if she could see him approaching her so I assumed he was doing as I asked. There was silence. Kathy was breathing hard, looking at something I couldn't see, smiling a little and then frowning. Dennis screamed.

"Holy mother fucking shit! That is the *last* time you are experimenting on me, woman."

"He can't cross it." Kathy's grin was huge. "Toss me my purse, will you? I need to get you a few things at the store and take Sheba home."

Dennis was moaning now like he was in pain.

"Crying like a *little girl*. Shake it off, man. You're tougher than that." I shook my head. "Poor baby."

"Umm, Tara?" Kathy had turned around to talk to me again. "I wouldn't taunt him if I were you."

"Why not?" And then I felt it, like a freezer walked through the center of my body. For a brief second I couldn't hear anything but the blood roaring through my ears and then Kathy's laughing.

"That's why."

"What'd he do?"

"He walked through you. He was trying to touch you, fell and stumbled, but the end result was that he passed through you."

"Oh *ew*. Never ever do that again!"

"Never laugh at me again, bitch." Dennis sounded really pissed. Huh. Whatever.

"Fine."

Kathy left and I decided to do laundry. Judging from Miss Good Voodoo's past wardrobe choices I wanted to be a little stylish at least.

CHAPTER TWENTY-SIX

Miss Good Voodoo Returns

BY THE TIME Kathy came back, Howard had returned with Sam and Derrick in tow. She had a huge jar of mastic gum and made me swallow two of the five hundred milligram pills.

"This will raise your psychic energy."

Whatever.

The rest she broke open and added to a jar of goo she made from several herbs she brought with her. In the trunk of her car, which I have now dubbed the arboretum, she had a dozen huge rosemary plants and a dozen smaller basil plants. The guys placed them at even intervals around the porch.

She hammered a braid of garlic up at each door and window. I thought this was a little much, but when I voiced my doubts everyone ignored me. Kathy updated all of them about the dog, which she had taken home for safety.

When she unpacked a box of sharp knives, I sighed.

"I called your cell phone to see if you needed me to pick

up anything while I was at the store. Derrick answered and said you didn't have any knives so I pick up an el cheapo pack so you'd have something until I can get into Miami to get you a decent set."

I sighed again and went to lay on my bed with Precious.

Kathy peeked in on me once in awhile, but for the most part they all just left me alone. If nothing happened tonight, we were all going to feel pretty stupid. Hey. I'm just sayin'.

I wondered what damage mastic gum will do to my digestive system and then I tried not to think about it. I smelled candles and incense and after awhile I dozed off. Falling asleep was probably only the first of many mistakes I would make tonight.

I learned from the Loa's little help session last time that a basic out-of-body experience without the aid of LSD is a fairly simple transition. When I relax, while concentrating on one simple thing, it's like rushing through a dark tunnel and then losing touch with gravity. In my case, it happened by accident. I was fixated on finding a way to get the hell out of dodge before Miss Good Voodoo arrived for her final showdown and suddenly, she was standing right in front of me.

"Yes," said Miss Good Voodoo. "You'll make a few more mistakes for me."

I was there and not there, much like the dream in the shack. Only we were standing right outside the bungalow. Darkness had fallen and Kathy had four fires positioned on the North, South, East and West corners of the building. They were set in cheap charcoal grills. I turned and could see Kathy and Howard moving around the bungalow, oblivious to the danger outside.

"She's still asleep," I heard Howard say.

"Let her be," Kathy answered.

"Come to me, closer." Miss Good Voodoo curled her fingers, motioning me closer. "You don't want them to get hurt. They can't help you anyway."

There were no other night sounds. No frogs were chirping. No cicadas singing. Nothing. I could feel the pea gravel beneath my bare feet and a wind was whispering through my hair. But it wasn't a natural wind; it was like an electric current racing along my scalp. I recognized it as fear.

"Time is running out for you," I taunted her. I'm guessing this was my second mistake and she confirmed it almost immediately. Her eyes blazed red for a brief second and she slammed me with an electric shock. I flew back and felt my heart stop in my chest. I was flat on my back gasping for air and wondering what hit me when I saw her staring down at me.

"You thought I was here in body?" She laughed. "I am no more here than you. But as you can see, I can hurt you even so."

My breath came back to me in big gulps and I pushed her back as I stood up, causing an electric current to pass between us again. I noticed that we were both standing inside the salt line and smiled.

"I liked you better when you were a dog," I said, for no particular reason other than to piss her off.

"You wouldn't have liked me as a dog if I had succeeded in mauling you."

"Well, you suck as a rabid dog. Who would have guessed it? You can't do much of anything right, can you?"

"It would have been just another stray dog attack. I was hoping to at least scar you for life. Darius only loves beauty. You would have been hideous if you had survived. I wanted to kill you, but after Dennis I need a cleansing period before I kill again."

"Dennis will be thrilled to know he requires special after-death consideration, I'm sure." Where the hell was Dennis anyway? Wasn't he supposed to guard my cowardly ass from Miss Good Voodoo? Dennis is fired.

"I wasn't willing to die myself. Your friend with the gun looked like he would have shot me. If I'd died as the dog, my body would die. And then you called Dennis to you. So now I have to find another way." She grinned. Obviously she's not too broken up about her first plan failing.

"So what's stopping you?"

She didn't answer. She just circled me slowly, muttering something under her breath so I couldn't hear it. She was trying to bind me again. I'm not sure what that does to a person's soul, but I didn't want to find out first hand.

I ran toward the docks and hit the salt line. Holy mother fucking shit! Dennis was right. That hurt like a son-of-a-bitch. It took me all of a minute to get oriented again and turn back to face her.

"You're trapped here. You can't get out." Hallelujah. My first break of the day has arrived.

She kept chanting

"Fuck that. You come for me in person or call it a night." I willed myself back in bed and suddenly I was there, wide-awake, sweating. For just a minute I wondered if I was still dreaming, because I could see Dennis standing next to the bed.

"It's going to be a long fucking night," I said and sat up. "Where the hell were you?" I asked, getting up and heading for the door.

"Watching you sleep." He laughed and followed me. I looked at him as he passed me through the door. He made eye contact and he paused. "You can see me?"

"Sadly, yes."

"Cool."

"Don't get your hopes up. You are leaving when this is over."

He just gave me a cocky smile and stepped into the living

room, passing through Sam deliberately as he headed into the kitchen. Sam shivered and looked around like he'd been pole axed.

"What was that?"

"Dennis."

He shivered and shook it off. "Jerk."

I caught Kathy's eye and nodded for her to follow me out onto the porch.

"What?" She asked.

"She's here."

She didn't say anything for about a minute, thinking that through. "Like the dream?"

"Yup."

"You're stronger than she is that way. She was just hoping to scare you into doing something stupid."

"Yeah." No way was I volunteering just how stupid I actually was, like challenging her to come back to finish me off in person. Nope. I took a deep breath. That little stupidity I will keep all to myself. "I think that was her big show. I think it's over."

She gave me a sharp glance. "What makes you say that?"

What did make me say that? Fear for Kathy's safety? Fear for everyone's safety? Yeah. That was it. For a fact, Miss Good Voodoo is trapped, and without her body, her ability to do damage was contained. I wondered, briefly, how long she could survive that way.

"I sent her screaming into the night." Screaming in rage, but Kathy doesn't have to know that.

"You did?" She didn't sound like she believed me. Now that hurts.

"Yes. Yes I did," I confirmed.

"Then how do you explain that torch coming our way?"

I looked in the direction where she was now pointing and damn if there wasn't a torch wending its way up the path from the beach. Time's up. It's show time.

Darius was carrying an unconscious Miss Good Voodoo in his arms and a mountain of muscle was holding a torch up, walking behind them, they stopped at the line of salt. Instinct? Chance? You decide.

In honor of the occasion, he had put on a loose, red, long sleeved button down shirt. He hadn't bothered to button it and stiletto pendant played peek-a-boo as Miss Good Voodoo's dress shifted in the wind, teasing his stomach and chest. She looked dead. I wish. And, Darius looked devastated.

"You've won, beloved. I have stood watch for over twenty-four hours and she is truly gone."

Call me crazy, but I did not want Darius to take that one last step over the line of salt. Bad things would happen. But now I was in a quandary. It's not like I'm Miss Nice-Nice and want to see the Queen of Hell reunited with her body, but, if she doesn't, will she die?

"She's still breathing." I said.

"Not for long," he answered and there was a sad quality to his tone. "Her mother says that if she can't find her way back in a day or less, she will fade to nothing and her body will die."

I'm thinking mama doesn't know her daughter very well. Miss Good Voodoo was far from fading away.

"Help her?" he pleaded.

"What makes you think I can help her?" I was so going to hell for this shit.

"Your magic is stronger than hers. Help her and I will send her home to Haiti." He buried his head next to hers and kissed her cheek.

Crud. He loves her. Of course he loves her. She's a murderous bitch and he's a psychopath. But you know, there's someone for everyone according to Kathy and who am I to pass judgment?

He stepped toward me and over the line. We were in very big trouble. Miss Good Voodoo stirred in his arms and kissed him back full on the lips. He set her on her feet and she turned to face me, putting her hands into hidden pockets at the sides of her dress.

"The day isn't over yet, Darius. I haven't lost yet," she said and walked up to me, taking her hands out of her pockets. I could see if she'd taken anything else out with them, but odds were good that she had.

Darius's muscle man moved up next to her. It looked like Darius had instructed him to get between us, afraid of what she would do.

"She saved you, Gigi. Leave her be now. I made a promise to send you home."

"She didn't save me. You did. And I'm not going home, ever. I am going to make her wish she had never been born."

You know. That's a great threat and all, but I've regretted being born for most of my life, so it's no biggie to me. My angst and not your problem so don't sweat it.

"I'm not afraid of you. Do your worst." That was the third stupid thing and counting.

She smiled and reached her hand out to trace it along my lips. "You have a big mouth. Let me close it for you." She turned her palm up and I saw the powder just before she blew it at my face. I ducked and turned, causing most of it to miss me. A sudden gust of wind blew it to the side and the man standing next to her took the full brunt of the powder. He fell down immediately, paralyzed.

"Zombie powder?"

"He'll live," she said and tried to grab my face. I backed away and wagged a finger.

"That's not polite." I turned and looked at the guys behind me. "Plan B. And don't try to help." I turned back and taunted her again. What can I say? I have a death wish. "Missed me. Missed me. Now you gotta kiss me." I blew her a kiss, turned and ran like hell for the front door. She was hot on my heals and through the door after me before she realized that *she* had just made the biggest mistake of the evening. Not me. Hah, take that. The bungalow lights began flashing on and off as knives flew from every direction. We ran the gauntlet all the way through the kitchen where the knives stopped and Dennis was standing in front of the back door.

"Nice to see you again, *Gigi*."

She froze in horror and started backing up, remembered the knives and froze.

"I'll be coming home with you tonight. We have a lot to talk about."

She started chanting in Creole and ran for the front door. Dennis winked at me and followed. "Thanks. I owe you one."

"Anytime." I said. Whatever he was going to do once she got him home, I didn't want to know about. Not my ghost, not my problem.

Several cars roared up the path in response to Darius's call from his cell phone. He held a shrieking Gigi in his arms and threw her into the nearest car.

"I will send her home, Tara," he promised again.

The men who had come with her picked up the fallen body guard and left. Miss Good Voodoo was gone and, I suspect, will be busy for a while.

Game over. Score one for the Tara team.

"Now was all the shrubbery and stuff really necessary?" I asked as Kathy and the guys came inside. She had the grace to shrug and look chagrined.

"Um, Tara?" Derrick was turning pale, staring at me.

"What? Another ghost?"

"No." He was standing away from everyone else to the side of me. I looked down my arm to see what he was staring at and saw a knife protruding from my waist and blood dripping down to the floor.

"Aww shit," I said, and passed out.

```
// Thought for the day on the Home Page of
Revenge-Gifts.com,
scheduled to load on Wednesday.

<script language="JavaScript">
<!-- This figures out what day of the week it
is, and prints a quote. -->
<!--
  Sys_Date = new Date();
  var DayofWeek = "";
  var TaraQuote = "";

  if(Sys_Date.getDay() == 3) {
          DayofWeek = "Wednesday";
```

TaraQuote = " 'Ernie, your whole family was killed by cows.
How can you maintain such a cheerful attitude?' And he smiled
and said something that I will never forget. He said, 'Drugs.'
So I fired him." — From the article Another Pet Peeve by Tim
Chitwood, Columbus Ledger-Enquirer";

```
  document.write (DayofWeek + " : " +
  TaraQuote);
  // -->
  </script>
```

CHAPTER TWENTY-SEVEN

Stitches

AILEEN, I SUSPECT, had been going for the stomach and missed by a few inches. Sheriff Jim briefly arrested everyone and, after I explained what really happened, rudely suggested that I might want to consider moving a few islands south, for my own personal safety.

"How do you feel?" Howard was snuggling up on my good side. They had defanged the bungalow before I returned and solemnly promised to never, ever provide Aileen with weapons again.

I sniffed piteously. "I'm damaged."

"I know, baby. You'll heal. The plastic surgeon swears there won't be any scarring."

I sniffled in response.

"Can I get you anything?" He fluffed my pillow and I smiled a secret little smile. "You were very brave, you know. It all happened so fast. It was over in less than a minute."

"It seemed longer." I scooched down into the pillows a little farther. "I want to go to the funeral."

He bent down and kissed my cheek. "The doctor says you shouldn't."

"I know but I promise I'll be good. I'll sit in a comfy chair and let everyone wait on me hand and foot."

He smiled and I noticed dimples, of all things.

"Yoo hoo!" Chanté was at the screen door hooting. Please, God, let it be a reasonable sized bouquet from a normal person this time. It wasn't. Over Howard's protests, I struggled out of bed and met her just as she was coming in and setting up another monstrosity in the middle of my dining room table.

"There's a note this time!" She said happily. "It says, 'She is Gone.' Do you know what that means? Who is 'she'?"

"I have no idea." I went to the seasonal urn slash piggy bank on the coffee table and got her a tip. "Thanks, Chanté."

"I heard you got hurt, but you look the same as always to me. Oh hi!" She bubbled at Howard, standing behind me. "You must be the hunk I read about in the paper. My name's Chanté of Chanté's Creations? You've probably driven past it a thousand times. Anyway, welcome to the Keys." She offered him her hand to shake.

"Who sent them?" he asked quietly.

"No name, same as the last bunch."

He hefted the tower of flowers up and took it out on the back porch, setting it next to the other one. Chanté looked from him to me when he came back and grinned.

"Hey. It's none of my business what you do with them after I get paid. The money's all the same to me." She grinned.

"UPS." Nick was at the door.

She grinned even wider and I suddenly knew she had timed her delivery for Nick. Yeah. Big shock there—everyone wants a piece of that.

Derrick had stacked the orders next to the door and restocked the guest bedroom from storage. Business was still booming.

"I can't talk today. Gotta get my route finished in time for Dennis's funeral. You coming, Chanté?"

"Wouldn't miss it. I'm making a small fortune off of it today." She smiled and headed to her own vehicle. "I'll see you there."

They were both gone in record time and Howard picked me up, like I weighed nothing, and put me back in bed; a few seconds later he put Precious in bed with me.

"Get some rest. I have a few things left to handle at the boat. I just remembered that the flowers will be arriving at two and the boat won't be back at the dock until four."

"It's hot as hell out there. Put them in the walk in fridge at Crusty's."

"Thanks. I'll do that. Rest," he admonished and then he was gone.

The pain pills knocked me out and before I knew it, it was four PM and Sam was standing next to my bed, looking worried.

"What?" I asked.

"Nothing. You just looked so peaceful, I didn't want to wake you."

"I'm awake anyway," I grumbled. I struggled to sit up, but the drugs were wearing off and my side hurt like a son-of-a-bitch. Sam sat next to me and put a hand behind my back to support me.

"What can I get you?"

I reached over and opened the pill bottle, spilling one into my hand. "Diet Coke please?"

He laughed and shook his head. "Amazing. Hang on a second." He went to the kitchen and grabbed one out of the cupboard. When he came back he was popping the top for me. "Here." He handed it to me and I swallowed the pill along with several chugs of warm soda.

My dress was hanging on the back of the closet door. I had ironed it yesterday and I didn't want it to wrinkle in the closet. I was wearing white undies and I needed to change into black before putting on the dress. "Out."

"I can't help you change? What if you pull out a stitch?"

"Out."

He sighed a happy little sigh and went out into the living room to wait. I creaked and groaned my way around the bedroom, getting dressed, braiding my hair. You know, girl stuff. When I was ready, Sam drove me to Crusty's.

The dock was full of people waiting to board. Sherry was looking frazzled, trying to direct Kay and the rest of the staff to handle all the orders from people waiting, with nothing better to do than have an appetizer and drink while they waited. On Sam's arm I made my way through the crowd and into Crusty's and found Howard in the kitchen directing two men on where to take the floral arrangement. Riqué and his cousin were cooking as fast as they could but I could see the orders piling up.

"What else needs to go on board, Howard?"

"I'm waiting for Jack to finish setting up. We couldn't do anything until the fishing customers had gone, so now we're playing catch up."

"Where's the band?"

"Setting up on board. How are you feeling?" He looked at me, concerned, but I knew he didn't need even one more thing to worry about.

"Where's Dennis?"

He looked at me like a light just went off. "Shit."

I smiled. "Sam and I will go get him. Don't worry about it." I went out the way I came in and grabbed Sam. People stopped me on the way to ask how I was doing and I put them to work. Nick and several of his friends were now in charge of clearing paths in the crowd and getting people settled and out of the way until they could board. Derrick I sent back to the main wait to prep the orders after Riqué and his cousin finished cooking them. Sherry and Kerry I tucked behind the bar. They'd be safe there, in a familiar spot until it was time to leave. Kay, relieved of bar duty got back to riding herd over the rest of the wait staff and conscripted a few of her relatives to put on an apron an take orders.

"You just get scarier and scarier every day that I know you," Sam said as he tucked me into his 'vette. Did I mention that Sam drives a red 1978 Corvette convertible, not a speck of rust on her and she purrs when he starts her up. I glanced over at my sadly abused cruiser and mourned for a bit. Maybe a detailing shop could get the pee smell out of the seats. I should have let Miss Gigi die.

"Where are we going?"

"The funeral home." There's only one funeral home, so I don't have to elaborate. Not that many people die in the Keys, in spite of what you may have heard about the AIDS epidemic and the highly concentrated gay population. I think the alcohol pickles them and the heat keeps people mellow and less likely to stress. Stress kills more people than AIDS. I'm sure of it.

It turned out that the funeral home was going to deliver, so we let them. Kerry and Sherry had picked out a seasonal urn from the Summer Pagan collection with a nude man and a woman doing it under a full moon. Their bodies were entwined with nightshade and night blooming jasmine. There was a knife between them. The top of the knife twisted open to open the container inside. The statue was actually two in one. The man and the woman came apart to form two containers. That particular series had three others in very similar veins. There was one for each change of seasons. I figured, if Aunt Jane was a bible thumper, this would be a great resting place for her ashes. I'm not anti-Christian; I just hate people who pretend to be Christian while all the while cursing you out in the name of God. It leaves a bad taste in my mouth. This particular series was requested by email. I never got the whole story, but the idea appealed to me, so I did it for him.

It came out beautifully. Dennis would have loved it.

The funeral director and his wife followed us to the dock where the crowd had already thinned as people boarded. The captain and crew were counting bodies, making sure they weren't overloaded. Some of the people were there with their own boats.

When we got out to the three-mile limit, the captain stopped the boat and the one or two private boats that had started out following us had turned into a massive floatilla. Sherry waited while everyone rafted up and then said a few words over the loud speaker. It was beautiful. Kerry. Now Kerry was going straight to hell for her speech. She read the death poem by W. H. Auden. I love that poem, but it was so wrong for Dennis, which proves that Kerry never really knew him at all.

"Stop all the clocks, cut off the telephone. Prevent the dog from barking with a juicy bone. Silence the pianos and with a muffled drum, bring out the coffin, let the mourners come." She paused and the silence was astonishing. For this many people to shut up and listen was nothing short of miraculous. I'm not sure if they are all shocked that Kerry is literate or if they just like the poem. Me? I liked the poem.

"He was my North, my South, my East and West, my working week and my Sunday rest, my noon, my midnight, my talk, my song; I thought that love would last forever: I was wrong."

What the F? She's skipping verses. I hate that.

"The stars are not wanted now; put out every one. Pack up the moon and dismantle the sun. Pour away the ocean and sweep away the woods; for nothing now can ever come to any good." She smiled a shy, cute little smile. Relief because she

was finished and lightning hadn't struck her dead? Drunk? You decide.

She stepped down into the arms of her date and headed in to the open bar.

We stayed there, all of us, until the wee hours of the night. It was a hell of a send-off for a guy almost everyone hated, but that's the Keys. Any excuse for a party will do.

The marine patrol boarded us several times and finally stayed permanently tied up with the rest of the flotilla.

Not my funeral, not my problem. I hoped that Dennis was getting his revenge and I prayed even harder that Aileen, having taken her pound of flesh, was done haunting me.

All I really know for sure is that the need to get even rules us all no matter how much we deny it. And as long as that's true, I'm in the right business.

A preview of

Colliding Forces

by Constance O'Day-Flannery

Coming in October from
Tor Romance

CHAPTER ONE

"RESIDENTS OF CENTER City were certainly out in full force today as everyone took advantage of the unexpected summer-like weather this close to Thanksgiving. Should we be defrosting our turkeys, Jim, or pulling out our barbeques again?"

"I'm afraid, Deborah, this has only been a tease," Jim Carter answered, picking up his cue as he stood in front of the blue weather screen and faced the camera. "The warm weather is already on the way out . . ."

As Philadelphia's top rated weatherman began his report, D. leaned back in her chair at the anchor desk and tried to concentrate on the pages in front of her, the same lines that were on the teleprompter over the camera. Another soft story. This must the tenth in two weeks. She found that her back teeth were grinding in annoyance and relaxed her jaw. They were feeding all these tug-your-heart stories to her because of that last *focus group*. Just thinking about them had the ability to raise her blood pressure. This time they said she wasn't feminine enough. Too tough. She didn't have any softness. One of them even had the balls to say he couldn't imagine her being affectionate! If they wanted The Pillsbury Dough Boy to read hard news then they should have hired him. Affectionate! She'd exploded in her boss' office two weeks ago when Dan, along with the station manager, tried to tell her she needed to soften the edges a little. Why were they brainwashed by a group of obvious morons who had completely missed the point that she reported hard news . . . politics, wars, murders, hit and runs, kidnappings, robberies. What was she supposed to do? Dab at her eyes with Grannie's lace handkerchief while telling the tri-state their news in order to please a handful of people they had pulled off the street?

But it was the affectionate remark that seemed to linger in her back teeth, like an irritating kernel of popcorn that couldn't be dislodged. Immediately, her brain ran over the last time she'd been *affectionate*. Hah! They should have seen her then . . .

The encounter with Marcus Bocelli still had the ability to warm her body whenever she thought of it . . . the two of them walking on the beach, how he casually took her hand, wooed her with his voice, his sensuous eyes, until she was actually preening just being in his presence. A kiss had led to being held in his arms, pulled against his lean hard body and, for the first time in a very, very long time, she had lost control.

It played back in lightening flashes . . . her pulling him into a cove, her back against a stone wall as his mouth explored her and her hands tore at his clothes. She couldn't remember the last time she'd made love with such abandon. She could picture Marcus' hands sliding up the skirt of her Versace dress as she clung to him, became one with him. It had seemed as though nothing existed in that space of time except a man and a woman doing the most primal thing in the world . . . bumping each other like wild monkeys. It was only days later that she wondered if they'd reacted so crazily because they each seemed to have lost something at that wedding. Maggie. D. knew Marcus loved Maggie, or had loved her at some point. And Maggie would no longer be in Philadelphia after she married Julian. Not having many friends, D. hated to lose Maggie, even if it was to love and marriage. Still, the whole encounter with Marcus had left her stunned and craving more. So far, she hadn't heard from him and—

"Deborah?"

"*Deborah!*" she heard in her earpiece, the floor director jerking her back from a magical tropical love fest to the dark television studio in center city Philadelphia.

"Sorry, Matt," she breathed with a smile to her co-anchor. Squaring her shoulders, she looked into the camera and tried to soften her facial expression. "We all know dogs are man's best friend, but what happens when your precious, furry friend disappears without any warning? When we come back we'll find one woman's answer, and we'll tell you how she fought City Hall to reclaim her best buddy."

They went to commercial and Matt Jordan laughed. "Now that's the first time I've caught you lost. Where were you, D.?"

She grinned. "If I told you, Matt, the rest of your hair would turn gray with shock."

"Good or bad?" he asked as the makeup crew came up to the desk and blotted sweat off his forehead.

"Neither," she answered, waving off the hair stylist who wanted to make her brown wisps even more defined. Having no desire to appear as a talking whisk broom, she said, "Thanks, Sheila, but the hair is fine as it is." And she had no intention of telling anyone about her personal life, or why she'd lost her focus. "Sorry, Alan," she called out to the floor director. "Won't happen again."

Alan nodded as he stretched out his hand to the news desk

with his fingers splayed. Everyone waited in silence as they came back from a short commercial. One by one, Alan's fingers curled into his palm, until he was pointing at her. Picking up her cue, she tried to appear sympathetic. "And now we'll go to Andrea Miller, for the story of one woman's struggle to reunite her canine family, a story of persistence and love."

"Thanks, Deborah. Judith Zink's best friend had recently given birth to triplets, no easy feat for human or animal, and Judith couldn't have been more happy to welcome the adorable West Highland Terriers into her family. That is, until Junibelle went missing. Was it merely a question of a mother needing a break, or something more sinister?"

D. hated the cutesy copy, was grateful she didn't have to read it, and she truly attempted to pay attention to the feature reporter, a young fresh faced woman who seemed to ooze softness and sympathy and probably was as affectionate as one of the puppies whose footage was being telecast out to the viewing audience. Despite the image, D. knew Andrea would stop just short of murder to sit at the six o'clock anchor desk. D. knew about ambition and acknowledged it came with the job description. She'd watch her back and the pretty blonde, who wouldn't hesitate to stick her high heels into D.'s shoulder blades to climb the corporate news ladder.

Her mind wasn't on job security or even on the reuniting of Junibelle and her puppies as Andrea's piece continued. Instead, it flirted with daydreaming as her thoughts took her back to that beach in Bermuda and to a great looking Italian who had apologized to her on the walk back to the party, telling her he hadn't meant for things to get out of hand. She had still been buzzing with electricity, feeling like she could walk on water, and had thanked him for getting out of hand and had told him anytime he wanted another play date to give her a call. She'd meant it to be casual, maybe even flippant, but secretly she wanted him to take her hand again, to walk her back to the wedding party, stay at her side, and fly with her to Philly, instead of New York, so they could continue exploring each other. It had been a long time since she'd felt that need. And that's what burned inside of her now. Need. She didn't just want to see him again. It was as if her body had a need, a hot flaming condition, an itch that required relief.

God, she was becoming pathetic.

Forcing herself through the rest of the newscast, she unplugged her mic and walked back to her office. She simply had to forget Marcus Bocelli, she thought as she sat down at her desk and began to log onto her computer. It was simply a crazy fling, not her first unfortunately, and could be filed away. Should be filed away, she mentally added, and yet her brain could easily conjure him up . . . flashing his face across the screen of her mind. She could see those dark, probing brown eyes, staring into her own as if he had some special pass beyond them into her soul. Even now she could actually feel a shiver of electricity pass over her skin as desire welled up within her again. Before she'd left Bermuda, she'd handed him her business card with all her phone numbers and her email address. The ball was in his court. She couldn't even talk to anyone about her ridiculous obsession with Marcus. The only person would have been Maggie, but Maggie was out of the question. Maggie had warned her off Marcus numerous times, telling her she'd only wind up heartbroken. Well, her heart wasn't broken. Her heart wasn't even involved. It was her body. That Roman god had put a spell on her.

It was up to her, alone, to find a way to remove it, she determined as her phone rang. No man, no matter how gorgeous, was worth becoming pathetic and jeopardizing her focus at work was out of the question.

"Deborah Stark," she automatically answered.

"Debbie, hon? This is Aunt Tina."

Immediately, she sat up straighter as all her internal alarms began buzzing. "Hi, Aunt Tina," she answered in a surprised and cautious voice. No one from her family had ever called her at work. "How are you?"

"Oh, honey . . . I'm so sorry. I don't know how to tell you this. It's your mom. She . . . she's passed, Debbie. About an hour ago. They say it was an embolism in her brain. She was talking to Anna Devers about Thanksgiving, her turkey, how excited she was that you were coming home for the holiday and . . . and then she just stopped speaking and went down. It was that quick, the doctors said, and . . . I'm so sorry to tell you like this over the phone, but I didn't know what else to do." Her paternal aunt began crying.

Numbness descended over D.'s body like an invisible shield as she tried to find her voice. Her mother. Dead. An embolism. She felt like her whole world was tilting at a dangerous angle and she gripped the edge of her desk to stay centered and not fall into a chasm of guilt. "You did the right thing," she whispered as she looked at her Gucci purse and envisioned her cars keys inside. "I was planning on driving up tomorrow morning, but I'll leave tonight. I'll be there tonight."

"Come to my house, honey. Stay with us."

She had to focus. "Yes," she murmured, running over in her head everything she'd have to do. Dan would give her the time off. Go back to the apartment and pack different clothes. Something black. "I might not be there until really late. Maybe it's best if I just go . . ." she found she had to force the word from her lips. ". . . home."

"Nonsense. You come as late as you like. We'll be up."

"Okay, then . . . I'll see you tonight. I should get started here and . . ." her words trailed off.

"I'm so sorry, Debbie. Even though your mother was my sister-in-law, she was like a real sister to me."

"I know," D. answered, picturing her father's sister staying in their lives, trying to make up for the fact that her brother had abandoned his wife and child. "And mom knew that too. She loved you, Aunt Tina."

"You be careful driving, Debbie. All that holiday traffic."

Debbie. No one, not even her mother, had called her that in decades. "Right, I should get going. I have to speak to my boss about getting some time off."

"I love you."

She felt the first stirring of emotion as tears welled up in her throat and burned her eyes. "I love you too," she answered, watching her hand as she hung up the phone.

Her mother. Dead. Gone . . .

She sat for a moment out of time, stunned by the news delivered by her aunt. Her body didn't feel capable of moving as years of regret and guilt swept over her. How fucking ironic that this was the first Thanksgiving in three years that she had arranged to spend with her mother. Within seconds her brain fired off reasons, good reasons, for not seeing more of the woman who had given her life . . . but deep down, in a place she wasn't ready to explore, Deborah Stark knew she had relegated her mother to the past, a place she rarely wanted to visit.

It hit her with the force of a bat to the back of her knees, bringing her down to reality. It was time to be the adult. There was no one ahead of her any longer being sensible and grown up. All her life other people took care of things like this. Births, deaths, weddings . . . when her mother had informed her of family news she'd called a florist and sent a huge arrangement of flowers, but her lifestyle and work had kept her from anything more personal, like showing up in person.

She couldn't back out of this one or expect anyone else to take care of it. Now it was up to her. She wished for a moment that she believed in a Supreme Being, someone to call upon for assistance, but in truth she only believed in herself. Long ago she had learned the lesson of depending on another for answers or help. She was too intelligent to blindly place her faith in anyone's dogma, but for a moment, a split second, she wished she was a religious person who could lay their troubles at the feet of a savior.

That wasn't her. She had already laid the foundation for her life and now she had to walk her talk. She had to be strong, push away the pain and also the guilt. She had to pretend to be what everyone expected, what she had worked so damn hard to make them believe.

And now . . . now she truly was alone.

MARCUS BOCELLI CLOSED the lid of his wireless phone, disconnecting his call, while looking out the window of his apartment and watching a squirrel deftly climb the delicate limbs of an maple tree, moving quickly, only stopping momentarily to test the strength of the next link on his journey. For a moment he thought that's what his own life has been like, moving quickly, only stopping briefly as he tested his next course of action. He placed the tiny phone back into his trouser pocket and knew he'd made the right decision. The last place he'd wanted to be was Senator Burke's farm in Maryland.

Maggie would be there. And so would her new husband. It would be a family Thanksgiving dinner and, even though Gabriel's invitation had been sincere, Marcus knew he wasn't family. Not really, and not anymore. Not with Maggie discovering Gabriel was her father. This Thanksgiving should be a private celebration for them.

He liked the American tradition of taking one day to be grateful. It was at times like this he yearned for his own family. His mother and sisters and all his nieces and nephews crowding the family home in northern Italy for holidays, creating noise, laughter and love to bounce off the old plaster walls. He missed his home, his family . . .

At thirty-seven, he'd seen enough of the world to realize how blessed he had been to have been born to his parents for he had grown up surrounded in love. This American holiday was a time to take stock and to be grateful. And he was, very, very grateful.

He was the only son in a family of four sisters, along with eight aunts and more female cousins than he could count. His father, an international banker, had spoiled him and was gentle with his discipline, leaving him to the females in the family to raise . . . and Marcus, being cherished by all those around him, came into manhood with a great fondness for the feminine gender. His early life had been a great influence, for he'd matured loving the way women smelled, the softness of their skin, the sound of their voices, the miracle of their bodies to create, sustain and nourish life. At eleven he found out about the pleasure and joy they could bring him. From that time on he had spent his time devising ways to be in their presence. By seventeen he'd had multiple affairs at the same time, in Italy and across the border in Monte Carlo. It hadn't mattered to him if the women were married or single, young or older, rich or poor. He had loved them all. And he had especially loved to see how they would blossom into fragile, fragrant flowers, offering up their unique, innate beauty under his expert hands. His skill with women had come naturally and he'd perfected it with each encounter. Romance had been his natural high, pleasurable and powerful. He'd been, to put it simply, a ladies man and life had been gloriously sweet until the summer he'd left for university.

Even now, twenty years later, just thinking about his father caused his body to tense with grief and regret. Returning home from his bank, Emilio Bocelli had been cruelly assassinated by remnants of The Red Brigade, an extreme leftist terrorist organization that had been intent on destructuralization of the capitalist economy by kidnapping and killing scions of Italian government and business.

Marcus' idyllic life had been shattered the moment he'd heard his mother's scream of horror upon being given the news. The house of grieving females had nearly stifled him. Hell bent on revenge, he'd gone to university and joined a student movement whose undercover motives were to separate Italy from the western alliance and promote its withdrawal from NATO. He had thought if he could infiltrate the group he would find his father's murders and exact justice. And visions of that justice was what had kept him sane while he sank deeper and deeper into the underbelly of a fanatical political movement.

It was hard for him to now remember being that young man, bitter and secretive, so bitter that his mother had contacted her husband's good friend in the United States. She had begged Gabriel Burke to save her son's life, to take Marcus away from Italy.

And Gabriel had saved his life, and his sanity.

He'd brought Marcus into his home and began tutoring him in the ways of the world, showing Marcus that answering violence with violence only creates more violence and there was another way, besides killing, to gain justice. Through the influence of Senator Burke, members of the Red Brigade were captured in a severe crackdown of the organization and imprisoned, including the killers of Emilio Bocelli. Many of them turned informer, leading security forces to other members and hastening the group's slide into obscurity.

Under Gabriel's tutelage, Marcus gradually regained his personality and finally, thankfully, his love of life. He'd had been an excellent student and was soon learning about the mysterious foundation that helped to balance light against the darkness of the world. He had attended college with Gabriel's son and was welcomed into the Burke family while being schooled in the traditions of the foundation. He learned about power, real power to bring about change. And, since he was fascinated with the sciences, he eventually learned about the structure of life . . . pure energy. The ability to shape shift came easily to him and he later learned his grandmother had also possessed that gift. He learned of the power of love in a much different way than he had used it in his youthful days. When he graduated from college he came into his inheritance and through Gabriel's guidance invested it wisely. He then began working for the foundation full time, using his ability to help heal damaged hearts and facilitate change in the world, one soul at a time.

He never questioned his purpose in life or his place within the foundation. Not until Maggie had married last month. Somehow, perhaps foolishly, he had believed he and Maggie were two of a kind, that they would grow old together, each serving in their own way, meeting up and enjoying each other for however long the pleasure lasted. They had understood each other, taking their leave before the pleasure led to possession and ruined a great relationship. But she had married another and he had witnessed her great love for Julian McDonald. He had made a mistake with Maggie, never realizing how much she'd wanted a husband and family, and he had lost the only women he had let into his soul.

Turning away from the window, he looked down to his desk and saw the business card of Maggie's friend. His finger traced the engraved printing. That had been another mistake. Deborah Stark. He never should have weakened and used her to wipe out the image of Maggie and Julian leaving the wedding reception. Never mind that she had been more than willing. She was Maggie's friend. He pictured her in his mind . . . tall, lovely, short dark hair, brown eyes that burned with ambition and a smart biting humor.

He closed his eyes and could almost sense her again . . . her breasts crushed against his chest, her mouth deliciously mating with his, her hips meeting each thrust with a challenge for more. Even now, he could feel his body become aroused by the memory of her passion.

How long since he'd had a fling?

His new assignment would begin in two weeks. That left this holiday weekend free.

Grinning, he wondered what Deborah Stark's plans were for Thanksgiving. It had been so long since he'd had fun for just the sake of it. No strings attached, no assignment. Just pleasure. Deborah Stark was the kind of woman who could appreciate exactly what he wanted.

Giving in, he took his phone out from his pocket and picked up her business card.

Look for

Dark Horse

by Patricia Simpson

Available November 2005
from Tom Doherty Associates

Look for

Hawkes Harbor

by S. E. Hinton

Available October 2005
from Tom Doherty Associates

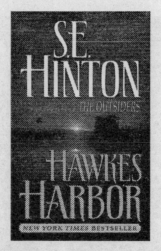

"Vampires, pirates, and lusty French socialites: now that's a recipe for a good time. Hinton has written an "adult" novel that can awaken the rough-and-tumble child in anyone. Hinton's ability to engage hasn't faded." —*The New York Times*

"Erasing age and genre barriers, prize-winning, bestselling YA author Hinton turns out a dark, funny, scary, suspenseful tale that will entertain mainstream and adventure/horror readers alike." —*Publishers Weekly*